Nobody Does the Right Thing

AMITAVA KUMAR

Nobody Does the Right Thing

a novel

Duke University Press

Durham and London

2010

© 2010 Duke University Press
All rights reserved
Printed in the United States of
America on acid-free paper ♾
Designed by C. H. Westmoreland
Typeset in Quadraat
with Rockwell display by Tseng
Information Systems, Inc.

Library of Congress Cataloging-in-
Publication Data appear on the last
printed page of this book.

An earlier, longer version of this
novel was published by Picador
India in 2007 under the title
Home Products.

for Ila

CONTENTS

. . . .

ACKNOWLEDGMENTS

Without Ken Wissoker, no reader outside the Indian subcontinent would have been doing the right thing. I am very happy that this novel has found a home at Duke University Press. With this book's arrival in these parts, Manto will visit cities whose names he had probably never heard of, and people who have long known George Orwell will learn about the town in India where he was born; Arthur Miller, after his brief stay in Patna, along with Tennessee Williams, following a performance in Bombay, are for a while returning home, a little bit changed. All of this is a matter of great satisfaction to me.

Thanks to David Davidar who first told me why and how what I was writing should be turned into fiction; to Manoj Bajpai, who agreed to make the journey back to the places in our past every time we talked about the ambition to act; and to my agents Gillon Aitken and Ayesha Karim for their commitment to what I write. Most of my gratitude is reserved for my editor at Picador India, Shruti Debi, who with such scrupulous attention and grace helped me find the novel's voice.

In Bombay: Naresh Fernandes, Neeraj Priyadarshi, Jerry Pinto, Nandini Ramnath, Shabana Raza, and Nira and Shyam Benegal. In Delhi: Uma and Ashis Nandy, Raj Kamal Jha, Sujata Bose, Karan Mahajan, Pragya and Siddharth Chowdhury. I am grateful to the Dean of Faculty at Vassar College for funding a research trip to Bihar and Bombay in 2005. To the members of my family, especially those who will find bits of themselves in this story, my love and wholly inadequate thanks for years of encouragement and support.

I have used for my narrative about battle scenes in a documentary, Lt. Gen. S.K. Sinha's study *Veer Kuer Singh: The Great Warrior of 1857* (New Delhi, Konark, 1997). For a report on the condition of Orwell's birthplace, I have relied on Luke Harding's "Shadows of Orwell" (*The Guardian*, January 24, 2000). The words quoted by a character to an interviewer from London are taken from Nasreen Munni Kabir's *Bollywood* (London, Channel 4, 2001).

A list of the planet's afflictions quotes from the "Findings" column in *Harper's* (December, 2003).

This is a work of imagination and does not claim to deal with facts. The reader will find that although this is a novel, it sometimes uses real events and the names of real people, especially in the Hindi film world, to tell its story.

PEOPLE AND PLACES

Mala Srivastava
A small-town poet in the news, murdered by her
politician-lover in Patna

Patna
An old city on the banks of the Ganges described by one writer
as "the subcontinent's heart of darkness"

Binod Singh
A journalist in Bombay who, like many others we know,
wants to write a real story

Bombay
The city now called Mumbai, home to the Hindi film industry
also known as Bollywood

Vikas Dhar
A popular Bollywood director who specializes in sleaze,
asks Binod to write about the death of Mala Srivastava

Baba
Binod's high-minded father, a documentary film-maker in Patna

Ma
Binod's mother, a school teacher

Rabinder Singh
Binod's cousin, in Hajipur Jail, who aspires to
produce a Bollywood film

Delhi
A city where, Binod is informed, people use crude language
"because they have had the sword of history repeatedly
thrust up their backsides"

Iraq
A far-off place from where news of war arrives
rich with rumors

Bua
Rabinder's mother, Baba's sister, a prominent politician in Bihar

Bihar
Binod's benighted home state, in eastern India,
with Patna as its proud capital

Bettiah
A small town north of Patna, where Rabinder grew up,
a place famous for kidnappings and extortion

Neeraj Dubey
Rabinder's classmate from Bettiah, a Bollywood film-star

Arpana
Binod's former wife

Roma Banerjee
Rabinder's illicit lover in Patna, married to a bureaucrat

Benares
Ancient city, where on getting off the train with funeral ashes
Binod first sights the poster for a film *Korean Kama Sutra*

Neelu
Binod's sister

Shatrughan
Neelu's husband, once rode in a car with Steven Seagal

Lalji
Bua's husband, housed in a mental asylum in
Ranchi till his death

Manik
Lalji's nephew, part-entrepreneur, part-criminal, part-politician

Ratauli
Baba's village, near Motihari

Motihari
Another town in Bihar, Baba's birthplace, where Gandhi
started the anti-colonial freedom struggle

George Orwell
A British writer born in Motihari

Ulan Bator
An imaginary place conjured by a man on his marriage-bed

I

The Car with
the Red Light

1

Mala Srivastava's mother lived in a two-room flat above a tiny kindergarten institution that called itself Harward Public School. Binod didn't know this; he stopped at the school first and was pointed to the narrow stairway that led up to the second floor. Rows of dark, feral faces with slightly scared but inquisitive eyes followed him from the window where the teacher had paused in the lesson he was giving. The door of the flat was open and lying on the dirty floor beside it was a steel plate with half a dozen freshly washed potatoes and a knife.

A middle-aged woman came out of the room at the back. Binod stopped knocking and, in the semi-darkness inside, the woman stopped too. She began to cover her head with her cotton sari when Binod introduced himself. He had brought a copy of the editorial he had written about Mala. The woman took it from his hand but said that she couldn't read without her glasses. Binod was still standing at the door. He said, "I didn't have your phone number. I couldn't call you before I showed up like this. Could you talk to me for a few minutes?"

The woman said, "My daughter . . . my second daughter . . . will be back from college. She will be able to answer your questions."

That must be Mala's younger sister. It was she who had first spoken to the media after the murder about Mala's affair with Surajdeo Tripathi. Just a day later, inexplicably, she had withdrawn the charge. She said that she had been misquoted in the press. But the police had done the tests on the fetus. Surajdeo and his wife were arrested within days, after Mala's servant had identified the hired killer.

Binod said, "I don't really have any questions. I came from Bombay just yesterday. A local journalist gave me this address last night . . ."

The woman didn't move or say anything. She looked past Binod into the street outside. She said, "I don't even have tea in the house. The servant went to his village last Monday and hasn't returned. I'm here by myself."

"Mataji," Binod said, folding his hands dramatically, "you need not concern yourself about me. I don't need tea. I have just come from my parents' home here in Patna. Please give me a few minutes of your time. That's all I ask."

He was seated on a wooden chair that the woman had dragged close to the door for him. She sat on a stool halfway across the room. The woman's hair was gray, but her face was largely free of wrinkles; it was a round and heavy face, tired looking because of the dark circles under the eyes. The face remained expressionless as Binod read aloud. He would read each sentence, putting great emphasis on those words where he seemed to be praising Mala's ambition, and stop to look at her. He faltered once he got to the closing lines about the children of film stars—what did it have to do with Mala anyway?—but he didn't pause in his reading. He had planned to ask her if she saw her daughter's journey as a terrifying trip to the heart of power, but the blankness of the woman's gaze made him hesitate. He began to justify what he had done. He said, "I didn't want to deal with details of the scandal. That wasn't of interest to me. I just wanted to comment on what it meant for a young, fatherless girl to make her way in the political world."

But it didn't matter.

The mother said, "The press printed reports that she was pregnant. How could that have been possible? People have insects in their brain . . . I had just seen her. She was wearing churidar kurta that day. Would it not have been obvious to everyone?"

Binod remained silent. After a while, he asked, "What did your daughter want to become when she grew up? I mean, when she was a child, what did she dream of becoming?"

The woman said, "When she was a child, she played, she went to school. What does a child care about how she is going to survive when she grows up?"

There must be wisdom in this response. That is what the shaking of Binod's head was supposed to mean. It might have suggested to someone else that he was actually shaking his head in despair.

The woman spoke again. "Her father passed away when she was only fourteen. I didn't have a son. Mala grew old almost overnight. She was the breadwinner now. She was my son. Who will—"

The old woman's hand went up to her throat and her plump lips fluttered for a second. She seemed to sigh but actually she was crying; she would catch her breath and then let out a small moan.

Binod wanted to ask her how Mala had discovered literature. He didn't

4

interrupt the woman's crying, however. And then it was too late. Mala's mother looked up with alarm and began to wipe her eyes. Binod turned and saw that a young woman was standing on the landing and behind her was a tall, dark man in a black shirt. The young woman pressed her lips and without saying anything to Binod made a circle around his chair and entered the flat. She put her hand on the old woman's shoulder and then, still not looking at Binod, asked her loudly, "Is it right to cry like this — in front of strangers?"

This was the sister. She had no interest in the editorial that Binod was holding out for her to see. But the tall man took it from Binod's hand. While the fellow was reading it, Binod said, "I wrote that editorial. I'm a journalist working in Bombay. But I'm from Patna."

The man said, "But what do you want here now?"

It didn't occur to Binod then, or even later that day when he kept returning to this question, to tell them that he was going to write a story for a film about the murdered girl. The dark man had a thin gold chain on his chest. Binod looked at him and then at the old woman, whose face, now emptied of grief, had once again surrendered itself to blankness. He felt he should say something about how difficult life was — and how he had felt that Mala had been unconventional. But it was clear that the girl wanted to speak. The younger sister. Her name had been in the papers too, but for some reason Binod couldn't recall it right then. He looked at the tense, thin fingers that she had placed on her mother's shoulder.

The girl, all fury suddenly, spoke up in English. "I think you are a lawyer."

"Lawyer," Binod asked loudly, doing his best to look hurt. But he was genuinely surprised. A lawyer? Did they think he was a lawyer, perhaps here to entrap them, and is that why there was such suspicion and anger?

The girl took a step toward him. "You are a lawyer. Get out." Her thin finger described a ridiculous arc through the air. Binod turned away. It wasn't until he had reached the bottom of the steps that he realized that she had actually been calling him a liar.

....

Binod did not know the woman but after her murder she had been everywhere in the papers. The stories repeated themselves and were often smudgy with their details, but the headlines told their own unambiguous story: "Bad Art, Worse Life," "Death of a Small Time Poetess," "Couplet of Ruin," and, given the eternal allure of alliteration, "Mala, Mahatva-kanksha, aur Maut" (Mala, Ambition, and Death).

Her name was Mala Srivastava and she was from a small town near Patna. She had been in the local papers even earlier because she used to recite poems at public meetings. Her poems mocked the manhood of Indian leaders; she called upon Indian youth to cross the border and slaughter the people in Pakistan; she wanted the national anthem inscribed on the body of Benazir Bhutto. Mala was only twenty-one when she died. People said that she was pretty. Those who had seen her performing said she was arrogant and wanted everything from life. A couple of the press reports after her death mentioned that during a visit to Bombay she had been arrested briefly for having stolen gold jewelry from her host's apartment.

When Mala had still been in high school her father was killed in a road accident and the family had fallen on bad times. But at the time of her death she had been living for a year and a half in a large house in Buddha Colony. The story went that Mala did not need to pay rent on that house in Patna. Her neighbors said that white cars with red lights would deliver sweets and gifts at her door whenever the festivals rolled around. Politicians and officials were regular visitors to her house at different times of the day and night.

The autopsy report revealed that Mala was pregnant when she was shot, and it was accepted that the father of the unborn child was Surajdeo Tripathi, a former minister in the state legislature who had done a brief stint in prison. Several corruption cases in which he had been charged were awaiting the attention of the honorable High Court. Tripathi was a married man; his wife, one of the six accused in the murder, had surrendered to the police. Tripathi had been arrested and then released and then arrested again.

The world had been busy at the time of Mala Srivastava's death. The American president had climbed into a green flight suit and flown in an aircraft onto the deck of a naval carrier to declare that war had ended in Iraq. In the Congo, the rear door of a Russian-built cargo plane had burst open in flight and 129 passengers had been sucked out into the open air. There were fears during those weeks of a new infectious disease having come from China. In Pune, a bride who was infected with SARS had insisted on getting married in church and was taken to the hospital in the middle of the ceremony. Both the groom and the priest were quarantined together in a hospital that was then forced to shut down.

The Supreme Court in Delhi ruled that the people in Jharia town in Bihar were to be relocated by the government. Seven of Binod's more distant relatives lived there, including his cousin Munni and her husband, whose teeth were falling out because he was addicted to the wrong tooth powder. Three decades ago in Jharia, Baba's old roommate from college had disappeared into the ground along with the postmaster's chair and desk at which he had been sitting. An underground fire had been raging there in the coal mines for nearly ninety years. It had started because of a spark from a Davy safety lamp in one of the mines. The fire had now spread to more than seventeen square kilometers. Every once in a while roads collapsed—and houses and the people in them disappeared down caves that suddenly opened up in the earth. A public-interest suit had been filed in the courts a few years ago and now the judiciary had directed the government to relocate all the affected families to a safer area. The news about the world's largest and oldest fire competed with the details of the private life of Mala Srivastava.

In the world of Bombay cinema, matters that were also in a way about life and death had forced Binod to go on an assignment to Surat. He had only recently arrived in Bombay, transferred from Delhi, and was expected to cover the city's film scene. Arrest warrants had recently been issued against the parents of an actress. The police said that they had used members of the Bombay underworld to extort money from a sari manufacturing company in Surat. Binod spent a day watching on video all of her hot dance numbers; then he caught a train that would take him north to Gujarat. By the time he got back to Bombay, Mala Srivastava had been buried under new names and new print, and it wasn't till the first anniversary of her murder that Binod wrote an editorial about her.

Eight hundred words on what he called the tragedy of small-town ambition. He quoted the actor Om Puri, who had told a journalist that in India there was poverty even of ambition: "Hamaare yahan iraadon mein bhi kangaali hai." Puri had been born in Ambala, which is a place only on the way to somewhere else, smelling of the diesel from the army trucks leaving for Kashmir. The real argument was not about character but about place. In Motihari, where Binod had been born, the evening's amusement came in the form of a walk to the railway station with your friends for a cup of tea. If you were a young woman and lived in a house with a court-yard or access to a roof, you always had a piece of the sky even though you were denied the rest of the world. It is doubtful that Mala Srivastava was a poet of any importance but her journey to the heart of power must have been as terrifying as a trip to the North Pole. When Binod wrote this, he was conscious that he was probably exaggerating and, therefore, in an effort to sound more restrained he had concluded with a more local sentiment. In Bombay it is usual to see the children of film stars easily stepping into the shoes of their parents and being handed one film contract after another. But if you happen to be from nowhere, it is not simply that you don't know anyone else—the truth is that you don't even know yourself.

The editorial came out on a Monday. On Tuesday evening, he was in the newspaper office downloading a wire story on Iraq when there was a phone call for him. The loud voice on the phone sounded familiar.

The man said, "Binod Singh?"

Binod said yes slowly, taking his time to place that voice, and the man said, "You're not sure?"

The caller laughed at his own joke. It was Vikas Dhar. Binod felt a rush. Dhar's *Rome* was the biggest hit of the year. His heroine's open-mouthed laugh next to a fountain spurting water in a piazza in Italy was plastered everywhere on the giant Bombay billboards. Binod heard him saying, "What you have written is not an editorial, it is actually a very powerful testimony. You should write a story about this. Write the story that is behind this editorial. I think a good film can be made on this story."

And he said, "Come and see me in my office tomorrow at five o'clock."

Binod said that he would do that. He had fought to keep the uncertainty out of his voice, but he was in a calmer state of mind when he went to Juhu to meet Dhar the next evening.

There was a sofa in the office that curled around the wall and the filmmaker, wearing a black kurta, lay sprawled on it, his right arm stretched out on the desk alongside. He was relaxed and friendly. Tea was brought. The lamp above the sofa was shining on his bald head. His face, still handsome and boyish, was framed between white sideburns. A small puppet of George W. Bush squatted on the desk close to him. Bush's pants were pulled down and a pencil rested snugly in the presidential asshole. From time to time, while he spoke, Dhar would meditatively wiggle the pencil and make the puppet twitch. The man who had brought tea returned and asked whether he wanted a vegetable patty; Binod shook his head although he felt a slight sensation of hunger spiral up his gut.

Dhar was frowning in thought. He said, "Do you write exclusively in English? You're from the cow belt, you must . . ."

The question was both unexpected and generous, and in the comfortable air-conditioned space of the office, Binod found himself telling Dhar about his past.

When he had come out of university, he wrote in both Hindi and English. He used to file all news reports in English, but his more reflective essays on Sunday were for the sister paper in Hindi. These essays were filled with nostalgia and protest, and reflected perhaps the loneliness he had felt while living away from home in Delhi.

He had once attended a week-long seminar on journalism at the Ashoka Hotel and in the afternoons he would go and lie down on the grass in Nehru Park. He rarely saw poor people from places like Bihar walking on the green grass—had they turned into machines of flesh and bone in the new factories of Noida and Ghaziabad? In prose made lyrical by homesickness and longing, Binod wondered if those who had left behind their small homes had turned to stone in this strange land and were laid down as slabs on the pavements of the city's wide streets.

The essays appeared under the heading *Aayeena*, which means "mirror" in Hindi. After a few months of this, Binod's editor told him that he needed to look in the mirror and decide what he wanted to be, a journalist in English or Hindi. The choice was easy. There were more readers for the Hindi papers but the money was in the English.

Nevertheless, while writing entirely in English, Binod found that he could not talk very easily about villages and small towns. He lacked the idiom to express his feelings directly about harvests or heavy rains that led to flooding, the excitement and then the numbing that followed the news of another caste massacre, the familiar bare roads that cut through fields and shone at night under the moon's light, the sound of a woman's bangles coming across a pond in the dark. He wanted to talk about the routine of travel during Holi and Diwali in the unreserved compartment of third-rate trains like the Shram Jeevi Express—but who among the readers of English newspapers in Delhi would find any appeal in such things? There were only so many times that he could remind his reader that you could not understand the pain of the man who brought your milk or drove your car unless you too needed to go back to your village every six months to find out whether the child who had four milk teeth last time had now learned to call your name when shown your photograph.

Binod was saying all this because he wanted Dhar to say that he did understand, but the man didn't say much. He was listening and smiling softly, and nodding his head as if he were a spiritual guru on television.

When he was asked to move to Bombay, Binod was happy that he worked for an English newspaper. The city supported the Hindi film industry, and hundreds of Hindi films were made each year, but the actors gave all their interviews in English. Twelve million people in the country watched films in Indian languages every day, but on the set everyone spoke in English except when barking commands to the unwashed workers tilting lights from the trees. Even the scripts were written in English and translated later into Hindi. Binod knew that it would have been humiliating to be a Hindi-language journalist. The film industry would have given him even less respect.

At a premiere one night, while drinking large quantities of the free Johnnie Walker served at the party, a film journalist who worked for *Dainik Bhaskar* began telling him about Mehboob Khan. Mehboob had become famous in the 1950s for making films like *Mother India*. The journalist said that Mehboob had been working at a tea stall when he had been hired as an assistant by a director. Even as a well-known auteur, Mehboob was unable to read any script brought to him, and he would sit back on his chair and ask the writers to narrate the story while he chewed his paan. An illiterate man had become India's legendary director!

The journalist talking to Binod used tobacco, which is why his teeth had turned black. He was from Benares. As Binod listened to him, he felt that people told stories like the one about Mehboob over and over again, although they bore only a slight resemblance to truth, because it made everyone think that they could do anything they wanted. This too was a Bombay specialty.

What Binod had learned after moving to the city and having to deal with the film world was that even the man who cut your hair had dreams. You would be sitting in front of the mirror under the pictures of stars like Sanjay Dutt or Shah Rukh Khan, hair falling down on the filthy sheet wrapped around your neck, and the man who was snipping the scissors would straighten his shoulders under the polyester shirt and say to you, "You need luck, no doubt, but you must have a plan. You have got to make your own destiny."

Binod told Vikas Dhar that the newspaper for which he worked had the highest circulation in India and he confessed that he regularly mentioned the paper in his conversations because people recognized the name.

Dhar asked, "What are you ashamed of?"

"I have not ever been of use to anyone as a journalist."

"Why?"

"I can think of countless other professions in which one can be more useful. I have nothing but the most basic knowledge about computers. It would be great to be friends with someone who can take a computer apart. Ditto for a banker, a businessman, an official in the railways. A travel agent. Even a karate instructor."

....

At nine, Dhar got up from the sofa and yawned. Binod took the local train that would bring him back to Yari Road. In the half-empty compartment, watching the swaying metal handrails that hung from the ceiling, he began to think of a book he had read in which a writer living abroad had mocked Indian melodrama. He couldn't recall who it was exactly, Rushdie or maybe even Naipaul, but he remembered the scene vividly. A character in that book had gone to watch an Indian dramatization of a play by Jean-Paul Sartre. In Sartre's play, a man is kneeling at the keyhole of his front door. He is peeping into his own house because he suspects his wife of infidelity. He has told her that he is going away on a business trip, but he returns a few hours later to spy. Then, he feels a presence behind his back, and when he turns he sees his wife looking down at him with revulsion and disgust. The scene was about shame.

In the Indian version, however, the kneeling husband, surprised by his wife, got up to confront her; there was shouting, there were tears, and, following an embrace, there was the inevitable reconciliation.

It is possible that the point of this comparison was to suggest that Indians were incapable of a sense of tragedy. They are rescued from having a single genuine emotion because of their attachment to melodrama. Knowledge comes to them only in the form of a film story with seven songs.

But Binod didn't feel any sense of shame about Indian cinema: even at its most imitative, it had its own rules and it survived by fulfilling the public's expectations. He admired that. At the same time, he could not imagine how the story about Mala Srivastava could be turned into a Bollywood film. He attempted to embrace the enigma of the dead woman. He began to invent a character just like himself, a young man who had been her lover once, and who could call her back sometimes to what she had left behind. Their paths have now diverged; they have gone in different directions. That man would perhaps be sitting late one evening in a half-empty train compartment and he would come upon the story of the murder in the day's newspaper. The film would follow in the form of a flashback.

Dhar had told him that he would call within a week and they would meet so that he could explain what he wanted in the film. A week passed but he didn't call. One week turned to two. A worry began to gnaw at Binod's insides. Then, while lying in bed and reading the newspaper, he glanced at the horoscopes and came across this forecast for his week ahead: "Change is in the air. However, your perspective needs adjusting; you should have a more positive outlook. For the most part, luck will be on your side. But when you find yourself running out of luck, remember that you must go looking for it. Saturday is especially good." The thought didn't come immediately to him but within half an hour he had decided that he would travel to Patna to meet Mala Srivastava's family.

If he could get a reservation on the train for the coming Saturday, it would be a good omen. But the agent said that there were no seats left for Saturday. Still, he was determined and, in the end, having paid an extra 150 rupees, Binod got what he wanted.

2

Binod became a journalist because he had been made to read George Orwell in school. What drew him to Orwell, more than the lucid essays about killing an elephant in Burma or the argument for clarity in the English language, was the happy discovery that the British writer had been born in Motihari. Orwell's mother had given birth to him in 1903 in the same hospital where Binod had arrived several decades later. This knowledge made Binod think of Orwell as someone who was related to him, as if the two of them belonged to the same caste.

But the reason that he began to write editorials had more to do with his father.

There was much that irked Baba. A wind from Antarctica was sucking all the rain out of Australia. Frogs had fallen from the sky in the state of Connecticut in America. A man in China had been arrested for poisoning a reservoir of drinking water in order to boost sales of his water purifiers. In Azamgarh, a man had been declared dead by his uncle, who wanted his property. But the man had fought back. He had formed an Association for Dead People and added the suffix "Mritak" or "Deceased" to his name in all his petitions. It had taken him eighteen years to prove in the courts that he was actually still alive. Baba took note of such things.

He listened to the radio and read newspapers and magazines, despite his bad eyes, in an organized effort to find out everything that was wrong with the world. And then when his own body began to harbor the illness, when he realized that death was what was corroding the planet, a deadly cancer turning the earth's landmass to a putrefying mess, changing the color of its rivers and oceans, he refined his search. He now spoke of the democracy of death and comforted himself by showing how it touched everyone big and small.

On the train a year back, when returning to Patna from Delhi where they had gone to see a doctor at the All India Institute for Medical Sciences, he told Binod a story about Mahatma Gandhi's death. There was a goat whose milk Gandhi drank each morning. The day that Gandhi was killed, no one in the country cooked any food. In Birla House in Delhi, the servants' quarters overlooked the garden where Nathuram Godse had pumped three bullets into the Mahatma's chest. Dough had been rolled in the kitchen earlier for rotis and then left untouched. During the night Gandhi's goat pushed its head through the kitchen door and ate all the dough. By morning the goat was dead from a bloated stomach. Its eyes had popped out.

On that journey, Baba was telling Binod this story in a rattling train carriage, his wasted body spread out on the berth. There is nothing louder than a train compartment, but the passengers around them spoke in soft whispers and listened quietly when Baba spoke. Binod hated the knowledge that he saw in other people's eyes and the way it made them behave differently with his father. But Baba was happy, it seemed, bringing the news from the other side.

Now Binod was returning to Patna with a secret ambition in his heart. He had fallen asleep on his berth, lulled by the motion and the cool night air. The train had stopped in the dark but because nobody was selling anything, no one asserting at two or three o'clock at night his fundamental right to sell you a crooked miniature stone replica of the Taj Mahal or badly made tea in a clay kulhar, he had woken up with the bizarre thought that they had been held up because someone on the train had died.

There was nothing to do but keep lying on the berth listening to strangers snoring or coughing in the compartment. The night was full of sighs.

At home, Baba was on his back, a sheet from the day's newspaper pressed close to his face. The ashen look on his unshaven cheeks hadn't been there before and his left arm was swollen because of an allergic reaction to some new injection. Binod waited inside the doorway, the suitcase on the floor beside him. When he went closer to his father and touched his feet, Baba began to talk almost immediately about what he was reading. So much uncertainty had entered Iraq; to add to the confusion of war, there were rumors everywhere. Smelling of the train, Binod just sat on the chair and listened.

"When we were children," Baba said, "we would hear about Baghdad in the stories from *Arabian Nights*. The cruelty of the king and the stories told by the vizier's daughter. Who can tell what is true or not in Iraq today? In Baghdad, people are saying that the Americans have been burning Iraqi currency and there will be no money left in the country. There will be no

14

business and no work. The tigers kept as pets by Uday Hussein are running loose in the streets."

There was the rumor that Israelis were buying real estate in Iraq just as they had done in Palestine. This was reported in the news as a story that was definitely not true. Baba had heard on BBC radio that there was a riot in Pakistan following a report that American soldiers were selling porn to Iraqi schoolgirls.

Binod cleared his throat. But Baba didn't look at him. He said that journalists should write why people resort to spreading stories. He wanted to know what Binod thought about torture in Abu Ghraib—and then didn't wait for an answer. Perhaps mistaking Binod's silence for disagreement he had begun to speak more loudly: "There must have been talk on the street long before the world heard about them. But even those who had believed the rumors couldn't have imagined the grinning face of Lynndie England. Her hands cocked at naked prisoners, her hands on her breasts, the interpreter asking the Iraqis to masturbate."

Binod was certain that his father had never in his presence used that last word before. It made him sad to think that these are the small ways in which a grown man discovers that his father is dying. He wanted to ask his father if the pain in his chest had increased or if he had been taking his medicines regularly. But he didn't because it would mean that he was acknowledging that Baba was in need of care and he himself wasn't there to help. He ought to tell his father about his interest in Mala Srivastava, he thought to himself, and then decided against it. Baba had made a few government-sponsored documentary films in his life; his interest in the song-and-dance routines of Hindi films was close to zero. How could Binod mention Vikas Dhar to him?

Baba would have much preferred that Binod be a writer. The models he had in mind, like his clothes, were more than a little worn out. The rest of India might be full of talk about young writers like Arundhati Roy but Baba's admiration was reserved for Munshi Premchand. He was the man who had given birth to realism in Hindi writing—and he had failed as a scriptwriter in Bombay! Premchand had died within a year or two of Baba's birth, but it was as if he had become even bigger after his death. In fact, Baba believed that Premchand could have won the Nobel Prize for his stories if the Swedish Academy had known of a language called Hindi. But it wasn't simply the language; the world's injustice went deeper. Baba also could not understand why Winston Churchill had been awarded the

Nobel Prize for literature and not Jawaharlal Nehru. Nehru's *Autobiography* and his *Discovery of India* had sat on a shelf in the house in Patna all through Binod's youth. They had only one bookshelf and it was placed in the living room. A visitor would sometimes step closer and look at the books there. Bertrand Russell, Gandhi, Nehru, Mulk Raj Anand, Hazari Prasad Dwivedi, Mahadevi Verma, Pearl S. Buck, Hemingway. On more than one occasion, Baba would turn to a visitor and declare, "Nehru's fluency in English was unmatched by any other Indian before or after Independence."

While Gandhi's body lay surrounded by mourners at Birla House, Nehru had addressed the nation on All India Radio. His speech was delivered in English and without any notes: "The light has gone out of our lives and there is darkness everywhere. Our beloved leader, Bapu, as we called him, the father of the nation, is no more. The light has gone out, I said, and yet I was wrong. For the light that has shone in this country was no ordinary light . . . For that light represented something more than the immediate present; it represented the living, the eternal truths, reminding us of the right path, drawing us from error, taking this ancient country to freedom."

....

The next day Binod went looking for the house in which Mala Srivastava's mother lived. But the astrological forecast on which he had pinned his hopes hadn't held true. The visit didn't go well. Mala's younger sister had been suspicious, and Binod had been able to say nothing to quiet her fears.

Later that same afternoon, Binod went to see Bua. She was Baba's younger sister and a prominent politician. Her son, Rabinder, was in prison in Hajipur and Binod wanted Bua to arrange a visit. He didn't tell Bua that he had heard that Surajdeo Tripathi, Mala's paramour, had been sent to the same prison in Hajipur after his arrest.

The minister for home and prisons in the Bihar cabinet was Kishen Murari Thakur. Bua knew him well from his days as a student leader. She called Kishen Murari's secretary on the phone. Her voice was louder than usual because that's what happened when she pretended that she was being ingratiating, especially in conversation with those whom she regarded as her social inferiors. Later, she said to Binod that the minister was in his forties and had been an agitator twenty years ago. There was something mocking in her tone. "He belongs to the barber caste," she said with a thin smile. "His father still has a hair-cutting place in Siwan."

Before dusk, Binod arrived at Kishen Murari's bungalow. He was taken inside and asked to sit on a metal chair in the living room. Outside on the verandah, there were other men waiting quietly with the uncertain look of poor relatives at a wedding. After a while, a small man with glasses returned and without saying anything handed Binod a letter in a brown envelope, and with that simple act erased the humiliation and anxiety that had remained with Binod ever since he stepped off the stairway that had led to the flat above Harward Public School.

....

In bed that night, Binod decided he would first stop at the Hanuman Mandir in the morning to pick up a box of sweets for his cousin.

Rabinder loved the laddoos from the temple; they were exceedingly sweet and likely to crumble easily in the mouth. He was devoted to Hanuman. Even inside InTouch, the cybercafe he owned, which was described in the Patna press after his arrest as an "Internet brothel," there was a gilt-framed picture of his favorite deity. You entered through the front door and found you were looking at a large, horizontal, full-length painting of the airborne Lord Hanuman. The puffed cheeks and thin forehead under a gold crown; the brown eyes staring resolutely ahead; a muscular left arm, bristly with yellow hairs, supporting a huge round club above which curled the long tail; silken shorts drawn tight over the private parts of the divine simian form. On his upturned right palm, Hanuman bore aloft a whole green-colored mountain on which grew a magical plant; small silver sequins were stuck to the plant and they winked in the light.

Rabinder prayed each morning and, on Tuesdays and Saturdays, which were special to Lord Hanuman, he prayed also at night. That is what Binod always remembered when he thought of Rabinder. Sitting in a corner in the different rooms that they had shared during their youth, his voice rattling in a quick, subdued monotone. Rabinder never turned his head while at puja, yet his eyes would be alert and mobile, noting everything that Binod was doing. He would rock back and forth slightly, never pausing in his chanting of the prayer, his voice rising and racing whenever he stumbled over his lines.

Over the last several years, Rabinder had made a habit of coming up with a fresh scheme every few weeks and he always consulted astrologers about auspicious dates. During his more frantic phases, Rabinder would appear wound up and anxious, making countless trips to the homes of political leaders and senior bureaucrats and, deep into the night, haggling on the phone with middlemen over amounts to be paid as bribes. When a particularly important plan was to be hatched, his wrist would be bright with red and yellow strings tied by the head priests of all his favorite local temples.

3

His father's driver was taking Binod to Hajipur Jail.

At the mouth of the bridge over the Ganges, there was a long line of cars and buses waiting to pay the toll. In the distance, on the other side of the river, banana fields stretched in both directions. The morning heat had formed a thin blanket of mist over the green leaves of the banana trees. A bus moved up and parked next to the Maruti and men got down to stretch their legs or to urinate by the roadside.

Loud music blared out from the bus. The song was in Bhojpuri and it had been set to a popular Hindi film tune. "Kaka hamaar vidhayak hauein, Nahin daraaib ho / Eh double chotiwaali, tohke taang le jayab ho!" (My uncle is a legislator, I will have no fear / You, with the two plaits, I will snatch you, my dear!) The song went on jauntily. The singer, the would-be abductor, was telling the girl that he had a lot of money and police protection. He would take the girl on a trip to Russia.

Then all at once a line of Jeeps and motorcycles roared past. The Jeeps had flags fluttering from the front and posters of Sonia Gandhi hanging on the side. A couple of the men on the motorcycles were holding guns. The ruling BJP had lost badly, and the Congress was lining up its allies. It was likely that the next day Sonia would become the prime minister. These men were headed to a rally. They didn't need to pay the toll.

It was a little past ten when Binod arrived at the large metal gate of the prison. He had the letter that he needed to give to the jail authorities. The head constable said that the superintendent, Mr. Prasad, prayed longer on Tuesday mornings and would be late.

Binod was asked to wait in the office. There was no one else there and it was as if he had been given a refuge. The heat was no longer bearing down on him, and the noise came as if from a distance, the voices of the guards calling out to prisoners who had visitors.

The room was bare except for a large desk and two chairs, and a faded portrait of Mahatma Gandhi. The moisture from the wall had seeped into the frame, and it hung over a sign that had been painted on the wall in black: *I am only a prisoner of truth. M. K. Gandhi. Father of the Nation.*

More than thirty minutes passed.

Binod fought the temptation to eat a laddoo from the box that he had brought. Once or twice, a head would appear at the door and then retreat wordlessly behind the curtain. Metal clanged. The heat grew, like a headache, gaining intensity. The voices of the guards still called out the names of prisoners. Mr. Prasad came presently. He was a middle-aged man with thick sideburns, wearing a printed red shirt and trousers that flared. At first, Binod thought that the superintendent had a thick layer of talcum powder on his face and neck, but it soon became clear that he had an ailment and had applied a white cream on the fiery red patches on his skin. While reading the letter he nodded his head a few times, as if he were listening to someone speaking in his ear. Then, after a long pause, he pressed the green tab of the bell on his desk and asked a guard to take Binod up to Rabinder's cell.

....

Rabinder gave a short laugh when he saw Binod, and then said, "Live from Bombay! Our film reporter Binod Singh!"

Binod laughed too and then looked back at the guard. Rabinder asked the man with a smile, "Khan sahib, under which offense have you arrested and brought this good citizen?" The guard was dwarfed by Rabinder's size. He folded his hands in a humble greeting and retreated from the room.

The cell was a dormitory room. There were no chairs or beds, only blankets rolled against the wall. It is possible that at night at least a dozen people slept there; four men, huddled at the opposite end of the room, got up and left when Binod entered with the guard. Rabinder's mattress occupied a large corner on the floor next to the window. There were film magazines and a Hindi newspaper stacked near his pillow. Binod's eyes stayed longer on a book that lay with its face down on the bed. Its glossy cover had the title printed in bold yellow against a background of black—*How to Make a Habit of Success.*

Rabinder looked healthy. His white kurta was a concession perhaps to the uniform of the prisoners. Rabinder was four years younger than Binod; in imitation of his older cousin, he called his own mother Bua. This was a childhood habit. He called Binod's parents Ma and Baba. He asked about Baba's health. And then he said, a bit awkwardly, pausing more than once, "Baba tries hard to be patient with me, at least most of the time, but Ma loves me the same way that she loves you."

Rabinder began to tell a story. A year or two after he had left Bettiah and begun going to school in Patna, he failed in two subjects. English and math. Bua was away at that time. When Rabinder showed the report card to Baba, he took off his glasses and calmly predicted that he was going to end up as a beggar on the street. That same evening, when Ma came back from her work at the school, she began to help him with his homework. They were reading a story by Tagore in class. Ma pointed out to him that the great Bengali writer had his name.

"I remember it very clearly because it was the first time," Rabinder said, "that anyone had told me about the Nobel Prize." There was no trace of self-consciousness about the setting in which he was telling Binod this story. He said, "She taught me that I could do anything I wanted."

Binod said, "Baba is dying and he has begun to look like Saddam Hussein when he was arrested."

Baba didn't allow the barber who came to their house during the illness to shave him regularly. His hair was also unkempt. Back during Dussehra last year, he had gone with Binod to the Kalyan Clinic and Hospital, and doctors there had shone torches in his mouth and eyes and ordered more tests. Binod was trying to tell Rabinder that when you are in love even the sight of ordinary things and ordinary people reminds you of your beloved. It is the same when someone close to you is dying. Ever since Baba had started undergoing chemotherapy, every object and person in the world seemed radioactive with death's eternal presence. The sight on the television screen of a former dictator opening his mouth to be examined by an American military doctor had moved Binod to tears.

Rabinder sat listening quietly with his eyes lowered, looking at the pattern on his bed. His broad mattress was covered with a bright, floral bed sheet. The sunlight flooded in and striped the bed with the straight lines of the window bars. The geometry of light and shade relieved the gloom in the room.

....

Binod had been surprised to see Rabinder holding a mobile phone in his right hand; it was tiny and silver in color. He told Rabinder that he didn't know prison rules permitted mobile phones. Rabinder said, "They don't. Let's just say that this is a very expensive phone. But low roaming charges, of course."

Rabinder held up his mobile in front of his face. He said, "Most of the people in the world have never made a telephone call in their lives. But the world is changing . . ." There was a bright future in telephones in India, especially mobile phones because it took such a long time for the government to provide phone lines. "When I get out of this bahenchod place," he said, "I'm going to buy a phone agency in Patna."

Rabinder asked Binod when he was going back to Bombay. Rabinder said, "I want to discuss an important matter with you, but first—" He took the box of laddoos and placed it in front of a small shrine he had made near his mattress; there was a picture of Hanuman, and small postcard-sized painted pictures of Durga and Shiva. Rabinder shut his eyes and bowed his head. Scraping some of the vermilion off the box with the ring finger of his right hand, he applied the paste to his forehead. He offered Binod a laddoo before putting two together into his mouth. He was happy and smiled easily. He said, "When you go to Bombay, I want you to think about an idea I have."

Rabinder always had ideas. He nursed wild fantasies that came pre-packaged with promises of fulfillment. Even when they were kids, Rabinder's optimism scared Binod. He remained silent but Rabinder barely seemed to notice that his cousin was again holding back. Rabinder said, "I have a proposal for a television commercial. If I am going to put money in the phone business, I'd like to sell my idea to some big mobile phone company. If truth be told, but you must keep this a secret, I want to use this opportunity to learn about how films get made in Bombay."

Binod felt a jolt. The script had been reversed. It was as if Binod were hearing an echo of his own voice, a few times more powerful, and he flinched a bit as if from a hurt. He had come to Rabinder to talk about Vikas Dhar. Binod was going to write the story for a film. It was his secret, and he had wanted to share it with his cousin. But it was Rabinder who had boldly made the demand.

The commercial would begin with a shot of a blue-green planet afloat in dark space. Then, with instant thousand-fold magnification, the camera would digitally zoom into that part of the landmass in the northern hemisphere that lies above the Indian Ocean, the subcontinent flecked closer to the top of the screen by the white crest of a wave representing the Himalayan snow-covered peaks. The camera would veer right, coming closer to the ground to reveal, for one-five-hundredth of a second, the muddy expanse of the Ganges, and then fanning above it a city visible only as a dirty wash of miniature roof tops, their color a uniform gray. Binod saw very clearly in his mind the spreading delta of underdevelopment; almost despite himself, he smiled.

And Rabinder, getting more excited, said that the camera would be at ground level now, approaching a heavily loaded Ashok Leyland truck on the highway: as it got close to the truck, a white Maruti would zoom out from behind the truck. A few drops of rain would fall on the lens as the camera swerved, forcing a policeman on his bicycle into a puddle. The man would be wearing his khaki uniform and a red cap. The camera would avoid hitting the bicycle and, almost within that same instant, its eye would pick out a large yellow building. There would be a short pan along the length of a tall wall before pausing at a barred room in which would be a solitary man, sitting. The film would cut to a shot from above: the top of the man's head and, pressed to his right ear, a mobile phone. The place would be a prison near Patna.

"What do you think?" Rabinder asked.

Binod said that the idea was a good one but asked why the prison was necessary.

Rabinder had a question in return, "Honestly, can you think of any place where a mobile phone would be more needed that it is in prison?"

After a moment, Rabinder asked Binod to think of filmmakers in Bombay so that the commercial could be made as soon as he got out of prison. It seemed that he would finance the production himself. There was no doubt in his mind that the best man to act in the commercial would be his friend, the actor Neeraj Dubey. Rabinder and Dubey had been classmates in KR School in Bettiah since they were eight.

Rabinder also had a great enthusiasm for the romance depicted in Bollywood films. He said that the commercial could show a woman at the other end. Her face would first become visible through a glass pane that was streaked with rain, like tears running down a face. She would half-turn her face away from the camera and part her lips to say something that the viewer would not hear because of the sound of the music beating like waves on a beach. The woman's role would go to Manisha Koirala — or even Raveena Tandon because she had acted with Dubey many times and they had developed a rapport. The song on the soundtrack, filled with yearning and promise, would be A. R. Rehman's hit from Mani Ratnam's popular film Bombay. "Tu hee re, Tu hee re . . . tere bina main kaise jeeoon."

4

A teenage boy with shiny eyes brought them tea. He returned later with plates of food, looking almost like a waiter in his convict's clothes. It was a vegetarian meal and had been cooked on a small coal chulha in the corridor outside the wards.

While they were eating, Binod asked, almost casually, "Is Surajdeo Tripathi inside here?"

Rabinder waited a second before replying. "He is in Block Four . . . A born prick. If a dog could be dressed up in a silk shirt and trained to work as a pimp, you would get Surajdeo Tripathi."

Binod said, "I take it he's not your friend."

Rabinder's face showed dismay. Binod quickly explained that he was asking only because he had run into a problem. He told Rabinder about his experience with Mala's sister. Rabinder said, "It is a misunderstanding. I'll arrange a meeting. No problem." He added, "I could get you inside Surajdeo's cell today. But he'll tell you nothing. He'll only talk of conspiracy, he'll tell you lies. You'll come away with a bagful of empty words."

Rabinder had finished his meal quickly and was sucking on the lime pickle on his plate. Binod had still not mentioned Vikas Dhar's phone call and the reason why he was interested in Mala and Surajdeo. He was thinking about how he would broach the subject when Rabinder said wrestling bouts were held in the prison every Tuesday and Saturday.

Those days were chosen because they were consecrated to Lord Hanuman, who was of course worshipped for his strength. The bouts were held in a small akhara that had been dug to the right of Rabinder's cell block. He had been one of the main supporters of the idea and had spoken to the officials. The matches would begin in the afternoon; it was something for them to look forward to as soon as lunch was over.

Then, hesitantly, as if he himself didn't believe it, Binod began to tell his cousin about the real reason he was in Patna. Rabinder's eyes twinkled. He patted his stomach and emitted a low giggle. He said, "Bhaiya, this is a very good period. Jupiter and Venus are coming together soon. You must not let this chance get away from you!"

He took off his kurta and sat down on the mattress, his legs neatly folded in a lotus posture. His right hand raised as if he were delivering a sermon, he said, "Surajdeo is just a two-bit pimp. He made his money through railway fraud. I had met Mala a couple of times. She was just a girl on the make. If I found her boring after two minutes, why will the audience love her for three hours?"

Binod listened carefully.

"Do you understand what I'm saying to you? There is no need for you to meet Surajdeo. You want to see what a criminal looks like? Take a walk on any street of Patna and look at the people around you. I'm not saying everyone is a criminal—but surely you know that a murderer also has a nose and eyes and ears . . . You must write a story for Dhar. But it should be a romance. The people in it should have some weight, but they should also have the lightness that everyone finds so very appealing. Two young people singing songs."

Binod nodded. Rabinder, satisfied, took his arm. "Let's go and watch some wrestling."

When they were coming down the staircase, Binod noticed the tall brick wall with razor wire nearby. Rabinder smiled. He said, "The female wards are on the other side. It is easier to escape from this jail than to cross over to the wards where the women are."

Although Rabinder had been imprisoned several times, people would often come to Baba with marriage proposals for their daughters. These parents of young women calculated that, given his political connections, Rabinder would always have money. They might have reasoned that once he was married he would settle down.

In Patna, where he entered college after returning from Delhi, Rabinder always had admirers among his female classmates. The real surprise for Binod was that in a place like that, Rabinder's interactions with girls had a quality of ease. Timid nineteen-year-olds in his class, girls who had probably only ever spoken to their male relatives, called him at home and wanted to know if he had watched the new Govinda film or if he had any idea what questions they would be asked in the political science exam.

There was the incident with Sujata Nanda. She was the daughter of a prominent orthopedic surgeon in Patna. She organized small get-togethers in the restaurants on Fraser Road and Rabinder would join her friends for a couple of hours. Binod had once asked Rabinder if Sujata

had ever been his girlfriend and he had said, "No, no. She is a good girl."
One day Rabinder learned that a classmate called Amit Suri had started
leaving love letters for Sujata on her desk in college. Suri was a fashionable young man with odd, golden-brown hair. His family owned the Brite
White Dry Cleaners on Jagjiwan Ram Road. The matter took a more serious turn when one day Suri caught hold of Sujata's wrist just as she was
about to get into her car. He wanted to know why she hadn't replied.

Sujata was too scared to say anything to Rabinder, but he heard about
it anyway. The next day he waited at Gopi's tea stall located just inside
the college gate on Ashok Rajpath. When Amit Suri arrived in his cream
Esteem, Rabinder went up to the car and asked Suri for a matchbox. Instead of lighting one match, Rabinder lit all the sticks in it and thrust
them into Suri's nostrils.

Binod remembered that it was Arpana who had told him this story.
She had laughed at the look of horror on his face. This was a little before
Arpana and Binod had ended their marriage. She had said that she really
liked Rabinder. When he asked her why, Arpana said Rabinder did not
ever hide his feelings.

Standing alongside his cousin at the edge of the wrestling pit in Hajipur Jail, Binod found himself thinking of what Arpana had said, and
he couldn't help observing to himself that all around him right there
were people who had been unable in one way or another to hide their
feelings.

....

The pit was fairly small, about twelve feet by fifteen feet. Yet, at least forty
prisoners were sitting on the ground around it and the rest stood three or
four deep in a large, engulfing circle. Half a dozen bare-bodied men were
standing in the sand, at the pit's edge, rubbing mustard oil and fistfuls of
dirt on each other. A transistor was playing loudly in the distance. Binod
could not see a prison guard anywhere.

A small Hanuman temple was under construction in the very center of
the prison's main yard. To its right was a guard post that was currently
empty. Rabinder dragged out a tiny desk and chair that had been inside
the post and placed them under a neem tree. Binod stood on the desk
while Rabinder balanced himself on the chair. They were shaded from the
sun and eager for the match to start.

A heavily built young man with a crooked jaw appeared beside them
with a whistle in his mouth. This was apparently the referee. Despite his

crooked features, his face had a boyish charm. The man had been a history student in Delhi but had fallen in with bad company. Rabinder said this in a tone that was intended to illuminate life's deep and amusing mysteries. He told the youth that if he ate less he would arrive at the events on time. The fellow asked in response, "Bhaiya, did you hear about the batsman in the Zimbabwe side who was mocked by an Australian? I think it was McGrath. He would send down a ball and then ask the batsman, 'How come you are so fat?' At last the man replied, 'Because your wife gives me a biscuit every time I fuck her.'"

Rabinder laughed loudly. He said, "Okay, go now. Let's start."

Two men had already stepped into the pit. Both of them were well built, but one was at least a foot taller than the other. Brown dust coated their dark bodies. Even their eyebrows and moustaches had dirt on them. When the referee blew the whistle, the two wrestlers circled for a while and then leaned into each other almost casually, one hand placed on the opponent's neck and the other intertwined with the other's hand.

It was a kind of lazy ballet. But the men were sweating profusely; there were dark patches on both bodies where through the dirt the skin glistened with oil and sweat. Binod could hear their labored breathing.

Rabinder said, "See the short one. He is a prison guard. The other one is a Kurmi who killed a Naxalite peasant." The murdered man was an untouchable; he had only been demanding his legal wage. Binod had expected the crowd to be cheering for the prisoner but there was no display of partisanship. Rabinder said that the guard was popular among the prisoners because he was a very good wrestler. He had once made it to the Asian Games trial. Rabinder said, "He was getting ready for the flight to Kuala Lumpur. But they sent another man from an akhara in Delhi."

After all the wary circling and the heaving and the grunting, the bout was decided very quickly. The guard had got his opponent's upper body in a tight grip: the struggle was now over the lower half of their bodies. The shouting increased. The taller man had long, powerful thighs, and it was his right thigh that seemed to have become the pivot of the struggle. Binod realized this only when he saw the man's leg buckle a little and then watched the quivering muscle of the thigh. A moment or two later, the man was down, flat on his back.

A big cheer went up.

The crowd of spectators had magically doubled while the match was in progress. Rabinder stepped down from his tiny perch. Binod jumped down too. Rabinder said, "Well-fought match. Last week, our champion had hurt his shoulder and I had some fears that he would disappoint you, but he did well."

Two men passed them carrying buckets of water to wash down the wrestlers. A fresh bout involving lesser fighters would start in a little while.

The late afternoon sun was still very hot but a breeze stirred the leaves of the neem tree. The contest they had witnessed had left both of them feeling excited and even a little elated. Rabinder was smiling. They walked a few paces in the yard and then Binod said he must soon be going. Rabinder stopped in the middle of the yard and faced his cousin. He said, "While we were standing at the pit, I was thinking about what you must do. If you consider what Vikas Dhar wants, a story about the life in small towns and a woman's lonely ambition—shouldn't you be writing Bua's story instead? I'm not saying that because she's my mother. But just think—"

Yes, yes, Binod said to himself. But lightness? And romance?

He stayed silent.

Rabinder smiled and said, "The only problem with this story would be that you wouldn't get to use your imagination. And how much fun would that be? Anyway, let's go and—"

He rapped on the small metal door. A face peered from a window and then the door swung open. In the cavernous hallway, naked bulbs were suspended from the roof from dark, coiled wires. Guards in khaki shorts stood quietly in the shadows as if it were they who were the prisoners. Rabinder accompanied Binod to Superintendent Prasad's office to help him sign out. Rabinder's smiling, coercive presence meant that Mr. Prasad had to be friendly with Binod and urge him that during his next visit to Hajipur he should save time for dinner. Then he was back on the road to Patna, the car's windows down, the wind bringing him the smell of rot from the river.

....

Ma had always been of the belief that it was Bua's entry into politics that had turned Rabinder into a thug. Baba wanted to defend his sister and dismissed such suggestions. Baba believed in character and, more than that, in destiny. To prove his thesis he would just as regularly repeat the details of the incident of the little girl in Siwan.

Rabinder must have been twelve at that time because Binod remembered that he himself was about to finish school in Patna. Rabinder's father, Lalji, was still alive at that time and in the asylum in Ranchi. The man who was getting married was Lalji's nephew, and Bua had taken Rabinder and Binod with her to Motihari. She stayed back there but Binod and Rabinder went with the rest of the male relatives in the baraat party for the wedding in Siwan.

In the wedding procession, as was customary, the band played in the front, and then the youths followed in a group, dancing and setting off crackers. There were also a few people with rifles and guns, and their responsibility was to fire in the air at regular intervals. The groom followed in a white flower-bedecked Ambassador. There were one or two other vehicles behind them, but most of the other two hundred guests made their way on foot, using the light from the dozen Petromax lamps in the procession to avoid the piles of rubbish that were spaced like sentries on the narrow street.

The baraat party was staying in that venerable institution of lower-middle-class hospitality called the dharamshala. Built by religious-minded Marwari philanthropists fifty or more years ago, their unassailable dullness in each small town in Bihar was a rebuke to the ambitions of the discipline of architecture. Along with the others who had come from Motihari, Binod and Rabinder spent several hours that evening in the designated dharamshala in Siwan. There had been a delay. The bus that had been contracted to bring the baraat party had arrived on time, but the Ambassador had developed some engine trouble on the way. It reached Siwan at last but first it had to be washed. Fresh garlands of tuberose and marigold woven with little threads of tinsel had to be draped over its sides. As a result, it wasn't until nine in the evening that the wedding procession began to make its way to the bride's house.

During the entire bus journey from Motihari to Siwan, Rabinder had been very pleased to hold a twelve-bore gun that belonged to one of Lalji's cousins. He repeatedly passed his finger over the place where the manufacturer's name had been engraved. W. W. Greener, England. Its owner, Shravan, was a lab assistant for a physician in Motihari but had bought the weapon to scare the peasants who worked on his land in the village.

Once the procession had set off from the dharamshala, Rabinder had to give up the gun. But just as soon as they were in sight of the bride's home, its walls lit up by the bright bulbs and the fluorescent tubes wrapped in colored transparent foil, Rabinder couldn't hold himself back. He had no desire that evening to join the dancers; he wanted to use the gun just once. He said to Shravan, "Chachaji, can I have the gun?"

Shravan was a very tall, thin man with a large Adam's apple. He had been drinking at the dharamshala while waiting for the Ambassador to arrive with the groom. When he looked at Rabinder, he probably saw an orphan, which is what a boy whose father had long been locked up in a mental hospital must have meant to him. Taking pity on the boy, he gave the weapon, only saying, "Be careful."

All around them firecrackers exploded in loud bursts. One of Rabinder's relatives, a youth in an orange shirt, fired a round from a double-barreled gun. Rabinder was holding the gun the same way he had seen dacoits and gangsters handling them in Hindi films. But when he squeezed the trigger, the gun jumped and swayed. He saw the sparks above him but did not hear what Shravan was shouting because of the ringing in his ear.

The sparks were actually from an electric transformer high on the poles above the street. The bullet had been deflected to the transformer after passing through the gullet of a seven-year-old girl who had been in her father's arms because she was scared of the firecrackers. She was the daughter of another of Lalji's nephews, a man who was a teller in the Muzaffarpur branch of the Punjab National Bank. The girl's name was Sushma and she was dead before she reached the hospital. When they took her away, Binod heard her father say repeatedly between sobs, "What face will I show her mother?"

The firecrackers were still going off in loud bursts ahead of and behind them. Many people in the wedding procession didn't know about the accident, and the elders in the party decided that there was no reason to make a general announcement. The bride's father was not in good health. Their family had been interested in arranging the marriage quickly so that everything could be over before his situation worsened. And it was the people from the bride's family who then helped deal with the hospital and also the law. The bride's older brother-in-law was a road-building contractor. At his request, the local MP, Rizwan Ahmad, made a call to the director-general of Police and ensured that no police case was filed. Everyone was grateful for the help.

Many people from the groom's family left the town the next morning by train, everyone returning to their own homes in different parts of Bihar. Binod and Rabinder returned in the half-empty bus to Motihari where, from the expression on Bua's face, it was clear that she had already been told about what had happened. She said nothing to Rabinder and perhaps as a result of that he felt he could not ever speak to her about it. Later, whenever Binod thought about what had happened, he realized that although he had been a witness to the incident, even he had never once heard Rabinder talk about it.

II

‹❋›

Ulan Bator

at Night

5

At dinner that night, Ma sat at the table with him, barely eating, listening to what he told her about Rabinder's plans. She sighed and said, "He changes his mind all the time. Just before he was arrested he told me that he was going to start a health spa in Patna."

Binod laughed. It probably wasn't Rabinder's fault. There were so few things in Patna and so little certainty that if you thought of yourself as an entrepreneur you were bound to be drawn by all kinds of possibilities. Each prospect appeared tantalizing. A gym, a health spa, an ice-cream parlor, a video-lending store, telephone booths, a travel agency, a place to buy books.

Ma said, "I had taken him to a pundit who recommended that he wear a topaz. He has it on a gold ring but I don't see it doing any good."

Then she said that Bua had called and wanted him to visit her house before eleven that night. At ten, Bua's Ambassador, white with a red light on its roof, arrived to take Binod to her place. The traffic was thin on Bailey Road and, as was his habit, he checked the Amul butter billboard there. The new ad was about Sonia Gandhi listening to her inner voice. Bua's house was only five minutes from there.

Bua was twelve years younger than Baba. Another daughter had been born to their parents in between, but she had died from diphtheria when she was a year old. Bua was only twenty-two when her husband, Lalji, fell ill and then she moved to Patna with Rabinder, who was very young at that time. During the first year of Lalji's stay in the mental asylum in Ranchi, some money came to Bua from his family, but then it stopped. It was as if in the middle of the afternoon someone had turned off a switch somewhere, and you had to wait with dread for the hours of the evening when darkness arrived. Manik, Lalji's nephew, had tampered with the court records and had got nearly everything transferred to his name. Bua now owned nothing that had belonged to her husband. Baba made more than one trip to Motihari to ask for what he felt was rightfully Bua's but he didn't have much success and he stopped going.

Bua also grew opposed to such missions. This was because on one of the trips to Motihari, the bus in which Baba had been traveling met with an accident. The driver had been sick with malaria; it was the conductor who was driving. He was nervous about the task and had therefore got drunk. The bus went off the road and smashed headlong into a peepul tree and the peepul's trunk got buried six feet inside the bus. Eleven passengers died. Baba escaped with a broken arm and an injury on the head from a small tin of Dalda oil. Ma heard the news from a relative who used to commute to Patna. The news unhinged her. She blamed Bua, saying that she had brought ill luck. Bua had made herself a widow and was now going to do the same to her. Because Binod used to sleep on the same bed as Bua and Rabinder, he heard her crying that night. She sobbed as if she were alone. This was nothing like the crying she did when she watched films in the cinema hall. She would wear glasses at the theater, and her cheeks would glisten with tears. But on the bed that night a different noise came from her direction; it resembled the sound a person made when trying to blow a paper boat on water.

....

The industries minister Parshuram Singh and Bua were on the sofa facing the door. A man who was responsible for the construction of irrigation canals all over Bihar was perched on a seat next to them. The hangers-on were not so large in number. There was a Maharashtrian officer, a Dalit, who headed the Handicrafts Department, and three others who looked familiar but whom Binod didn't remember meeting. He went up to Bua and touched her feet. He then bowed to Parshuram and touched his chest in a vague gesture that was meant to be respectful.

Bua got up and said, "Binod, come with me for a minute . . ."

In the hallway outside her bedroom, she asked about the meeting with Rabinder. Binod smiled. He said that Rabinder had looked good. Bua nodded but remained quiet. On the wall near his face, tribals danced with flowers in their hair, their arms interlinked, a picture of the perfectly happy nation. After a moment, Bua said, "Okay, then. I know you're leaving tomorrow and I'll be busy all day. The political situation is . . . well, you know how things are at the moment. But call me on my mobile if you need anything. It's not too late yet. Sit down with us for a bit before you leave."

Back in the living room, Bua turned to Parshuram and said that Binod was doing well as a reporter in Bombay.

Parshuram nodded and said in a low, world-weary voice, "It is a wonderful profession. It is the only way we have to keep a check on politicians."

Parshuram was from a land-owning family, the token upper-caste member of the cabinet. In his youth, he was a follower of the socialist Lohia. A bit of bohemia clung to him still: he kept his white, wavy hair long, and liked to keep a silk shawl on his shoulder. The people in the room listened to him with quiet respect and, during the silence that followed his remark, Parshuram reached over to where Bua sat, took the corner of her sari in his right hand, and began to rub it on the lens of his spectacles.

Binod turned his gaze away. There had been talk about a relationship between Bua and Parshuram for the past four or five years — she had been a widow for nearly two decades now and he had been a lifelong bachelor — but neither of them spoke about it or had acknowledged it by getting married. Bihari society was conservative; it was also corrupt, hollow to its core; you put a finger on its thin, distended skin and it split under your touch, revealing white worms. But Binod could never gather the courage to ask Bua why she encouraged gossip.

There had been an incident two years ago at a head-shaving ceremony of the grandson of the police inspector-general. Baba had been among the hundreds who had been invited. He ran into Lalji's nephew, Manik, the same man who now owned Bua's property in Chapwa. Manik had become a businessman, a contractor who took on government projects; like everyone else, he did little work on those projects and shared the profits with the bureaucrats and politicians. At the party Baba was perhaps surprised by his unexpected meeting with Manik: he spoke impulsively to the young man about what was on his mind. He said, "Bhai, when are you all going to get tired with the business of playing around with a widow's property?"

Manik's eyes hardened. He smirked and asked, "Widow? I heard that she has married our honorable industries minister . . . Or have they not been married yet?"

Baba must have been shocked by the remark. But he persisted. He said, "You can throw mud at her. But the fact remains that she has rights to the money you have denied her all these years. Remember there is such a thing as law in this country."

Manik had leered some more. He said, "I respect you but please do not threaten me. I am not a criminal like your nephew Rabinder. Everything I own is legally mine. And unlike Rabinder, my life is not in danger."

Binod imagined the shame—and alarm—that his father must have felt. He was told that Baba had said something about God and justice, and Manik had laughed and walked away. Baba had never spoken to Binod about the incident. It was a relative of theirs who had told him the story. It was the same man who brought Binod the news that Manik had bought an AK-47 from a Nepali dealer and given it as a gift to a legislator friend of his. This legislator, a man with murder charges against him, had been helping Manik acquire road-building contracts in Champaran and Siwan.

This relative of theirs said to Binod with an air of mystery, "Your father has been plotting against Manik for a long time." It thrilled Binod. He saw his father as a fighter and a strategist. But the man said, "Nothing however will come of it. Baba hopes to use the law, and the law is of course useless. The only answer to Manik is Rabinder, but he will have nothing to do with it either."

Defeat was the most likely outcome then, but not without its consolation. It made the vanquished appear noble. Rabinder could now be seen as someone full of restraint and with a strong desire not to see his mother humiliated.

Binod felt that he was back in his village of Ratauli, watching in the white light of the Petromax lamps the enactment of scenes from the Mahabharata. A widow in the public eye and her brave but flawed son were on the one side; ranged in battle against them on the other side was a young and uncouth enemy, a blood relative, who was full of guile and hidden strength. There were other characters too. The widow's paramour, a politician of some importance, and the widow's brother, an old man who used words like culture and justice. Everyone was caught up in the play of larger destinies. So too were the spectators who stood in the shadows, people who were in real life friends and relatives of the ones who moved around on the stage. All night through, like the light from the Petromax lamps, the drama would flare bright and then die.

When Binod was about to leave and saying goodbye, Baba asked him if he had been successful in finding the answers to the questions that had brought him to Patna. Caught by surprise, he said that yes, he had. His mother was crying and he told her he would return soon. She made him lick the bit of curd she was holding on a spoon, the sugar on the top already turning dark.

6

It was past one o'clock but the train didn't move. There was a handcuffed prisoner, a young man with a scruffy beard, sitting on the side berth. Shoulders hunched, he sat between the two constables accompanying him. The youth bought orange lollipops for himself and his companions. A manacled hand went to the breast pocket of his dirty shirt and plucked out a note, and then one of his escorts leaned out of the window and paid the ice-cream vendor. Binod was watching this transaction and therefore didn't notice the dark man till he had come to a stop in front of him, bowing and smiling.

Binod's immediate response was of fear. It was the man from Mala Srivastava's house. He was being deferential now, still in the same black shirt, saying something about Rabinder having called him. He said Usha would have come too but she had already left for college when Rabinder's call came. Of course, that was her name! Usha Srivastava. The man, his mouth red with paan, was saying, "I was supposed to go to Barauni today but I changed plans and came looking for you. It was a misunderstanding, two days ago. Please excuse us."

The man stepped a little closer. The handcuffed youth, licking his orange lollipop, was looking at them. The dark man didn't seem conscious of the other faces looking at him, but his voice dropped to a confidential whisper. He said, "You see, over the past two or three months, Surajdeo has been sending all kinds of people around to the house, with inducements and threats. We didn't know you. And then Rabinder bhaiya called."

"I understand entirely. Please don't worry," Binod said.

The man took out a crumpled piece of paper and held it out. He said, "This is a number. You can call and give them a time. Usha and her mother will be there to answer any questions you have."

Binod thanked the man. He didn't yet know his name. The train lurched, but it was a false alarm. In any case, the man seemed to be in no hurry. Binod said, "It will move soon. I think you should get down."

"Okay," the man said and folded his hands.

Once the train had started moving Binod was glad that he was alone again. He told himself that he would perhaps never call the number. If he was now going to write the story about Bua, as Rabinder had suggested, there was nothing that Usha Srivastava or her mother could tell him about his own aunt.

....

Binod remembered when Bua got married to Lalji. The wedding took place in Patna—he was eight years old—and the groom had arrived on a horse. Lalji was wearing a suit and tie; he sat on the horse with a pink mayur on his head, its silver tassels obscuring his eyes and face. The rest of the evening was a blur. What remained clearly etched in Binod's mind were the horse's head and eyes and its black lips.

He either remembered or had been told that the wedding procession arrived very late at night. He had woken up the next morning and was excited because he was going to accompany Bua to Lalji's house. He had heard that the house was in the middle of a mango orchard.

A man sitting outside on the verandah in their house in Patna was playing the shehnai. Binod could see the man from the window, and also the piece of open ground that stretched behind him, where three men were taking down the shamiana under which Bua had gotten married. A small pile of carpets had already been loaded on a rickshaw. For a moment, he was afraid that they had forgotten about him and that Bua was already gone. But then he saw the green Fiat that belonged to the groom's family parked in the driveway.

Bua could not have left alone with Lalji. A grown-up had probably explained to Binod that the custom was to send away the bride with an ayah and a younger male relative so that she didn't feel lost in the house of her in-laws. Her husband was likely to be a stranger but with her own relative it would be easy for the young bride to cry. Last summer he had accompanied two of his elder cousins to their new homes. He was right for the job because he was well-behaved and as he was studying in an English-language school he was likely to leave a good impression.

Bua's husband, the newest groom in the family, was a man of medium height, with plump, swarthy cheeks and a thin moustache. A month earlier, he had been traveling in a Jeep with his maternal uncle and had met with an accident. A dog chased a small goat onto the road, and a boy ran after the goat to save it from the approaching Jeep. To avoid hitting them, the driver swerved to the right and the Jeep took a tumble. Lalji's uncle had broken his right arm—although, marching in the baraat on the wedding night, he had used his cast to rakishly prop his rifle against his chest and fire the weapon in the air. Lalji had suffered a different kind of injury. His left cheek had been gouged and when he came for the wedding a purplish scar remained on his face despite the diligent application of an ointment every morning and night. More prominent than the scar on Lalji's face, however, were his bulging eyes that, because of a blood pressure ailment, were always streaked with red.

As he had been trained as a veterinarian, everyone called Lalji "Doctor sahib" to his face, and "Ghoda dakter" or "Horse healer" behind his back. Everyone knew that Lalji did not really practice his trade. His family owned a cold storage unit near Sugauli and also grew potato and sugarcane on the surrounding land.

Binod remembered that on the morning after her marriage, when Bua was brought out to the green Fiat, she looked beautiful in a red silk sari and heavy gold jewelry. Her eyes were downcast but you could see that she was weeping. The customary redness of Lalji's eyes gave the impression that he too had been shedding tears all morning.

Ma spoke to Bua in a gentle voice as she led her slowly to the car. All of the relatives were packed into the narrow verandah. Binod was already sitting inside the Fiat. Three steps led down to the driveway and Baba raised his voice and cautioned Ma as she brought Bua closer to the car. Hearing his voice, Bua called out to Baba and fell sobbing against his chest. Binod saw his father's eyes fill up with water.

Baba said to Bua, "Binod . . . Binod is going with you. Everything will be all right." His voice sounded like a woman's.

Bua was not consoled and she continued to cry in the car as it wound its way to Mahendru Ghat where they had to wait for the ferry to take them across the Ganges. Binod was disappointed with the wait; he did not want the trip to be delayed. Bua's crying made it difficult for him to show his enthusiasm for the journey.

In the car, Bua's face wasn't visible anymore: the red, richly embroidered sari was drawn down over her eyes like a veil. He hadn't seen her face hidden like that before, and he felt a great deal of tenderness toward his young aunt.

They were parked beside a truck loaded with new Vespa scooters. Lalji and the driver, along with a distant relative of Binod's who had come to help them get cheaper tickets, stood outside the car talking. Lalji prompted Binod to ask Bua if she needed tea. She shook her head instead of saying no. There was nothing more to be done. Binod stepped out of the car to look at the stretch of the Ganges before them. The water from that distance looked a pale green. Small white clouds drifted in the sky above. He made up his mind that as soon as the ferry had left the ghat, he would ask Lalji to buy him the breakfast of boiled egg and toast that was served on the steamer.

....

Bua said very little all day. In two hours, they were on the other side of the river, the car leaving the sandy riverbed behind. But the roads were bad and the car bumped and swayed, and every time it did that, Binod was thrown against Lalji on one side and Bua on the other. They drove past small fields with green paddy standing in the water. When they crossed tiny towns and hamlets, Binod noticed the boys and the girls, kids his own age but with thin, dark bodies and ragged clothes, milling around in the dirt by the roadside. He felt strangely enough a tinge of envy.

Beside him, Lalji gazed out of the window at the passing scenery and, when he thought Binod wasn't looking, picked his nose with a calmly attentive air and then extended his arm outside into the wind. After a while, Lalji fell asleep. Binod looked at the sleeping man's face as if he were seeing him for the first time. The lips trembled slightly whenever he exhaled and gave the impression that he was trying to whisper something in his sleep. The ointment on his cheek was dry and the tilak that Ma had put on his forehead had begun to flake. The tunic that Lalji was wearing exuded a sweet odor, a mixture of attar and scented cardamom.

Binod turned to look at Bua. The thin strands of gold that feathered the hem of her sari fluttered in the breeze. Her hands, with fresh henna embroidering her skin, were clenched tightly in her lap. Rosewater had been sprinkled on her in Patna when she sat down in the car. That scent lingered on her clothes but had become mingled with the sharper smell of sweat. Binod did not know whether Bua was sleeping too, but soon he began to feel drowsy and he leaned against her and slept.

....

When they were alone in Bua's room later in the evening, she asked Binod whether he had been fed. She told him that he was to come and ask her for anything he needed. That was the most that Binod had heard her say all day.

Binod ate beside Bua and then Lalji's mother took him to another room with a dark wooden bed on which three other children were already sleeping. He took up the remaining space. Nailed to the wall above him was a leopard skin. The leopard's head was supported by a small wooden shelf and its glass eyes were bright yellow. "You sleep here for a while," the old woman said, "and later you can return to the other room."

When Binod woke up, it was still night. He remembered a small table lamp glowing in the corner, just like the one that he had seen earlier in the evening in Bua's room. Its shade was red and much of its stem was made up of a transparent plastic column with small silver shavings floating in a red plasma-like liquid. The light from the lamp was just enough for him to be able to make out the mirror beside which the lamp stood and the shape all around him of a white mosquito net. There was no leopard in the room.

Binod heard voices in the dark. Bua was talking to someone in a very low voice. When he heard Lalji's voice, he knew that he should be sleeping. It was wrong to be awake. But sleep didn't come to him and he was afraid to move or change sides.

Lalji spoke to Bua in a loud whisper. "I looked at your matriculation mark sheet. No one scores so high in history and geography. You got more than I did in both Hindi and English."

Bua was saying, "Let me go."

Lalji shifted his weight and when he spoke again his voice seemed to come from a closer place. Bua was lying between Binod and Lalji; Lalji's voice sounded as if he were laughing. "But tell me your secret. How can anyone be so brilliant?"

The low laughter in his throat made Binod think of marbles being rubbed in the palm of his hand in the schoolyard.

There was silence. Binod had shut his eyes. The bed creaked again, and once more Bua said, "Let me go." Her bangles jingled in the dark. Perhaps she was sleeping closer to him than to Lalji. Binod knew that she was wearing thin gold bangles and new red and green glass ones.

He heard Lalji say "Okay, okay" in a reasonable voice. There was a pause and he spoke again. "People like me know that the capital of Nepal is Kathmandu or that the capital of Burma is Rangoon. But please tell me—what is the capital of Mongolia?"

He laughed but a note of pleading had come into his voice.

Bua rose to the bait. She said quietly, "Ulan Bator."

"Ulan Bator," Lalji said with great relish and laughed.

Binod was glad that Bua knew the answer because he certainly didn't.

He heard Lalji murmur happily in the dark "Ulan Bator . . . Ulan Bator" but it seemed that he had begun to run in bed. He was trying to catch his breath. Bua said, "You are breaking my bangles." But Lalji didn't say anything in response. He continued to run in the dark. And then it seemed that Bua was running too. They were panting with the effort and then Binod felt that they were tiring and he shared their tiredness and sometime later when the voices had stopped in the dark he began to dream of leopards in the forest and small birds with painted breasts.

7

Ulan Bator. Binod forgot about that night and then the memory returned and occupied a fixed place in his imagination for much of his adolescent years. The name of the capital city of Mongolia made him sit up in geography class when he was in the seventh standard and gave him a passion for the subject that he would not have imagined in himself. Binod returned to the conversation he had overheard in bed that night long ago; and he would often think of it in the years that followed, when Rabinder and he shared the small room with Bua while Neelu slept in the other bedroom with Baba and Ma. But on no occasion did the memory of that strange experience in the dark in Motihari stand out in his mind as vividly as on the night when it became clear that Lalji had gone mad.

Bua and Lalji arrived unannounced in the afternoon. Ma had come back from school and shut the bedroom door to take her nap in peace. Binod had tiptoed to the living room door and was looking out into the street hoping to see the two sons of the Electricity Board engineer next door. They were to bring the cricket bat with them for the game. Instead of the boys, Binod saw a rickshaw standing near the gate.

The rickshawala was looking toward the house, and Binod could see that there was a man sitting in the rickshaw.

Then Bua stepped out from behind the men and lifted the latch on the gate. Binod was surprised to see her but ran out quickly and touched her feet. She blessed him, but when he looked up he saw that she wasn't smiling. Bua asked if Baba and Ma were at home. When Binod told her that Ma was taking her nap, Bua said, "Let her sleep. You put on your slippers and come outside with me."

The afternoon's heat was at its peak. The man on the rickshaw was Lalji but he looked different. Taking a quick step toward him, Binod touched Lalji's brown sandals in greeting. Lalji did not say anything, nor did he make any move to get down. He kept looking at a small suitcase with a green canvas cover sitting next to his feet.

Bua pulled gently on her husband's right arm. His eyes were large and red like a water buffalo's when it steps out of a pond. Bua said, "Come, come." But Lalji did not budge. It seemed as if he hadn't slept for days. It was not possible to imagine that he could even hear what was being said to him. He looked at Bua as if he were seeing her for the first time.

The rickshawala asked Bua if he should climb beside Lalji and try helping him down. Bua nodded. The man began to speak to Lalji.

He put his arms around Lalji's shoulders and began to say, "Huzoor, you have now come home. I have brought you home, huzoor. Sir, please get down, sir."

In response, Lalji peered at the man's face with genuine interest. But he did not move. The rickshawala jumped down after a while and without waiting for Bua to say anything he wheeled his rickshaw inside the narrow gate. Standing near the open door, he resumed his pleading. "Come, sir, come into the shade. It is cool inside. Why are you sitting in the rickshaw? Come down, huzoor . . ."

Binod was conscious of a nervous trembling in his legs. He did not know what had happened to Lalji—but the rickshawala acted as if he did. He was a young man with thin sinewy limbs, and Binod suspected that he was a Muslim. From his cotton trousers that rode high above his ankles he drew out a soiled handkerchief and wiped his face. He resumed his gentle pleading. The voice and manner of the rickshawala fascinated Binod. Bua had decided to let the man take over from her; she simply stood to the side clutching a black purse in her hand.

Bua had red alta painted on her feet as if she were a bride. Binod suspected that the rickshawala with his earnest, overeager ways was trying to impress Bua. Even at that young age, Binod was conscious that Bua wore short blouses that left bare a large portion of her midriff, and he found the flare of her waist utterly bewitching. He would scarcely look at her, but the knowledge and the excitement was always there. That afternoon he wanted to reach out to his aunt but didn't quite know how. The rickshawala wanted to do that too. This realization made Binod wonder later on whether he had exaggerated in his mind Bua's helplessness beneath her quiet and composed exterior.

. . . .

"Who is there—who are you talking to?"

Ma had appeared at the door, her eyes still showing signs of sleep. She then saw Bua and understood immediately that something was wrong.

Lalji had not moved from his seat on the rickshaw. Bua put her head on Ma's shoulder and began to cry.

The rickshawala now stood aside.

Bua was saying to Ma, "He started talking nonsense yesterday, and now he doesn't seem to hear. He is sick . . ."

Binod's mother went inside the house and fetched a glass of water. Lalji took the cold glass and drank deeply, and then handed the empty glass over to Bua. Binod watched as the rickshawala walked over to the small tap in the tiny garden and, cupping the water in his hands, began to wash his face and feet. Then he turned his face, like the crows that sometimes took the water in their beaks from that same faucet, and drank deeply, his throat bobbing up and down.

Ma had always had a formal manner with Lalji, but she came close to him and said softly, "You are not feeling well. Come inside the house. Everything will be all right."

Lalji said to her, "There's a new line that has opened between Patna and Dhanbad. We will talk about the paddy crop . . . They are coming to get me." He spoke these words with slow deliberation and then, although this was difficult to watch, he began to smile.

When Binod looked at his mother he realized that her expression mirrored the one on Lalji's face; she did not seem to comprehend anything that was going on and her face revealed a frightened blankness. She reeled back toward the door and said to him, "Go next door and call your father."

The telephone in their house had not been working for the past week. Binod went to Mr. Gupta's house and called the Public Relations Department, but the man who answered the phone said that Baba had already left the office. On returning to the house, Binod saw that Ma had given a plate of food to the rickshawala; he was squatting with his back to the wall and eating the sweets that had been sent from a cousin's wedding.

The rickshaw now faced the door of the house. Lalji was sitting quietly on its seat and he watched Binod walking toward him. For a moment Binod thought that there was curiosity on Lalji's face, but when he stopped he saw that the dark, plump face was silent and expressionless. He stood at the door and waited for something to change.

Ma and Bua came out too after a while, and they were all standing near the rickshaw when Baba arrived. Bua didn't say anything and allowed Ma to speak to Baba. Lalji kept his eyes fixed on the two.

"Doctor sahib," Binod's father said to Lalji, "come down." Then, he added, "The rickshaw fare is going up. Get down at once."

When Baba caught his arm and pulled, Lalji tried to draw back into the seat. He said, "I will take care of each one of them. You go and tell them first. Nothing has happened to me."

Baba said, "Nothing has happened to you."

He repeated these words and then gestured to the rickshawala. Lalji was a heavy man but together the two men pulled him down. Then, just like that, Lalji became docile and walked into the house and sank down on the sofa near the door. But Baba wasn't happy with this. He and the rickshawala half-carried Lalji to the bed on which Neelu and Binod used to sleep. Bua stepped forward and removed her husband's sandals from his feet.

Lalji turned away to the wall—and Binod saw that he had become bald, the bare circle of skin at the top scored by two lines, scars from some old and terrible injury—and the adults returned to the living room to talk in low, hushed tones.

....

It was decided that Lalji should be taken to Dr. Sushant Sen's clinic in the morning. He refused to eat anything, however, and dinner became a tense affair. Baba tried to achieve a sense of normality by continually asking Bua about Rabinder and his performance at school. Bua looked at Lalji as if she wanted him to give the answer and then said that Rabinder had won a prize in the Hindi elocution contest. Baba was famous for his good memory and he now recited the poem by Sumitranandan Pant whose title Bua had mentioned. Lalji stared at his plate with enormous concentration.

When dinner was over, Binod was asked to sleep on the sofa in the living room and Neelu was transferred to the bed where their parents slept. Ma had shut the door, but Binod could hear his parents talking. Bua was still in the kitchen washing dishes. Then, Lalji began to chant. It is possible that he had been affected by Baba's recitation of Pant's poem, but the difference was that Lalji was speaking English. He was saying the same words over and over again in a loud singsong voice:

> For oft, when on my couch I lie
> In vacant or in pensive mood,
> They flash upon that inward eye
> Which is the bliss of solitude.

Daffodils! Binod recognized the lines after a while because he had been taught Wordsworth's poem in class. He wondered whether Bua knew those words too. It was she who was the poet; in a brown plastic-bound diary, she wrote short poems in Hindi.

When Binod had grown up and started going to college, Bua would sometimes show him her writings. Her poems hinted at the hidden romance in things—a torn shoe recalling the journeys undertaken over riverbanks and across many hills—and the ways in which small things told the story of the nation and humanity—a beggar-woman sitting with a child at a bus stop would also vote in the country's elections one day. But, on that night, Binod saw her sitting silently at the foot of the bed while Lalji, his back reclining against the wall, carried on his manic recitation. When Binod walked up to the door, Bua looked up at him and asked, "You didn't go to sleep?"

Binod stood on one foot, saying nothing in reply, and then returned to the sofa.

Lalji's voice rose again. Binod must have fallen asleep and been woken up by the noise. The door to his parents' room was still closed. It was not poetry that Lalji was chanting any more. He was detailing in a loud, unnatural voice the things he was going to do to someone who was threatening him. These things were new to Binod and it took him some time to understand what was happening. He didn't get up from the sofa. Lalji was saying that he would pour mustard oil in the vagina of the branch manager's wife and he would ask the honorable judge to suck his penis.

Binod was reminded of that night long ago when he had first learned the name of the capital of Mongolia. Ulan Bator was now a distant place. He had no idea what it was like in reality. And as he lay on the sofa in the dark, his imagination offered an image of a place where snow swirled in cold, deserted streets and where outside a barred door stood a nervous, shivering mare.

In the morning, Ma woke up Binod and asked him to get ready quickly. She gave him two rupees to buy samosas for breakfast and it was clear that she wanted Neelu and him to leave the house. Binod had the excuse of finding his shoes and he went into the room where Bua had spent the night. The window was shut and so the room was a little dark. Bua wasn't even there. Instead, Baba was sitting on a chair; he didn't say a word when Binod entered the room and looked under the bed for his shoes.

Lalji was lying on the bed but his hands were tied to the bedposts with the rope from the broken cot that was kept leaning against the kitchen wall. When he was older, Binod would ask himself whether he had really seen or only imagined the white sock stuffed into Lalji's mouth. There was also another question that appeared later in his mind. When Binod had begun working as a reporter in Delhi, he sat down late one night, alone in the newspaper office, to write down a short story. The man he found himself writing about goes mad. He begins to humiliate his wife by screaming out the secrets of their love-making. The setting of the story was a modern one. The couple lived in an apartment building in a city. As the hours pass and the silence of the night deepens, the windows of the surrounding apartments are being shut because people don't want to hear any more. They have always liked the woman who is their neighbor. One of the neighbors comes down and asks the woman to shut her window: in her confusion and grief she had not thought of doing this earlier. Sitting in front of the shut window, the man screams louder. He surprises his wife by what he says. She hears him say that when he was a boy he had often seen his mother at night with his uncle. The woman does not know if her husband is raving mad or telling the truth when he screams again and again that he is aware what everyone says behind his back about his being a bastard.

8

Bua came to Patna with eight-year-old Rabinder when Lalji was sent away to Ranchi. They arrived during the monsoons. Rains lashed the house, driving water inside through the cracks in the windows, making the wooden window frames swollen and gray. The ceiling in the bathroom turned green and began to drip. If the front door was left open in the evenings, frogs hopped in and took their place on the floor around the sofa, looking very much like well-fed but malcontent guests. The pages of the notebooks reserved for homework got stuck together and could only with some ingenuity be used to make paper boats. Binod and Rabinder would return from school with their hair damp and their clothes soiled with mud. Wet garments were spread to dry on every available piece of furniture and also under the sluggishly turning blades of the ceiling fans. There was a clothesline even in the kitchen. Most of the walls became furred with peeling paint and centipedes of different colors crawled on them and found their way onto beds and pillows. It suddenly seemed during those months that there was very little space in the house for its real inhabitants.

Baba took Bua to Magadh Mahila College and she became a student of Hindi literature, the same subject that both of Binod's parents had studied long ago. Baba wanted her to become a teacher, but if Bua had any ambitions at that time, she kept them to herself. She would go to her classes every day after drinking tea, and when she came back late in the middle of the afternoon, she helped Ma in the kitchen and with cleaning.

Widows wore plain white but Bua, dressing as a half-widow, had taken to wearing plain saris with thin, dark borders. Her elegance made her vulnerable. Binod had gone with his parents to a dinner party once and their host asked them why they had left Mother Teresa behind.

After Lalji's illness, Bua had withdrawn into herself; she spoke little but was capable of making cutting remarks about everyone. Ma used to repeat this fact during conversations so that people didn't pity Bua too much. Yet, to most people Bua was a mystery. No one knew what she thought of Lalji or his internment till her brief poem was published. It was a short poem with two stanzas. The first stanza repeated the story told about the poet Nirala—on a street in Allahabad at the end of his life, long-haired Nirala threw himself over the neck of a horse being whipped. The poet in Bua's poem was described pressing his damp cheeks against the hide of the poor horse, but in the second stanza, he turned into an unnamed being that was in reality Lalji. He had wrapped his arms around a terrible pain and had become crazy with grief. The whip had continued to fall on him.

Baba would show the poem to visitors and everyone would fall silent in sympathy. Those who did not know Lalji were most affected by it and the poem appeared in the Sunday issue of *Vishwamitra* and then again in the brochure *Half the Earth: Women in Bihar* released by the Chirag Cultural Group. A little while after the group had published her poem, Bua joined it and everyone thought that this was a good thing.

Bua was no longer interested in seeing films by the likes of Manmohan Desai, about brothers who had been separated at birth in a storm and found each other at the end. Now she took Ma to watch art films. Binod was twelve at that time and he went as their male escort. He barely understood these films, but they had a disturbing effect on him, and he often felt exposed when sad, beautiful women on the screen gazed into the camera for long stretches of time.

....

Bua and Rabinder moved into the room that till then Binod had shared with Neelu. His younger sister was glad to sleep in the same bed with her parents but he remained in the old room. After a few nights he complained to Bua that Rabinder kicked his legs at night and so Bua moved him to the other side. She slept in the middle now. At times, he would wake up with Bua's arm thrown around his body and he would lie still and think that he was in a Hindi film.

The bed was near an open window and during the daytime if they looked out they could see the leaves of the young mango tree almost touching the iron grille. At night, when the moon was out, the bed was bathed in a white light. Binod woke up once from a dream and Bua's face was close to his, close enough for him to feel her breath on his skin. When he woke up again the faint light of the approaching dawn had crept inside the room and he could see that Bua's eyes were shut and she was in deep sleep. After lying awake for several minutes, Binod drew his face closer to Bua's and laid his cheek against hers; her skin was cool, much cooler than his, as if she had gone out walking in the night and dew had fallen on her face. He remained like that, his cheek touching hers, and although he had wanted to lie awake, without moving and silent, he had fallen back asleep again.

A part of him did not care whether Bua was awake or not, and during the nights that followed he would sometimes put his lips against hers. When he woke up and rode his bicycle to school, he would lower his face close to the front wheel and try to remember the dizziness of those nocturnal moments. Months passed. Binod felt that he had grown up faster than the boys around him, but he did not speak about this with anyone, and in this too he began to appear older to himself.

During the day, Bua would be the adult who cared for Binod as a mother would, putting food on his plate or ironing his clothes when she returned from college. But at night, she would become someone his own age, a girl holding him in the dark. Once he put his hand on her chest but she turned away on her side. After that, whenever he would wake up at night, Binod was conscious of her body pressed against his back.

In the living room one evening, Binod was leafing through a comic book while Ma and Bua talked and had tea. Ma was telling Bua about a Hindi short story she had read in *Hans* (Swam), about a young woman who had renounced the world and gone up to a monastery in the mountains. Binod kept looking at the pictures in his book, but his attention was wholly absorbed by what his mother was saying. He had never heard his mother speaking about love before and he found himself trying to place in the story his still unexpressed feelings about Bua.

The woman at the monastery talked to a monk every day, discussing questions of faith and the mystery of the divine. She had never seen the monk's face because he hung a saffron sheet between them to screen him from temptation. The woman had guessed from the monk's voice that he was young; despite his youth, the monk appeared wise and his words held a calmness that never failed to answer a deep need inside the woman. One morning, the young woman's bed was empty. The inmates of the monastery searched everywhere but found no sign of her.

At the tale's end, the narrator described a woman's beautiful face framed by a bus window. The bus was leaving the mountains and was headed back to the plains. A voice was speaking inside the woman's head. It was the voice of the monk discoursing about the nature of the world.

Ma paused and smiled. She said, "The monk, despite his wisdom, hadn't imagined that love is like a vine that can flourish with the slightest support. The woman had fallen in love just with his voice."

Bua was nodding slowly while Ma went on explaining that love does not need a face or a body. It will grasp at anything and everything. But often such love is a delusion.

Binod felt his heart kick against his ribs. He was sure that these weren't the storyteller's words but his mother's—she was aware of how Binod would kiss Bua's lips at night. At night sometimes Ma had come into the room and stood like a pale apparition visible outside the white of the mosquito net. Now Binod knew why.

He was still holding the comic book open to a page that showed beefy men wearing helmets shouting "Achtung, Englander!" But his eyes were fixed on the two women. The older woman had a smile on her lips. The younger woman, perhaps aware of her guilt, wore a more serious expression on her face.

Binod considered the possibility that he was mistaken. Perhaps Ma was only teaching his aunt about the presence of temptation. Maybe all that his mother was saying was that Bua did not need her husband's body to be in love. She could be content with the memory of his voice.

"Achtung, Englander!" The need to cry out. To warn. He looked at the black letters on the pages of his comic book. It couldn't merely be a coincidence. His mother was warning Bua.

But he loved too much his aunt's touch, and the thumping of his own daring heart.

He knew, however, that what he felt was wrong, and he could be punished by failing in his exams and remaining in standard seven forever.

He could renounce temptation and yet receive a young woman's unspoken love.

The boy felt a sudden desire to wear saffron.

. . . .

Like the young woman at the monastery, it was Bua who left, moving away to live in the post-graduates' hostel. It was understood, of course, that Rabinder was to go on living with the family. It had become difficult for Bua to attend her classes and travel by rickshaw for two hours each way from the house in Rajvanshi Nagar. A friend of Baba's took everyone in his car to see Bua the day after she moved from home. Men were not allowed inside the hostel and Baba had to wait outside, but Rabinder and

Binod were let in, and this was good because they saw how Bua used an electric heater to toast bread.

She had kept a bottle of strawberry jam and a stick of butter in a bowl of water to prevent ants from getting to the food. Neelu and Binod ate toast with jam and butter, and ice cream was brought from outside for Rabinder. Ma watched Bua making tea for her and said, like a middle-aged actress in a Hindi film, "You are living the life I wanted for myself so long ago."

The whitewashed walls of Bua's room were damp and she had pasted newspapers on the back of her wardrobe. A small desk and a chair were placed next to the window. On the desk there were a stack of library books and two black-and-white photographs—one a studio photograph of Lalji, Bua, and an infant Rabinder, and the other a group shot of Ma and the two kids with Rabinder at an older cousin's wedding. Before they left, Ma wanted Bua to show her the bathrooms that were shared by the students on that floor. The two of them stood by themselves at the end of the corridor, their heads close together like schoolgirls, talking for many minutes in low voices.

Then it was time to say goodbye. On the way back home, Baba noted with satisfaction that the guard at the gate had been efficient at his job and not allowed males to enter the premises of the girls' hostel.

....

The Chirag Cultural Group that Bua had joined was a front formed— these were the days of Indira Gandhi's Emergency—by radical students in Patna. Bua had joined the group as a writer: she had wanted an audience for her poems. But that was to change with time. She found places on committees devoted to education and female empowerment. The men who would later become her political patrons, people like Lalu Yadav, were those she came to know during those days of struggle.

No one in her family really knew of the life that Bua had entered. Binod heard later that the only reason why Bua wasn't thrown into prison was because she steadfastly shunned the limelight. She was also aware of her shortcomings. Years later, she would happily tell everyone, "Before I became involved in that work in college, I hadn't even heard about a man called Ho Chi Minh, and I was already in my twenties."

She was a committed worker. Even her education now mattered more because she was becoming aware of the world around her and the lives that people led. Among her friends there was very little of the confusion that is often the bane of youth movements. This was because their enemy was the authoritarian government in Delhi, which had banned freedom of speech and the constitution. Its blatant presence made it easier for Bua and her friends to tell themselves that they were working for freedom from tyranny.

And then one day, a letter came from Lalji's family. It was attached to a page torn from the Hindi magazine *Dharmayug*. The magazine had printed a photograph of a political demonstration outside Governor House in Patna, and there was Bua holding a banner that demanded the release of nineteen students who had been jailed. The letter had been written by one of Lalji's nephews on behalf of Bua's mother-in-law. It was not only her own personal dignity but also the dignity of her husband's family that Bua was responsible for. Her guardians in Patna were not to allow her to lose a sense of herself as a respectable woman. The letter insulted Bua as well as Binod's own parents, but Binod looked at the picture and felt that Bua had become a film star.

Baba was taken aback by the photograph. So was Ma. They had been unaware of what Bua had been doing. But the letter infuriated them and there was no question of their not supporting her. Baba said to Ma that she was not to mention the letter to Bua, but Binod heard Bua crying in the kitchen while talking to Ma the next time Bua came to the house.

Bua had received no money from Lalji's family for a long time. There was talk that the nephew, Manik, was prepared to cut ties with her. It was he who had written the letter for Lalji's mother. Baba didn't know that Ma had already discussed the letter. During dinner, he made a remark about the old socialist politician Karpoori Thakur, who was coming back as a leader in Bihar. Bua didn't avoid the opening. She told Baba that she had sat on several meetings with the leader and she found that his views were very enlightened. The committees on which she worked had received help from Thakur. Baba was impressed. He stuffed more food into his mouth and kept chewing so that Bua would have no excuse to stop speaking.

. . . .

Perhaps others who knew Bua better and had seen her grow over the past three years might have found her emergence as a political entity unremarkable. But within her own family she suddenly came to represent everything that was dramatic. She embodied change and excitement.

In time, even the news that Bua would take part in the elections was accepted only as a part of that which had always been expected.

The Congress party had lost power in Delhi and fresh elections were announced in the states. Bua was given the Janata party ticket from Patna Sadar. A new, alien world was opened to Binod. He spent many hours in the small flat on Gardiner Road that served as headquarters of the campaign. At all hours of the day and night, the office would be filled with men whom he had never before seen in his life. They would look at him with exhausted, bloodshot eyes, and they would engage in talk that was filled with calculation. Binod was useful only for small tasks like carrying armloads of flyers and banners outside to the jeeps that stood festooned with the saffron and green party flag. One day he sat at the telephone, but the calls that came didn't make much sense to him. A caller wanted to know the name of the observer at SD Girls School. When Binod said he didn't know, the man told him angrily not to answer the phone ever again. The representative of a woman's organization called to complain that all of the party posters on Museum Road had been torn down by a group of goons. One man called and shouted in Hindi, "Turn on the radio! Turn on the radio!"

Bua lost her voice on the day before the election. But that seemed to be the least of the worries. On the day of the election itself, Baba complained of illegal voting and booth capturing by her opponents and hinted that the frauds committed by them would ensure Bua's defeat. But she won. She received sixty-five thousand more votes than her rival. For many years to come Binod would think of sixty-five as his lucky number.

He had grown up in a society in which your friends as well as your biggest foes were people within your own family. Bua had altered that. This was the first time that anyone Binod knew had asked to be judged by people outside the family. Bua's victory in the election was important because she had persuaded others of her worth; it also gave Binod a concrete sense of audience. More than anything else, however, her success demonstrated that one could escape one's past. This was a more important lesson than anything that Binod had been taught at school or at home.

It also remained a matter of amazement to him that in a place like Bihar there was very little mention of Lalji when there was a discussion in the press about Bua. Perhaps this was because Bua had emptied out her own details from the public story and spoke of women in India and in Russia, in China and in America, in homes and in war zones, in hospitals and also in factories. She wanted women even in villages to be paid in cash, and she campaigned for small bank loans to be granted to working women. In Bihar, Bua became a symbol of a form of independence that was still new in independent India. Binod couldn't judge, not even in later years, how much of this had been by design. He came to know women with rich husbands who had opened travel agencies or boutiques in big cities like Delhi and Bombay; he also had friends in Patna whose wives had started schools or even fashionable beauty parlors. In each of these cases, the women had access to money. Bua had had nothing. She got an education and then entered public life at a time and place where there were no women around her even to give her company.

....

When Bua was provided a flat by the government she asked Ma and Baba to give up the rented house so that they could all live together. Binod's parents were unsure about this plan, not least because Baba knew that there could be no guarantee about houses given to politicians. When the next election rolled around, they could find themselves homeless. They remained where they were and Bua moved on to a different future.

Lalji spent twelve years in the Conolly ward of the asylum in Ranchi. In the beginning years, Baba and Bua both visited him. Rabinder had also been taken there in the vague hope, perhaps, that the sight of his son would lift Lalji's spirits and do him some good. But something must have happened because Ma forbade any such visits in the future. Binod had gone to the mental hospital as a boy when Baba was shooting his documentary there. And then, when he was older and had begun to work, when he would travel to Dhanbad or Bokaro, he would be asked to make a detour and take clothes or food to Lalji.

The hospital was a particularly cheerless place. Its yellow walls, which would first appear in view through a thin curtain of eucalyptus trees, remained unchanging during all his adult years. The officials he needed to see on each occasion sometimes changed — once he learned that the head of the institution had shot himself, and then there was the case of the doctor who had himself gone mad and was locked up with his patients. The other workers remained the same, but there was little consolation in this. With each successive visit, it began to appear to Binod that the workers were trapped in their employment and they slowly began to seem indistinguishable from the inmates.

Over the years, Lalji's condition had so deteriorated that he didn't recognize even the men who washed and fed him. On at least a couple of occasions, Binod had felt that it was his arrival that had given his caretakers the only reason to bathe Lalji.

He would wait in the dark corridor outside the office of the head, and Lalji would be brought to him, his malnourished body slumped in the wheelchair, his eyes red and their gaze turned inward toward nothingness. Binod would be filled with unease, or maybe it was something more like fear, because he told himself that this could happen to anyone, even to Baba and to him. But there was little empathy in his heart. The sight of Lalji's sparse hair, the thin strands still wet from the bath and plastered to the side of the round head, filled him with repulsion.

One day he had handed Lalji a cardboard box given by Ma; it was filled with salty snacks and sweets. The attendant laughed, showing rotten teeth, and said in Hindi, "He only likes lollipop." More than once, Binod hadn't even waited to see him. He would make an entry in the register at the desk out in the front, give to the guard whatever it was that he had brought for Lalji, and flee.

For her part, Bua never took Lalji's name. Everyone in the family learned not to talk about him either. But if ever, for some reason, his name came up, Bua spoke of him always as a healthy, living presence. She laughed whenever she spoke about him with Rabinder. It was possible that she did this because she loved him very much, but it might also have been because she found it unbearable to face the sad and often hypocritical faces of her relatives. By the time Binod was old enough to understand this, he had become conscious of how power had isolated Bua. She was alone. The force of this realization had come as a shock to Binod, and it was certainly the reason why, after more than two decades, in writing for his newspaper about the murdered Mala Srivastava he had appeared so very sympathetic. In giving his editorial about Mala the title "The Car with the Red Light," he had in mind not the cars of the officials and ministers that used to stop outside the murdered poet's door. Instead, he was thinking about Bua, the discovery of ambition, and the price that she had paid for such achievement.

Bua's family could only pity her. But the truth was that for Bua her husband's madness hadn't been the great tragedy of her life. In fact, it had liberated her. However, no one in Bua's family recognized this. She was a mere widow. Everyone demanded a piece of Bua and wanted her to be grateful for being used.

III

❋

The Lady

with the Dog

9

"The textile strike of 1982 ruined many of the cotton mills of Bombay and it devastated many workers and their families. It is possible that if that had not happened, if money and muscle had not torn apart the fabric of working-class culture in the tenements of Bombay, then pogroms like those witnessed against Muslims in the early 1990s wouldn't have occurred. Today, more than two decades later, you can see the ghostly remains of the mills that still stand in central Bombay but many have been pulled down and given way to high-rise buildings where the rich live surrounded by slums that stretch for miles." That is how he had begun a recent editorial.

Binod had a friend who worked in a new office complex that had come up after the demolition of a mill. His name was Ajay Brahmatmaj. His office was in Lower Parel, on the fourth floor of what used to be Kamala Mills.

Ajay worked as a film journalist for a Hindi daily. The paper had no circulation in Bombay at all. Although it was the largest-selling paper in the country it was read only in the Hindi-speaking north. The majority of people in Ajay's office were there only to sell space to advertisers like Hindustan Lever that had an interest in selling soap in India's hinterland. This peculiar organization was the reason why Ajay could draw back from any immediate event or personality in Bombay and present the reader with the larger social picture. Unlike so many of the film journalists in Bombay whose main job was to report on the rumors of romance among stars, Ajay was likely to begin an essay with a line like "Hindi films are the primary means by which most people in India get to step inside a five-star hotel."

Ajay was less interested in telling you whether Hindi films are good or bad; instead, he tried hard to make his readers aware of the enormous importance these films had in their lives. In one piece, he had challenged his readers to deny that every one of them had a favorite Hindi film song. By way of example, he had offered that many Indian men, in the late

1970s and 1980s, looking for the first time at the faces of their brides on their wedding nights, recalled the scene from *Kabhi Kabhie* when Amitabh Bachchan lifts the veil and looks at Rakhee. "Kabhi kabhie mere dil mein khayal aata hai . . ."

More than once, Ajay had said that no one in India has as much influence as the Indian film hero: he runs the barber's shop simply by smiling from a photograph on the wall; he tells a woman what a man wants by looking into her eyes from the screen; he teaches a man how to cry when his mother dies; he gets voted into office and runs the country from his seat in the Parliament. And, as was clear during the textile strike, even Prime Minister Indira Gandhi on a visit to Bombay cared enough for the film star lying in a hospital bed at Breach Candy but not for the thousands of workers and their families starving because of lost wages and lost jobs.

When Binod went to talk to Ajay about Vikas Dhar it was July. A thin rain was coming down that afternoon and he got drenched after stepping out of the local train that had brought him from Churchgate Station. People were already leaving their offices even though it was nowhere close to five o'clock.

....

Binod had been back in Bombay after his visit to Patna for almost a month and a half. After his return, he had waited for the promised call from Vikas Dhar, but it hadn't happened. And then one morning, when he came to the office, there was a scribbled note on his keyboard. "Vikas Dhar. Call 9821888340."

The message filled him with elation, and he immediately thought of Ajay, because he would understand his excitement. His sister, Neelu, was in the city too, but he didn't want to call her because she would be disappointed if nothing came of it.

Dhar answered the phone himself. Binod gave his name and his newspaper's name and Dhar said hello in a singsong way and asked him whether he had the story. But he had thought that Dhar wanted them to meet first—and that he was going to tell Binod what to write. Did he remember wrong? He hesitated for a moment and then anxiety made him inventive. He said that he had written a sketch that he wanted to show him.

Dhar said that he was going to Goa on a shoot. The young man who was the director of the film that he was producing had been sick. Dhar had stepped in himself and was busy completing the film. "Let's meet in two weeks," he said. Binod felt a great sense of relief at this offer of time. For a journalist, two weeks can be like two years. He began to improvise. "Dhar saheb," he said, "I have changed the story a bit. I have made it more romantic."

The sound that he heard at the other end signaled enthusiasm. Then Dhar said, "That is good. That is what the people want . . . I want the viewer to be able to breathe the air of the small town, but it should also have a more universal feel to it. It should be a human story, you understand?"

"Yes," Binod said.

Dhar said, "It should have its own ethos, its own recognizable stamp of place, but you should be able to surprise me."

"Yes," he said again, growing more unsure.

. . . .

The plain fact is that a viewer in the city is surprised by something that a viewer in the small town isn't. In an interview with a writer from London, Neeraj Dubey had said that if you really want to enjoy a Hindi film, you should go to a theater in a small town in Bihar. "Small-town people tear their shirts open when they are feeling very excited. They do that when a hit song is on the screen. When some titillating dance is going on, you see coins being thrown at the screen. It's madness. They don't hold back any emotion, they don't care a damn what people think. If they want to cry, they cry or howl in the theater. In cities, audiences go to the theater with expectations. In small towns, they don't have any expectations, they come to enjoy the film and if you betray them, and you let them down and you can't hold them, then you'll see empty theaters the next day. They are extreme in their emotions; the city people aren't—I would say they don't know how to enjoy a Hindi film."

When he read those lines, Binod had felt love for Dubey. He saw him as someone who would speak honestly and in an unguarded way, even though when he thought about it more, he felt that Dubey's success as an actor was precisely in holding himself back while a part of him cried for full disclosure. It was that struggle between opposing emotions that gave his performances their particular tension.

In one interview, Binod had asked Dubey to describe his childhood. The first thing that came out of Dubey's mouth was, "I used to wet my bed." Binod was reminded of Orwell: "Soon after I arrived at Crossgates (not immediately, but after a week or two, just when I seemed to be settling into a routine of school life) I began wetting my bed." There was honesty there, no doubt, but also something more sophisticated, a performance of innocence. It was an act of confidence and a desire to win an audience.

....

After the phone conversation with Dhar, Binod sat down to write a story for him. He began with a group of policemen sitting at a Hanuman temple in front of a yellow building that serves as the police station. The men are wearing dhotis and singing bhajans. One of them is beating a drum and another handles a pair of cymbals. A small boy is squatting a little distance away, washing the clothes of these policemen. One of the policemen has lost a child, but he is cruel to everyone, in particular to the boy who washes and cleans for them.

Binod dawdled with this opening for quite a while but it didn't go anywhere. He let a day or two pass. Then he began afresh.

A young, well-dressed man is at a tea stall in a tiny town. He is standing with his glass of tea in hand because of the transistor playing there and he is interested in finding out the score in a cricket match. The young man has taken a job in that town or maybe he is only passing through. While standing at the tea stall, listening to the cricket commentary and sipping tea, he watches a tall Adivasi woman who comes there with a baby in her arms. She asks the owner of the tea stall for some medicine for the child. The man sitting behind the counter asks what's wrong with the child, and the woman responds by removing the cloth covering the baby's bottom. The young man sipping his tea can also see the sore that is filled with pus.

The owner of the tea stall takes out tablets from a tin and asks the woman how many he should give. The narrator sees that the medicine is Pentid-Sulpha. The tribal woman puts a crumpled note on the counter. The man gives the woman two of the tablets. She takes the medicine but keeps standing. The man asks rudely why she is still there and the woman says that the baby also has a runny stomach. In reply, the man says that he has medicine for that too; he asks for two rupees. The woman shakes her head to say that she doesn't have the money. The man says to her that he can give her the medicine for the diarrhea but she needs to choose whether she wants to treat the baby's wound or his stomach.

The young man signals to the owner of the tea stall that he will pay for the medicine. Before the Adivasi woman leaves, the fellow behind the counter asks her to thank the gentleman standing beside her. But she quietly takes the medicine and turns away with her sick child without uttering a word.

This had happened once in front of Binod. After he had written the scene down, drawing a portrait of the tribal woman and her child, he saw that it was too slight to be developed into a story, especially one with any romance in it. This time he let more days pass, and then he went to see his friend Ajay in his office.

He was offered green tea while he waited. Back in the 1980s, Ajay had spent time in Beijing working on Hindi translations, and whether anything else came out of the experience or not, green tea remained as an evidence of that past. Ajay was busy working on a story about Iraq. Three Indian truck drivers had been taken hostage there by a group called the Islamic Secret Army—Holders of the Black Banners. The matter had taken a new turn in recent days because the Iraqi tribal leader Sheikh Hisham al-Dulaimi, who was helping with the negotiations, had suggested that Bollywood film stars could appeal for the release of the prisoners and then the men would go free.

All of the actors that the sheikh had named had been famous back in the 1970s. From Ajay, Binod learned that Amitabh Bachchan had just given an interview clarifying his position on the situation. The actor had said, "If my words help, I'd consider it a privilege. Either the prime minister or the minister of external affairs should make an official request for my intervention. The request should be official." Ajay began to laugh as he read those words. He slapped the screen of his computer and said, "This is what I keep telling you about our line of work. The film star in our great republic is able to demand that he should be approached only by the PM or failing that the poor foreign minister."

Ajay also told Binod about a report he had found in a British newspaper—the story's moral for him being that the whole war in Iraq was like a bad movie in that it allowed bad people to mouth bad lines. A fat and shy fifteen-year-old Iraqi boy, who liked to sit for hours by the river with his birdcage, had been killed by the U.S. army. When asked about the details of the boy's death, the American division commander had said, "That person was probably in the wrong place at the wrong time."

Binod recounted the details of his conversation with Dhar. Ajay was encouraging but not too much. He believed that he was a better film journalist because he didn't harbor secret ambitions of becoming a screenwriter. The two of them were in his Maruti some months ago and Ajay had said to him, "If you are always trying to be someone else, you never know who you are. I am happy being a journalist. I feel no need to go around hawking a screenplay." But that day in July, in his office, he didn't mock Binod's ambition. Instead, he said, "Vikas Dhar's specialty is man-woman relationships and the murky temptations of sex. He must have liked the story of a murdered poet because of its sleaze." He added, "If you leave aside his small body of good work, Dhar's films are recycled Hollywood productions. In that way, he is typical of Bollywood. But you should learn from him. Why don't you rewrite a story you have liked in the past?"

....

Binod came back to his office after that, stopping to eat some cheap Chinese food. Then, for good measure, he helped himself to some kulfi sold by a bhaiyya standing near the building gate. In the office Binod sat down with three clean sheets of paper. Wasn't there something worthwhile, a classic tale of romance, that could be rewritten in an Indian setting? After a while, an idea came to him. He was thinking of the Russians. The stories written by the nineteenth-century Russian writers had always appealed to him. They could have been written in Hindi. The narratives meandered slowly, peopled by characters who drank endless cups of tea and rubbed their hands in front of the fire, their lives made sluggish by futile longing. The people that those writers presented could have been the members of his own large family in Bihar.

But Binod had something particular in mind. He was thinking of Chekhov's short story, "The Lady with the Dog." A married man, dissolute and cynical, seduces a young married woman while she is alone on holiday in a seaside town. The affair doesn't end with their return home. The man is surprised by his own passion and by the realization that he will never be happy without this plain, somewhat provincial, woman whom he has seduced and struggled to forget. But this realization doesn't bring happiness: "We are like two migrating birds, the male and the female, who have been caught and put into separate cages." The story closes with a sad, wistful sense that the two lovers, despite their desire, cannot see how their lives will end.

"A young woman with a small, four-year-old boy had rented a flat for a fortnight in the small town of Haridwar, which was popular among pilgrims." This is how Binod began his story, imagining Bua as a widow. Parshuram was a monk at a local temple, shaven-headed except for a lock of hair at the back that fell to his shoulders. The discovery of love, thrilling and disturbing to both of them, would not be without its difficulties. The two would talk of middle-class literature—a secular longing among all the religion around them—and they would come together because of the loneliness that they saw looming in their middle ages.

....

"The Lady with the Dog" ends with Dmitry Dmitrich Gurov and Anna Sergeyevna in a room in the Slavyansky Bazar Hotel. She is wearing her favorite gray dress. He has caught sight of himself in the mirror and seen that he has lost his looks. The two have grown to love each other "like man and wife, like tender friends." Chekhov is at pains to describe the change that has overcome Gurov. In the past, he has used logical arguments to soothe away any sadness in his heart, but not any longer; "now he no longer cared for logic; he felt profound compassion, he wanted to be sincere and tender."

The story showed the two lovers spending a long time talking about how they could free themselves of the "intolerable fetters" of distance and the necessity for deception. Gurov clutches his head and asks, "How? How?" And then comes the sublime end. "And it seemed as though in a little while the solution would be found, and then a new and glorious life would begin; and it was clear to both of them that the end was still far off, and that what was to be the most complicated and difficult for them was only just beginning." There is no solution, really, just as life offers no solution. There is no point of rest.

But what worked in a short story would not work in a film. The conventions of Hindi filmmaking demanded a satisfying closure. There was no clear place for Anton Chekhov in Amritsar. Binod had been working on the story for almost two weeks and was happy with what he had so far, but he needed to do more, and he tried to imagine a happy ending for the couple in Haridwar.

The audience would expect that much. Even in fairly realistic Hindi films, as for instance in one recent film about a Hindu man and a Muslim woman who are in love, the filmmaker had reached for magic. Everything before the end had been rather realistic but then, just before the credits rolled up, there they were, the two people who couldn't get married because they belonged to different religions, both of them brightly clothed and smiling, embracing each other above the fluffy white clouds in heaven.

Vikas Dhar had asked him to wait for two weeks and Binod wanted clues on what was to be added to the Chekhov story. He typed up the story and had it couriered to Dhar. He didn't have to wait long for the response; Dhar called him the same evening and said that he was leaving for London but they could discuss things when he got back.

"There aren't many films being made about middle-aged people in love," Dhar said, and added, "This story can fulfill a real need in the market."

Then he said that he wanted the ending to be changed; it was somewhat subdued right now, and it needed to be more emotional. Binod said, "Yes, of course, yes."

Dhar said, "I want you to think about one thing. The woman being a widow doesn't work because we don't expect her to want more from life. It'll be better if you think of her as an unhappily married woman. I think there are millions of those among our viewers."

They both laughed.

10

When Dhar returned from London, he was on all the news channels, talking this time about violence in Kashmir. But he didn't call. Instead, the person who spoke to Binod nearly every day was Rabinder. He would call from prison, mostly in the afternoons but also late at night, to check on the progress being made on the story. He wanted to discuss details. He was full of ideas.

Binod knew that deep inside Rabinder thought of himself as an artist.

When describing his own character Rabinder would often say that he was "sensitive" and therefore likely to be easily hurt. He had acted in plays in school and again during the short time that he spent in college. When Bua came to live in Patna after Lalji's illness, Rabinder was put in St. Michael's, the same school where Binod was studying. There was a tradition in the school of presenting an annual play. When he was in the ninth standard, the year before he was dismissed from school, Rabinder had acted in the school's production of *Death of a Salesman*.

The play was performed in English although in the past years Mr. Suresh King had translated the scripts into Hindi. Mr. King was a Christian convert from Bettiah. Rabinder played the younger son of the salesman, displaying a great deal of physical energy and even a touch of menace. He told everyone that what he liked most about being in the drama was that he wore a stylish black hat.

For much of the play, he was dressed in a long-sleeved cotton shirt and black slacks held up by dark suspenders. These had been provided by the missionaries. Father McCauley was directing the play and he had allowed Rabinder to adopt an American accent, which mostly meant that Rabinder decided to deliver all his lines with broadened, slightly nasal vowels. In one part of the play, Rabinder got into a conversation with two girls in a bar in the city. Both girls had been borrowed from the nearby Notre Dame Academy. The girls looked very modern in skirts and high heels. They also wore lipstick. When they had drinks together, Rabinder's manner with the girls was frank and casual. He had no experience of romance, and certainly not sex, but you wouldn't have felt it watching him. Or at least Binod didn't. This might have been because he himself knew nothing about women then—but the truth was that later when he talked to women in Delhi he mimicked Rabinder's manner on stage. He often wondered whether Rabinder remembered himself on stage too and therefore had never grown up. This he knew happened to men for whom the days spent in high school were the happiest part of their lives.

There was a time when they were in college in Delhi and Rabinder played with the thought that he would become an actor. This was after he had got into serious trouble in the attempted robbery case. He had been jailed in Buxar and when he came out and expressed an interest in studying in Delhi, no one opposed the idea. It actually came as a relief to everyone in the family. He had told Bua that he wanted to get a law degree, but then he found out that he needed to get an intermediate degree first. So he joined Khalsa College in Delhi. Binod rented a room near the university to make it easier for Rabinder to go to his classes. Their landlord was an older municipal employee, a Brahmin from Azamganj, who had an extra room on the roof of his house in Kamla Nagar.

One day, a friend of Rabinder's from Patna, a student with a face like the head of a horse, won the election for the position of the mess-in-charge at his hostel. His name was Vivek. To celebrate, he invited Rabinder and Binod for dinner at the Khyber restaurant. A loud group of young men, a couple of pink-turbaned Sikhs among them sitting like trussed-up bulls, was at a nearby table. One of the Sikhs was recounting a trip he had taken to the shrine at Vaishnodevi. The climb up to the hilltop temple had been difficult, and the man cursed several times as he described his ordeal. Some rich folks, he said, used ponies to get to the top. The abuse he used constantly—"behan di lund"—would roughly translate as "your sister's penis." Rabinder sat listening to the man quietly and then asked, "Why are Punjabis like this?"

Binod was taken aback because Rabinder's own speech was littered with references to the other person's sister. It was only the novelty of this piece of Delhi abuse that had shocked him so much. While Binod said nothing, their host, Vivek, slowly masticating his jaws, answered on Binod's behalf. He had a Bihari history lecturer from Dumraon who was taking the civil services exams. Vivek said, "Mr. Ratnakar told us that this is a part of the country that has suffered many invasions. All those Muslim bastards rode through this place. The speech here reflects that long history of violence. You and I have only come here to study, but think of those who are Delhi's most recent settlers. People who were fleeing Pakistan. They had witnessed the riots and the looting. The rapes."

Whenever Vivek opened his mouth, he exposed giant, splayed teeth. He rarely looked up while delivering his discourse. He bit into the tandoori chicken and kept spitting out small bits of sentences about the past. He said, "When the Mongols captured the kingdoms around here, they ordered that the native rulers be wrapped in the hide of cows that had just been slaughtered. Our former rulers were left under the sun. Maggots ate them alive."

Rabinder smiled. "So here we are, at a restaurant called Khyber. Eating chicken and lamb in the style of the invaders."

Vivek said, "You can't laugh. Take that lame motherfucker Timur, who wasn't a Mongol but certainly behaved like one. He left huge pyramids of dead bodies in these streets . . . The people in Delhi are very rough. Their language is crude. But that is because they have had the sword of history repeatedly thrust up their backsides."

Binod thought that Vivek wanted them to sympathize with the people at the adjoining table and at the same time feel a bit superior to them. And perhaps Rabinder was thinking of what Vivek had said that day in the restaurant when he announced to Binod, before a month was over, that he wouldn't be going back to Khalsa College any more. When Binod asked him the reason why, he shrugged and said, "Bahut Punjabi sab hai." "Too many Punjabis there." He wasn't going to sit in class with boisterous, abusive Sikhs and big-breasted women who laughed at dirty jokes. Those people hardly ever noticed him, but there was nothing that would prevent Rabinder from returning that contempt.

. . . .

One late morning, Binod was on his way to the khadi shop near Regal Cinema to buy cheap kurtas. While waiting at the bus stop he saw a group of actors performing a street play in front of the college. He walked over to watch and immediately recognized Neeraj Dubey among the performers. Dubey looked thinner and taller since Binod had last seen him in Bettiah. He wore a plain green shirt, its top buttons open, and a pair of cotton trousers, but on his head he had a policeman's cap and under his right arm a policeman's baton. He was performing with an engaging swagger inside the circle formed by the spectators. The university crowd was enjoying the show. They snickered knowingly as Dubey interrogated a tall dark-skinned actress playing a woman who had just burned to death her daughter-in-law. Every question that Dubey asked showed how ridiculous the law could be in the hands of men who were unjust.

"Did the girl tell you why she was killing herself?"

"No, she never spoke to me. She would just sit beside the stove and make tea for herself."

"She had no respect for others? She was a modern girl?"

"I don't know if she was or not. She never spoke to me. She put on silk saris and sat beside the stove drinking tea all the time."

"If she didn't speak to you that means she was modern. Do you think she wanted to kill you too?"

Binod couldn't stay to watch the whole performance, but when he returned to the flat he told Rabinder about having seen Dubey. This was welcome news for Rabinder; he had been morose for several days. His spirits must have lifted because he fetched the blue plastic bucket from the bathroom and began to scrub his feet diligently in the cold water. The two of them needed to go to the dhaba where, for a monthly payment of five hundred rupees, they would eat their dinner every night. But Rabinder was in no hurry. He went on washing his feet. Binod was sitting in the single cane chair they had in the room, reading something, maybe a novel by Steinbeck or Dreiser, people he had begun taking an interest in at that time, when Rabinder announced that he too wanted to become an actor.

The moment remained fresh in Binod's mind for a very long time. His cousin had remained bent over the bucket, quietly rubbing Lifebuoy soap between his toes, perhaps waiting for Binod to say something encouraging in response. After ten minutes, Rabinder placed his soles at the edge of the bucket and said, "I acted in plays in school. I enjoyed doing that. It has become plain to me that I should be doing something that I enjoy."

Binod felt his heart sink. He felt responsible. It seemed to him that just because he had mentioned seeing Dubey performing on the street, Rabinder had decided that he should be doing the same. He said, "Give the idea a little bit of time. If you continue to feel this way, then certainly we should find out how you could get a degree in drama."

Rabinder said, "Did you not like me in Death of a Salesman?"

Binod admitted that he had, and Rabinder said, "This is the time when we can change our minds. If I don't do it at twenty, when will I do it, when I'm sixty?"

During dinner the next night, Rabinder revealed that he had found Dubey. They had talked. Dubey was sharing a flat in Mukherjee Nagar with some other friends from Bettiah. The flat was only a couple of miles away. Rabinder had also met members of the theater group that Dubey had joined. He said that they were all bearded communists. But they couldn't say no to him. He had been told that he was free to come to their rehearsals every day at three o'clock on the lawns of the Law College.

He went. Every day in the afternoon, Rabinder fetched an omelet wrapped in a piece of newspaper; he would eat it sandwiched between the slices of bread they kept in the room. After lunch he dusted each armpit with talcum powder and walked over to the grounds of the Law College. The plays were improvised affairs; they were all in Hindi and they were fashioned as responses to current social issues. The idea was to educate the masses in an entertaining way.

Rabinder got more interested in the people performing the plays. There was a girl called Meera in that group and Rabinder told Binod that he liked her. He hadn't spoken to her yet. He said that her parents lived in Safdarjung Enclave. When Binod went to watch one of their rehearsals he knew that Meera was the pretty one in a mauve-colored cotton shirt. Her teeth were glinting and it took him a minute to realize that she was wearing braces. Meera was very fair-skinned and one would have guessed that she was wealthy from the way she laughed. She only spoke English. Dubey was there too, short in comparison to Rabinder, both of them with wiry beards on their cheeks. They both looked a little shabby, as if they had just arrived after a long journey on a train.

For many days, Rabinder was regular in attending rehearsals and he performed in a drama festival and also in some villages across the Yamuna. But then he stopped going. He told Binod that he had gotten into an argument with Meera and he didn't think that the communists wanted him anymore.

The same evening Rabinder confessed that he had told an actor in the group, a dull whining fellow called Trivedi, that he and Meera were likely to go together to watch the film *Massey Sahib*. There was no such plan, of course. Rabinder had till then exchanged no more than a few words with Meera. She was polite but they were not friends. It was just that Trivedi had appeared interested in Meera, and Rabinder had calculated that he might head off trouble early by suggesting that he was close to Meera. This fool Trivedi suspected that Rabinder was lying. He went to Meera and asked her about her movie date.

Meera came to Rabinder the next day. Trivedi was walking sullenly a couple of paces behind her. Rabinder denied having said anything to anyone. Trying to be emphatic in his denial, he ended up being curt with Meera. He could see that she did not believe him. The fact was that she was talking to him in English and it was difficult for Rabinder to be more at ease and tactful in his responses. Exasperated by his brusqueness, Meera said, "Either you are childish or you are just weird—and I have an idea that you are both."

Rabinder had nothing to say. He came back to the flat and lay down on the cot. Lying there silently in the dark, he played out in his mind various sequences, all of which involved his offering an apology to Meera and being granted quick forgiveness. When he closed his eyes and inhaled, he could smell her perfume. Everything would be okay. Both of them would talk. They would get past the misunderstanding and then inevitably fall in love. He would hold her the way one holds a Coca-Cola bottle and drinks from it.

But that didn't happen. Rabinder just never went back. However, he would meet Dubey often and they went out together to watch films. They would ask Binod to accompany them, but not always or very persistently, and he decided to stay away. When he returned to the room in the evenings, Dubey would be there, chatting with Rabinder. Many years later, when Binod began working in Bombay, he had written about one of those evenings in an article that was published in *Mid-Day*. Dubey was already famous by then and the feature was a piece of reminiscence about him. Binod had described an evening when he and Rabinder had sold the pile of accumulated newspapers to the raddiwala and then used that money to buy chicken and rum. On the way back to the room, they picked up Dubey. Binod cooked the chicken and the three of them got drunk on Old Monk. They sat outside on the roof, under the stars, and sang the Mukesh and Lata duet "Saawan ka maheena, Pawan kare shor."

Dubey told them that night that he had been living in a lodge in Bettiah just before he got a place in the hostel in the KR School. He was ten at that time. This was also the period during which Indira Gandhi had imposed the Emergency and there was a great deal of political unrest in the country. The toilets in the lodge opened on to the street: there was a hole in the floor and a bucket was placed beneath. It would be removed every day by the untouchable cleaner. Dubey would be sitting in the toilet during the cold winter nights and feel the chill air through the hole beneath him. The police outside made announcements from a van. The voice on the loudspeaker would reach him in the toilet: a curfew had been imposed and if anyone stepped out on the street he would be shot.

Dubey said, "I was too young to understand politics, but I was old enough to know fear. I was just a boy, shitting into a hole." In his mind, his fear was linked to the admiration he felt for his idol, Amitabh Bachchan. In those days, the film hero would make his entrance on screen and people would clap, because they knew that this man was going to make the villain's life hell. That was what was expected of a hero. If the hero spoke, the audience would listen. When Bachchan came into films, the movement against Indira Gandhi had already started. Did the boy sitting powerless in a toilet want to believe that he could become powerful? Dubey said, "Even a rickshawala had started reacting to mistreatment, so people recognized their stories in Amitabh Bachchan's anger. They wanted a leader, someone who could destroy anyone."

....

During their phone conversations, Binod couldn't bring himself to tell Rabinder that he was writing now about the romance between Bua and Parshuram. His reticence made Rabinder more emphatic. Whatever Binod chose to write, he needed to have hidden in it a romance. Rabinder would say, "Bhaiya, yeh hai anda ka funda—any hit film is in essence a love story."

When Binod had married Arpana, Rabinder became her favorite in the family. He would tell her stories about troubled romance in college. He would bring her small gifts, usually food that she liked from little-known places in Patna, and from the railway station he would pick up magazines and newspapers. Arpana would sit down with him and solve crossword puzzles in which you had to guess the names of cricketers and film stars. Rabinder had been opposed to the divorce but, unlike everyone else in the family, he had respected Binod's decision and said nothing. In fact, he was also the only one who had never asked Binod when he would remarry.

The love in Bombay films was sentimental, largely meaningless, and all over in three hours. If Binod found a film that departed from that model in any intelligent way, he experienced it as a form of euphoria. On the wall above the computer in his office, there hung a still from last year's early release, *Maqbool*. Critics had much to say about the film's adaptation of *Macbeth*, the drama transported ingeniously to the Muslim underworld of Bombay, but he had eyes only for Tabu. In the picture on his office wall, beautiful, warm, utterly human Tabu pointed a gun at her gangster-yet-to-be-lover played by Irfan, the man with the insomniac eyes, the one who like Macbeth would be unable to court sleep because of the nightmare of ambition planted in his mind.

"'Meri Jaan' kaho."

She had said, "Say 'my love' to me."

And when he did, warily, wearily—she asked him, the gun still pointed at his heart, "Are you doing me a favor? Speak those words as if you mean them. Say 'my love.'"

My love, my life. She dissolved into laughter when he said the words the way she had wanted. He snatched away the gun and slapped her.

It is tempting to think of truth being produced under the barrel of a gun. A gun held by a beautiful woman who wants your love. It is a pleasing deceit, the idea in the film that the woman who loves you will be your undoing, and not the other way around. After his divorce, after what he had done to Arpana, Binod could not lay claim to any innocence again.

He had been in love with Tabu since the winter of 1996. That is when she made her first major appearance, in Gulzar's *Maachis*, the only mainstream film to discuss the torture and the killings in Punjab. He remembered the film also for the soliloquy delivered by the leader of the terrorists. It went like this: "The country hasn't become self-sufficient. Yes, some people have. Electricity, water, housing, medical care, education. What has been made available to the common man? Sixty percent of the people still live below the poverty line. And they're not only poor, they're also unfortunate. It's been more than forty years since we got our independence. *Half a century!* How long are we to wait? I want my fair share, and that too in my lifetime. I want it *right now.*" This was an editorial of the sort that Binod wrote routinely—but made vivid and stirring by the actor Om Puri. His face was a rough map of disenchantment and rage. Tabu's was a fresh landscape where by the time the film ended pain had burned away all the tears. All the five rivers in the land were dry. Blood had been spilled in every home. You could look at Tabu's face and make the old mistake of wanting to read there your own destiny. Or, indeed, the fate of your nation.

Rabinder would meet Tabu when he visited Neeraj Dubey in Bombay. This would be at a party. All that he would say about her later was that she was wearing an orange poncho and looked sleepy.

Rabinder also claimed to have met the superstar Aishwarya Rai at a fundraiser. And at a cricket match in Delhi he had sat in the pavilion close to Anil Kapoor and Preity Zinta. One night, when shooting for *Barood*, Dubey had taken Rabinder along and he had seen Kareena Kapoor. The shot was being filmed on a highway close to Bandra. The police had shut off a whole section of the road that had been floodlit. Kareena had carefully used a thin maroon pencil to line her lips, pouting in front of the mirror, before turning her gaze at the camera. That was the detail that Rabinder tossed to Binod at breakfast. The scene he had described was, in Rabinder's mind, a bit like a woman dressing in public. It spoke to him of Kareena's confidence. The technicians and onlookers crowded around the shoot didn't exist for her. Rabinder bunched his lips together as if he were kissing. He said, "She is sexy. Definitely. Like a young lioness."

....

Binod had believed that Rabinder kept himself aloof from romantic and sexual attachments but then, a little over two years ago, just before Binod moved to Bombay, Neelu told him that Rabinder was involved with a married woman.

Everyone was in Patna for a brief holiday because Shatrughan, Neelu's husband, was beginning work on a high-rise building in Bank Colony. He wanted the whole family to witness the laying of the foundation stone. A band like the ones that you see at weddings in red and white uniforms had been arranged to play. There was a celebratory lunch with at least a hundred people.

The following night, a few of the guests whom Binod had seen at the event were sitting in the living room talking to Baba. The visitors had brought a marriage proposal for Rabinder; they had first gone to Bua's house, but she had sent them to Baba, saying that it was he who made all such decisions in the family. The girl lived in Dhanbad and her father owned a hotel and a petrol station. He was also involved in municipal politics. Binod went inside the room where Neelu was sitting, listening to the radio. He said, "It'll be good if Rabinder gets married. Bua will be happy."

Neelu said very quietly, "Rabinder is following in the footsteps of Lattu Chachaji."

Binod immediately thought of the maidservant in the house, Lily, a Christian Adivasi girl from Chaibasa. Was Rabinder using her?

Lattu Chachaji was Baba's first cousin. He had returned to the village after an unsuccessful attempt at acquiring a law degree in Motihari. Nevertheless, he was more educated than anyone else in Ratauli and had even tried to become elected as the leader of the village panchayat. But the lower-caste vote had gone against Lattu. He had lost very badly. Lattu had for a long while kept as his mistress a Kurmi girl who had worked in his fields. The girl's name was Girija and she was sixteen when Lattu had started sleeping with her. At first people heard that Girija had been hired to cook dinner every evening for Lattu, but soon she had stopped joining other laborers in the fields during the day. Just before evening fell, she would be seen walking to Lattu's large brick house. She would have freshly bathed. She wore bright saris and she put glittering rupee-sized bindis on her forehead.

The medical officer at the government hospital fourteen miles away was from the same caste as Binod's family and he had quietly performed an abortion on Girija. Later, Lattu Chachaji also had to give ten thousand rupees for the dowry when the girl's marriage was settled with a youth from a nearby village who had been working as a watchman in Calcutta.

But the truth about Rabinder turned out to be a bit more complicated.

Neelu said that the woman that Rabinder was with was the wife of a Bengali officer who was the deputy director in the Health Department. She was an educated woman. She lived in the same building as Bua. Recently the government had appointed Bua the head of the Women's Welfare Board as well as the Education Reform Commission—appointments that resulted in her being given a bungalow near the airport—but earlier she had lived in a flat in the government-owned building on Gardiner Road. The building had apartments occupied by legislators and mid-level bureaucrats. The woman with whom Rabinder was having an affair lived on another floor in that same building. The woman's name was Rani or Reema.

"Did Rabinder tell you all this?"

Neelu laughed. She said, "Everyone in Patna knows about it."

"Including the husband?"

Neelu gave Binod a look. But it wasn't clear whether he was being foolish because *of course* the husband knew or of course he *didn't*.

He repeated the question.

His sister responded, "Why does it matter?"

....

Both Bua and Rabinder were at home. Rabinder said loudly, "A visit from a member of the independent press!"

Bua said, "Baba called a few minutes ago. Can you show me the pictures?"

He handed her the two photographs. The prospective bride, wearing a silk sari, gazed into the half-distance under studio lights. Her face and arms had a rigidity about them which, Binod was convinced, studio photographers confused for a declaration of virginity. The other picture was a close-up of the young woman's unsmiling face. Both photographs had been taken on the same day.

Bua looked at the pictures and smiled, and then passed them to Rabinder, who casually glanced over them. Then, looking at Binod, he grinned. He asked, "What did Baba say? Did he demand a sample of her writing?"

"Show me her homework!" Bua said, laughing, and asked, "My dear, will you eat fish?"

Mutton cooked with lots of onion was Rabinder's dish of choice; fish cooked in mustard came a distant second. Binod had just eaten but he began to feel a sudden awakening of hunger. The servant stepped shyly into the room with the tea on a tray. Bua gave him instructions for lunch. The young fellow was to fry the fish first and show it to Bua before preparing the curry.

After lunch, Rabinder took Binod to his room so that he could smoke a cigarette in peace. There was a large map of Bihar hanging on one wall of his room and near the door there was a small picture of Shri Ramakrishna. There were two chairs, and a pile of law books were stacked on the desk. A somewhat squat but buff Lord Hanuman, attached to a blue-dialed alarm clock, sat on a low table next to the bed.

Rabinder placed himself on a chair and began to smoke. Binod lay down on the batik-print bedspread and said, "I understand that you have a woman."

The look of surprise on Rabinder's face lasted only for a moment. He grinned. Clapping his hands, he said, "You are a true journalist."

Binod said, "But not a very good one. I know very little about her."

The first thing that he learned was that the woman's name was not Rani or Reema as Neelu had thought, but Roma, short for Romola. Yes, she was a Bengali. She was short and fair and had beautiful eyes. She looked a little bit, in Rabinder's opinion, like the young Sharmila Tagore in *An Evening in Paris*, the object of desire for a rambunctious Shammi Kapoor. Roma was a singer and had performed at a couple of events organized by women's groups. Bua had been invited to such events and that is how Rabinder had first come in contact with her.

Yes, she was married. But, Rabinder added quickly, there were no children.

Rabinder thought that her husband was impotent. No, he didn't know for sure.

Yes, the husband knew. Knew about Rabinder? He must, Rabinder said, looking up at Binod as if for confirmation. He said that it seemed the husband deliberately absented himself whenever his wife wanted to be with her lover. Binod couldn't say for certain that he saw love pouring out of Rabinder's eyes that afternoon, but there was undeniable pride in his voice and he looked happy.

....

More facts emerged later that evening. Shatrughan brought home a bottle of Scotch in Binod's honor. He had already talked to Rabinder on the phone and they waited till he arrived, two big bags of tandoori chicken in his hand.

The men drank and talked. They could hear the television on the other side of the wall, Baba and Ma watching the news from America. Shatrughan was characteristically adamant that they have a very good time. He was becoming more than a bit annoying. He kept turning up the music and Neelu would come into the room from the kitchen to lower the volume.

Binod changed the subject. He looked at Rabinder and said slowly, "I have been thinking of our conversation this afternoon . . . I don't think he knows. I don't think Roma's husband has a clue about your sneaking into his house when he's not there."

Rabinder didn't reply. He lowered his eyes.

It was Shatrughan who broke the silence. He said to Binod, "It is you who know nothing. Roma's husband knows everything. Rabinder himself told him."

Binod looked at Rabinder. His eyes were still downcast but there was a faint smile on his lips.

The affair had started with Rabinder going down to the flat when the woman was alone in her house. Her servant was not there because Rabinder's friend Vishnu had stopped by a few minutes earlier and taken the fellow in his car to Rupak Cinema where the new film *Lagaan* was being shown. The boy was told he could choose to sit anywhere he wanted. He happily sat down very close to the screen in the front. The film was four hours long, so Vishnu gave him enough money to eat and drink and then catch a rickshaw home.

Rabinder began to grin.

Shatrughan said, "Rabinder had his way with Roma during the first visit itself."

This time Binod did not look at Rabinder. If he understood what Shatrughan was saying, Rabinder had raped her. Shatrughan was saying that this happened on a few occasions. Rabinder was pressing and rubbing a nub on the thick bedcover with his thumbnail. Had he so scared the Bengali woman that she had not even complained to anyone?

Shatrughan had been speaking with slow pauses. He raised his voice a notch and said, "The fun thing is that she likes him so much now that she misses him if he doesn't visit her for a few days."

Then he said, "You should meet her. Nice lady. She is modern."

In Patna, to call a woman modern usually means that she wears sleeveless blouses and can drive a car. Rabinder hadn't spoken a word. Shatrughan said that Roma cooked for Rabinder sometimes. She was a fashionable woman and wanted to open a boutique on Dak Bungalow Road in Patna. The two of them—Rabinder and Roma—often made plans for the future. Rabinder had wanted to go to the Kumbha Mela but she had suggested Mt. Abu in Rajasthan.

"Or is Mt. Abu in Gujarat?" Shatrughan asked.

All this while, Rabinder had looked up only once, smiling half-bashfully. His expression became suddenly serious when he saw what must have been a blank expression on Binod's face.

There was silence for a while. Then Shatrughan said that Rabinder had stopped Banerjee, Roma's husband, on the stairs of his own home and had invited him out for dinner. Banerjee had said they could go out the next evening, but Rabinder had insisted that the matter couldn't wait. It concerned Banerjee's job. They went and ate at the new Saluja restaurant. Rabinder drank Scotch and Banerjee agreed to have a beer. During dinner, Rabinder hinted that the man's boss, the health minister, was Bua's friend and that he had been asking them about their opinion of their neighbor Banerjee. The fellow had looked surprised but said nothing.

On the way back, while they were in the car, Rabinder told Banerjee that he was having an affair with his wife. Shatrughan used the English word "involved." Rabinder told the man that if he dared to speak about this matter to his wife, he would break his bones. And if he went to the police, Rabinder said that he would still break his bones but he would also make sure that he had made public the fact that his wife had come to him begging for sex.

That conversation had taken place when the affair had started. But now, Rabinder used it to blackmail Banerjee. Rabinder would send to him all his cronies who did business in pharmaceuticals or wanted contracts with hospitals. They always got help. When he finished delivering these details Shatrughan smiled and patted Rabinder's calf, like a wrestling coach showing affection for a boy who had a coveted prize under his belt.

Binod said, "What does Roma like about you?"

Rabinder suppressed a giggle. He said, "She doesn't like me. She calls me an animal. She calls me Junglee . . ."

"But Shatrughan says she misses you."

He said, "That is true. I went to Delhi and she called me every day."

"Why?"

"I don't know."

After a pause, Rabinder added, "I think she likes the idea of being in love with someone who is not her husband . . . I would marry her otherwise. Honest."

Even without knowing much about Roma, Binod felt both revulsion and desire.

. . . .

It was easy not to meet Roma because of the general disapproval of her. But he heard conflicting reports during his visits to Patna: the affair between Roma and Rabinder had cooled; the affair had revived and they had gone to Gaya together to see the new statue of Buddha that the Japanese were building; Roma had been seen shopping with Bua; Roma's husband was seeking a transfer; Bua had told someone that Banerjee should be sent to the asylum in Ranchi.

Long before Roma's murder, which took place when Rabinder was in prison, it had begun to amaze Binod that the whole affair only remained a subject of gossip. No one really tried to find out the truth. When he got the news that Rabinder had been arrested, he had immediately assumed that Roma or her husband had finally informed the police. But he was wrong. Rabinder's arrest was entirely unconnected. In the days that followed, the attention remained focused on Rabinder's imprisonment and trial, and the Banerjees were forgotten, till the news appeared in the papers that Roma was dead.

11

There was a time close to the mid-1980s when Rabinder and his friends would shoot heroin into their veins and stand close to the railway tracks in Rajendra Nagar waiting for a train to pass.

A small two-story yellow structure owned by the railways stood a hundred yards away from the railway crossing: a man would lean half-out of the window on the top and wave a green flag when a train was approaching. These boys would step out from behind the building when the train came close. They wanted to feel the blast of air when the train passed inches away from their faces.

If your arms were still tingling from the sting of the needle, the effect of the cool air rushing like that gave you a special high. The boys were eighteen or nineteen. Binod had heard that Rabinder used to take off his shirt and stand with his arms raised. The train would come, whistles blowing, and that sudden sucking into a tunnel of air was like being swept into a trance.

One day there was an accident. A milkman was sitting near the door of one of the compartments of a passing train. He had his big aluminum milk cans next to him and his bamboo stave was wedged between the cans and protruded a full arm or two outside the door. The train came too quickly and anyway these boys kept their eyes shut. Rabinder's friend Paritosh was to his left and caught the stick on his ribs.

The blow flung him against his friends. Although there was no puncturing of the lungs, several of his ribs were broken. His left arm was in a cast for months. Many years later, in a theater in Delhi, Binod watched a film in English called Trainspotting and it showed boys in Scotland horsing around at the railway tracks. It was difficult for him to understand what they were saying, but there were people in the audience who were laughing. He thought of people back in Bihar traveling on the roofs of the trains, sometimes just for fun but mostly because there was no space inside, and he wondered whether in countries like England or Germany people would laugh if they watched a movie that showed a scene like that. And then he remembered being told about Rabinder standing beside the tracks in a trance. Who knows, perhaps it would look great in a movie if someone showed the hero, high on heroin, left swaying in the slipstream of the Rajdhani Express.

When all of this happened, Binod was in college in Delhi. Every day during the years that he was an undergraduate at Hindu College, the papers were filled with reports of the violence in Punjab. Rows of newspapers in the students' mess would be open to the same stories of massacres each morning. He would sit down for breakfast and read the news. Cold scrambled eggs with tomatoes in them always reminded him now of the demand for Khalistan.

The roads of Delhi, where he had first discovered the excitement of being in a large city, became a labyrinth of police checkpoints and military bunkers. Buses were frequently stopped and the luggage checked. At night, cops peered into cars; they held light machine guns in one hand and torches in the other. Then one morning Indira Gandhi was shot dead outside her home. October had nearly come to an end. Binod's roommate, Goel, returned to the hostel from Mukherjee Nagar after having beaten up two Sikh boys who had been distributing sweets on the street. Goel was the opening batsman for Delhi University, but he had hurt his hand while meting out the punishment, and he was upset that he had missed lunch.

Through the afternoon, classes continued to be held and Binod attended a lecture on Locke. By evening, there were reports of violence in the city and when night came, the horizon glowed from houses on fire. Goel climbed to the roof of the hostel in the morning. He said that dense black smoke was rising from all around the university campus. Everyone ran up to take a look.

Three days later Binod joined a group that was going to work in a relief camp. A young history professor took them to Kalyanpuri where all the Sikh houses now stood empty. In the streets all around them was the stench of spilled guts. They had to be careful not to step on the hair that had been cut from the men before they were murdered. Binod passed an open door. Outside the door was a patch of fire-blackened lawn.

Inside, a Hindu family was sitting around a table. No one was eating. Had these people seen a Sikh being burned in their garden? Binod didn't have the courage to ask. Back in the relief camp, he heard turbaned old men with long beards telling a female reporter about how their sons had been forced to drink kerosene before being set alight. That explained the smell in Kalyanpuri.

He only lasted another day in the camp. There was confusion about how they were going to team up, and he used it as an excuse to stay away. This was before his Orwell days: there was only altruism and guilt at that time, and these were easier to suppress than the curiosity that would come later.

There was someone called Rajji in their hostel; he shaved his beard and had his long hair chopped off two days after the riots started. Rajji was a Sikh from Hazaribagh in Bihar. When Goel returned from Indira Gandhi's funeral, he said that he felt sad. Then he confessed that earlier he had felt only anger. He spoke of Rajji. On that first day, when Goel had gone on the roof and seen the smoke, a man who cleaned the toilets in the hostel had told him that the Sikhs had poisoned the water supply in parts of Delhi. Goel had known that this was probably only a rumor. But he decided that if the report turned out to be true, he would kill Rajji. Two years later, both Goel and Rajji joined the civil services. Binod ran into Goel once at the Old Delhi railway station some years later. He was a deputy commissioner in Tripura and had two lovely daughters.

Classes resumed in late November but Binod fell sick. He had an acute case of bronchitis and Goel made him swallow a tablespoon of warm mustard oil each morning and night. He felt a little better after a fortnight and decided to go to Patna. The train was the Tinsukia Mail going to Assam and it kept getting delayed as it moved east; he stepped down on the platform at Patna, wrapped in a blanket, at three in the morning.

Passing the windows of the houses shuttered against the night, a rickshaw brought him home. Baba was the one who woke up and opened the door. Binod hadn't shaved for many days. When Ma came out, he saw fear on her face. She asked him why he had come back.

It was several hours later, after he had returned from a visit to the doctor in the morning, that he learned the reason for her fear. Rabinder was in jail. This was the first time that he would be imprisoned. He was barely nineteen.

....

Four boys had decided to rob a jewelry shop—Navlakha Diamonds on S. P. Verma Road. They arrived at the shop on two motorcycles. The boys had among them three kattas, cheap homemade guns.

Rabinder had walked into Navlakha first, seen that there was only one customer inside, and then come out and given the signal to his companions. He then seated himself on his motorcycle and waited. When his friends disappeared into the shop, a plainclothesman came out of the hair-cutting place next door and pushed a revolver into Rabinder's chest. Rabinder bravely revved his bike but received a blow on his face. He cut the engine and then heard the shots.

A man in Rajendra Nagar was their source for heroin and Paritosh, who was the son of a professor, had promised that he would soon pay off his debts. The dealer was getting impatient. When he arrived at Paritosh's house with a gun, the boy tried to reassure him that his payment was guaranteed. This was the day before the job. He and his friends, Paritosh told the dealer, were going to rob a jewelry shop. The man was pleased with this piece of news, and sat down for a hit, but before he left he forced Paritosh to be more precise about their plans.

A deal was struck that evening between the jeweler and the drug dealer. An hour later, the police had picked up the dealer from one of his haunts and taken him away; no case was filed against him so that the matter would remain secret. And that is why a team of plainclothesmen was sitting nearby when Rabinder and his buddies arrived at Navlakha.

A sharpshooter, also in plainclothes, was inside the shop assisting the jeweler as a salesman. The officer in charge was a young man from Kerala who, the newspapers said, was a martial arts expert as well as a Kathakali dancer. He sat in the store bargaining over a pair of earrings. He was an adventurous fellow and had put on a pair of spectacles and a Gandhi cap. There was no one else inside.

Paritosh ordered the safe to be opened and then tried to cock his gun. The cop pretending to be the salesman saw that it was a cheap katta liable to go off unexpectedly and decided he wasn't going to take any chances. He shot the boy in the face. Paritosh's family did not even claim his body.

But Bua wasn't like that. She said to Baba, "He will go mad in prison."

She spoke to various ministers and officers. Baba had also heard other reports. He told Binod that Bua paid the thana inspector to make some changes in the police report, and then he began to say that this was impossible because Bua did not have that kind of money. Bua was advised to get a new birth certificate made for Rabinder that would allow her to claim in court that he was less than seventeen years old. She did everything that needed to be done. Rabinder would be released in two months, one day before the case came up before the judicial magistrate.

....

Binod took a train to Buxar and went to see Rabinder in prison. The cough that he had brought from Delhi had not eased, and the smoke from the train affected him. He was often breathless; as a result, he was not able to talk much. The train that would bring him back to Patna would cross Buxar in two hours and he could spend only over an hour with Rabinder. But this was his first visit to a prison and he was excited.

Rabinder didn't say much at first and then while they ate oranges he said that he was sleeping a lot in prison. He slept even in the afternoon although it was winter and the day ended quickly. The smell of fish being fried in the market on the other side of the prison walls would draw him out of his sleep every evening.

A little later he said that he used to have odd dreams in his sleep. The previous day Rabinder had seen their grandfather in his dream — Baba's and Bua's father, who had been dead for ten years. In his dream, Rabinder was squatting on the floor of the bedroom while their grandfather, old and with the white mark of Vishnu on his forehead, sat in a chair looking serenely at him.

He smiled faintly, "What does it mean?"

Binod shrugged.

Rabinder laughed, "If you are in prison, you have a lot of time to think about useless things."

It was around this time that Rabinder told his mother that he wanted to study law in Delhi.

Rabinder's declaration had been surprising to Binod not least because Binod was filled with uncertainty about what he himself was going to do. There were exams that he needed to take in May and after that he would have to make up his mind whether he was going to appear for the civil services test. He wasn't sure whether he wanted to stay in Delhi or return to Patna. Often during those days, Binod suffered from the feeling that he was utterly adrift.

When Bua told him of her conversation with Rabinder, he felt a quick stab of irritation. Bua had forgotten what had happened the last time Rabinder had gone to Delhi; he had gotten into a fight and his own friend, a boy from Bettiah who had accompanied him, had tried to stab him. But

Binod's real anger was perhaps at himself for not having had a sense of purpose or the courage to move to Delhi to work.

A week later Baba announced that he was going to a place close to Buxar. He and a small crew would be collecting footage in Ara and then Jagdishpur. He told Binod that he could take a bus to Buxar and pay a visit to the prison for a few hours.

This time Binod was afraid that Rabinder might be sleeping because it was early in the afternoon, but his cousin appeared very quickly at the barred window outside the assistant superintendent's office. He had spent more than a month in prison and now appeared much more at ease. He was smiling. He said that a dog that he had often fed scraps from his meals was right then giving birth to little pups in the yard outside his cell.

It was a mongrel that roamed outside the ward—at some point in the past it had probably climbed in through the sewer when it was being cleaned. Rabinder said, "The bitch had been sullen all through the afternoon. But I hadn't known . . ." He had seen her pacing around the tiny clump of banana trees in the yard. Then she had vomited.

He said, "A little while ago, I saw her licking what looked like a bone. Then, I saw that it was a puppy. I think there are more to come . . ."

He smiled, and Binod did too.

In Rabinder's opinion, Baba should have come to Buxar and filmed the inmates. Rabinder gripped the bars of the window and smiled, "Jail life!"

They talked for a while and then Rabinder waved over a guard wearing a khaki uniform and dark orange sneakers. He put a twenty-rupee note in the man's shirt pocket. He said, "I have a guest. Can we get some tea? The rest of the money is for you."

He also wanted the man to get a saucer of milk and some bread for the bitch that had just littered. He laughed and said in a loud voice in English, "Dog is man's best friend." Then, shifting to Hindi, he said to the guard, "Please do this much. She too is the daughter of Mother India."

. . . .

While Rabinder and Binod sat drinking tea, Baba was a few miles away to the east of Buxar Jail, shooting the landscape on which a military encounter had taken place more than a century ago. The documentary was for the Bihar government archives. It was a tribute to the life of Veer Kuer Singh, one of the heroes of the rebellion against the British in 1857.

Kuer Singh had been a landlord from Jagdishpur, near Ara, and when the sepoys of the British cantonment revolted, they gathered around him and proclaimed him their maharaja.

It was only much later, after he had seen some of the writing that Baba had done, that Binod became aware of his real purpose in wanting to make the film about the rebellion. Kuer Singh was eighty years old when he joined the revolt. This single fact had inspired Baba. He wanted the old man's courage and strength to be recognized and praised.

In September 1857, the ruler in Delhi, Bahadur Shah Zafar, who was eighty-two, had been taken prisoner by the British and sent into exile in Burma. He was never to return but old Kuer Singh soldiered on. He embarked on an arduous four-hundred-mile journey to Kanpur, participating in battles and guerrilla attacks even during the monsoons. After a long march west took him to Rewa, Kalpi, and then Kanpur, Kuer Singh continued to harass the British well into the next year. In the last days of his life, in April 1858, Kuer Singh defeated the British forces at Azamgarh.

When the enemy turned on the offensive again, he conducted a brilliant withdrawal of his forces for over one hundred and fifty miles. Despite their superior firepower and their leadership, which had been tested in the Crimean War, the English soldiers could not capture Kuer Singh. He crossed the Ganges with his army and died in his home in Jagdishpur, his own golden banner flying from his rooftop.

Baba's film ended with the camera showing a large painting of Kuer Singh making the crossing on the Ganges at Shivpur Ghat. On April 21, 1858 the sepoys had succeeded in eluding the British infantry as well as the surveillance of three gunboats deployed on the Ganges. When the British forces arrived at the ghat, most of the rebel army had crossed over to safety on the other side. Kuer Singh was on a boat in the river, guiding the withdrawal from the enemy's advance. The Royal Horse Artillery and the guns of the gunboat *Meghna* started firing on the retreating army. One boat capsized and the boat on which Kuer Singh stood took a hit. His left arm was shattered by a cannon ball. Binod remembered reading in his history book in school that amputation was the only cure in those days. The painting that Baba used in his film showed the eighty-year-old warrior, having drawn his sword with his right hand, chopping off his left arm and letting it fall as an offering to the holy river.

12

A year ago in Bombay, Binod was sitting in the Café Samovar, sipping lemonade that smelled faintly of onions, and reading the previous day's copy of the Hindu. Nearby were the libraries and offices built of yellow Malad stone a century ago. Rainwater dripped from green leaves, washing clean the dirty marble busts of a business tycoon whose ancestors had come to Bombay from Baghdad. Binod was looking at an article on Vedic myths by one Sukumari Bhattacharji. Bhattacharji had written, "The spiritual life of the period exhibits peaks and lows. We have philosophical speculations of considerable significance in a few hymns. But simultaneously, there are many prayers for the destruction of enemies, of co-wives and rivals, and prayers for the safe abduction of a girl on a dark night, for her brothers to sleep soundly and for the dogs not to bark."

Binod tore out the paragraph and put it in his diary. The essay interested him because it presented a more down-to-earth view of what is thought of as an ancient and sacred Vedic culture. At first he thought he would show it to Baba but he knew that he wouldn't and he never did.

His father's sense of religion was edged with an annoying high-mindedness. Although Baba had a sharp and unsentimental sense of the world around him, he also believed in a pure realm that existed above and beyond the tainted domains of human habitation. Unfortunately, even in his work, he tried to convey the same idealism and as a result his documentaries seemed deprived of oxygen and were always without life.

Until shortly after Binod was born, Baba had been a lecturer in Motihari, and then he had started working for the state government in a low-paid job in Bettiah. After a few years, he had joined the Public Relations Department and had himself transferred to Patna. A friend of his from college had become a Hindi radio announcer on All India Radio, and he got Baba involved in writing speeches for politicians. While he was working in public relations, Baba also started producing scripts for short documentaries. These were the black-and-white government films that were shown in cinema halls just before the start of the main features.

You came to watch a drama about a man who is sent to London to study law and who comes back to marry a village belle, but first you had to sit through a five-minute documentary about how new locomotive engines had been designed at Chittaranjan near Asansol.

Everyone worked cheerfully in these films, contributing their mite to national progress, just like the many instruments combined in the orchestra that had provided the loud background score.

Baba's family was also recruited to do its bit. A film had needed to be made on farming and irrigation. Baba arranged for the film to be shot in their village. The government jeep took them to Bettiah and then an hour away to Ratauli. The film started with a view of the bridge on the irrigation canal where Binod had often stood during evenings, spitting into the water and watching the thin black fish nibbling on his spit. When the camera panned over a farmer guiding his two bullocks while hoeing his field, Baba told Binod to run in a diagonal line across the new rows that had been furrowed into the ground. In the documentary, Binod was a ten-year-old boy scowling at the sun and then running across the frame to the mixed beat of tabla and cymbals.

Two years later, Baba was given the task of coming up with a documentary on the rehabilitation of soldiers who had been maimed in the Bangladesh War. Viewers all over India watched documentary footage of a boy (Binod, hair freshly combed, his shirt buttoned up right up to his throat) intently studying the actions of a smiling man sitting in front of a bulky piece of machinery, the man swinging his arms rhythmically, weaving a long bolt of multi-patterned cloth (the camera zoomed back to reveal his amputated calves while the voice-over identified him as Sudama Mandal, a brave soldier wounded in the last war).

When Lalji went mad and was sent to Ranchi, Baba's superiors approved his proposal for a film about the progressive ways in which mental sickness was being treated in the government hospitals. A car was provided for the long trip. Binod made an appearance in that film too. Visitors to the hospital were shown waiting on benches under tall eucalyptus trees, and Binod sat among them, eating a snack that the cameraman shared with him between takes.

Baba had suggested that the documentary would encourage people to provide treatment to relatives who were mentally ill. In villages and small towns such people were commonly locked up in a small room. Binod suspected that the film was never released for viewing. Perhaps a bureaucrat in the Information Ministry in Delhi had found the film too cheerful. As it was, the hospital in Ranchi had acquired a slightly sinister reputation as a dumping ground for helpless people whose relatives put them there if they were interested in their property. Another story that had appeared in the press was that two Chinese men captured during the war in 1962 had been kept there because no one understood what they were saying. The men had by now learned a few words of Hindi. They could ask for tea and biscuits. One of them was slowly going mad. No government official thought that the mental hospital was in need of any more public attention.

....

From an early age, Binod had learned that Baba offered lessons for the masses. These were lessons that proclaimed India's march toward the rosy horizon of development. Baba wanted him to do well in school but could not be concerned about the lowly task of helping him with homework. On those rare occasions when he was unoccupied, especially on Sundays, Baba would want to know what he was learning at school. Whenever Baba tried to teach him, however, he would inevitably lose his temper, and, almost in anticipation of this, Binod would become nervous and make mistakes. Once when he was still in school in Patna, Binod was in the living room watching a film on television. This was in the afternoon when they would show art films or regional films in languages other than Hindi. That day Binod was watching a film in which Naseeruddin Shah played an Anglo-Indian named Albert Pinto. He heard his father calling him.

Baba was lying on the bed with the *Sunday Times of India* in his hand.

"What were you doing?"

"Nothing."

"Why nothing? Are Sundays only for wasting time?"

He stayed silent.

Baba nodded toward the paper and said, "Read this."

Binod took the newspaper and began to walk out of the room, back to the television where the film had gone on without him. From his place on the bed, Baba shouted, "Where are you going? I asked you to read something from the paper."

Binod put out his tongue to show him that he realized he had made a mistake.

He sat down at the edge of the bed and looked down at the newspaper. The ceiling fan was making a creaking sound with each rotation. The way

Baba was lying on the bed, if the fan fell down, it was sure to land on his body. The thought crossed Binod's mind that a person might die if a fan fell on him. If the blades were still in motion, which they probably would be, they could even possibly cut a person in half. It also occurred to him that a fan could operate like a helicopter, and therefore, even in the act of falling it could actually travel some distance. In which case, he too would be fair prey.

The newspaper article began with a quotation from a book by Louis Fischer on the life of Gandhi: "At Rajghat, a few hundred feet from the river, a fresh pyre had been built of stone, brick and earth. It was eight feet square and about two feet high. Long, thin sandalwood logs sprinkled with incense were stacked on it. Mahatma Gandhi's body lay on the pyre with his head to the north. In that position Buddha met his end."

Binod's reading did not progress any further. Baba asked him to read those beginning lines once again.

It was very common for Baba to complain of his failing eyesight and it seemed right to assume that Binod was being tested for the task of a reader for his father. He reread the lines, paying less attention to the words. He tried to make his voice more sonorous, like an actor's, and read through the passage with the right intonation and dramatic emphasis.

Baba asked, "Whose memorial is at Rajghat?"

Binod was surprised by the question and he stared hard at the passage in front of him. It was obvious that Mahatma Gandhi was cremated there. The last line mentioned Gautama Buddha. This must be the hidden clue that Baba wanted him to notice.

"Gautama Buddha," he answered quickly.

His father's voice changed as if he needed to clear his throat. He said slowly, "Where was Bhagwan Buddha born?" Binod now felt that he had probably answered right. He also knew the answer to the new question. This had actually been a joke in his school. Mr. Lall, the history teacher, had said during one of his lectures, "When the Buddha was in pregnancy in Kapilvastu, his mother had a dream with a white elephant in it . . ."

Binod said, "Kapilvastu."

Baba nodded and then said in an even voice, "And where did he die?"

"Rajghat."

Baba's right leg came at him with great force but not fast enough because there was time for Binod to become a camera installed in the ceiling. He observed from that height his hip being pushed off the bed and the rest of his body seeming to follow later. He was afraid that Baba was going to slap the face that he saw on the floor, but Baba only sat up on the bed and repeated the question he had asked earlier.

"Where did Gautama Buddha die?"

For the first time, doubt entered Binod's head. He had perhaps not read the passage carefully enough. He began to pass his eyes over it again but he was having difficulty because his eyes had filled up with what must be tears. He was thankful that he was reading only to himself, otherwise he was sure his voice would have cracked and embarrassed him. He heard Baba say, with some gentleness in his voice this time, "Tell me the name of the place where Gautama Buddha breathed his last."

Binod was midway through the passage when this question was asked.

In order to gain time, he now began to read the rest of the words out loud. But the answer was not there on the page. It was not in those words in front of him and, maybe to gain his father's sympathy, he began to sob.

Baba was not moved. He leaned toward him and caught hold of the hair on the side of his head. But it was the ear that he wanted and, with a second lunge, he caught and twisted his ear.

He said, "Unless you stop crying, how are you going to learn anything?"

The question made sense. There was also tenderness in Baba's voice. Binod saw his advantage and wiped away his tears and then brushed his short sleeve under his nose. He tried to concentrate on the newspaper and was conscious of his hands shaking.

"Have you heard of Sarnath?" Baba asked.

The name came from a distance, but it sounded familiar. In fact, he suddenly knew that that was where Buddha had died. Yet he didn't want to risk giving the wrong answer; he stayed silent. Baba said that he was a fool.

Once again, Binod said nothing and then his father said, "Buddha attained nirvana in Sarnath near Benares."

Binod was not certain that his ordeal had now ended. Baba asked him to pick up the newspaper. When he started reading those familiar lines again, Baba stopped him. He said, "Go. Bring your notebook." Binod hurried out to the living room where his school bag was lying on the floor. On the television, he caught a glimpse of Naseeruddin Shah riding a motorcycle near the sea in a city that must be Bombay.

The notebook for Hindi was the one that had the greatest number of empty pages. He took it to his father. Baba said, "Where is your pen?" and Binod went back out again. "Write," Baba said, when he returned. "The samadhi of the Father of the Nation is at Rajghat in Delhi." Binod was to write this five hundred times. The lesson was over.

IV

✳

Kiss of the

Spider Woman

13

Rabinder and Binod were both in Patna, home from college, eating mangos one evening when the news came of Lalji's death.

The trip to Ranchi was made by train. Binod and Rabinder were going to get the body. Bua had spoken to the speaker of the Bihar Assembly and he had made matters easier at the morgue. The following day was August 15, Independence Day, and the speaker had regretted that he could not provide his own official car for the boys. On the train, Binod watched Rabinder reading the new issue of India Today that had a cover story about the trial of Indira Gandhi's killers. They had not spoken about Lalji. When it was time to sleep he asked his cousin if he needed anything. Rabinder said that he was going to smoke and went off in the direction of the toilet. Ten minutes later, Binod also got up. Rabinder had unlocked the door of the coach and was leaning against the side with a cigarette in his hand. Outside, in the pitch dark, showers of sparks, caught in the smoke thrown out by the railway engine, flew past and died a moment later.

At seven the next morning, they hired a taxi. The man at the morgue wanted Binod to sign three copies of a form. Binod gave the pen to Rabinder but he silently shook his head. While he was signing the yellow sheets, Binod could hear the pigeons cooing outside. He had expected the room to be chilly and was disappointed that the sweat under his armpits wasn't even fully dry.

The attendant wore a Gandhi cap and was barefoot. He began in a whining voice. "It is August 15, sir. I was supposed to be on leave today . . ." He stopped to touch the pieces of cotton protruding from Lalji's nostrils—he was like a waiter in a restaurant straightening the cutlery on the white cloth. Then, he resumed. "But a phone call came from Patna and I have been here just for you—"

Rabinder cut him off. "I came here to take away a corpse, but I'll wait. Why don't you tear the flesh out first and eat to your heart's content?"

They sat in the front along with the driver of the taxi. The body lay in a wooden crate with a block of ice and soggy sawdust wrapped in sacks of jute. The crate had been put on the back seat. Binod could feel a coolness behind his neck because of the ice, but the Ambassador was fairly old and its floor had been corroded, and hot air from the engine poured onto his toes. Every now and then he would readjust his sandals, trying his best to cover with his soles the gaps in the floorboard. In his hands was a library copy of *The Road to Wigan Pier*. He would read a few lines and then the hot air would make him sigh and he would lift up his head.

Rabinder didn't say much. He sat next to the window and gazed at the passing landscape, flat red earth with tiny pieces of mica gleaming and sparkling in the sun. Small, seemingly stunted cattle stretched their necks to nibble on the leaves of short-limbed keekar trees. At short intervals, the car would come upon Adivasi men and women with weather-beaten faces sitting in the shade of rocks and trees. The walls of the huts that faced the highway were covered with a government slogan encouraging education for girls. There was nothing to distract Binod from the fact that the corpse had begun to smell. They traveled like that for six hours.

The reason Binod was in Patna when the call had come from Ranchi was that he had taken his exams in Delhi and was waiting for his results. He had begun reading George Orwell and he told himself that he would try to write; but even though he wrote a bit and felt pleased when he put words on paper, nothing very good came of his efforts.

In school they had read an essay by George Orwell called "Politics and the English Language" and at first it had not made any special impact on Binod. But he read it again, by chance, in the same old school textbook and, as a result, decided to give up the use of a dozen words that had till then distinguished him from his classmates. ("I am *sanguine* that you are in good health"; "the *cerulean* sky"; "if we meet in the afternoon, we can share a light *repast*"; "the landscape around Barauni is full of *verdure*, and, albeit infested with dacoits or armed *brigands*, the area boasts several *picturesque* spots"; "full of *poppycock*"; "*verily*, the air in my native village Ratauli is quite *salubrious*"; "*saturnine* aspect," "our *pusillanimous* politicians"; and so forth.)

The exam results came out in July. Binod hadn't done well but this didn't bother him. He began to tell his parents and everyone else that he would take a job at a newspaper in Delhi. He read *Homage to Catalonia*. In Delhi, for a whole week after his exams, he had watched a retrospective of six films by Shyam Benegal. Binod wanted to write reports on the social realities that those films depicted. But for that he needed to leave Patna. The terrible things that were to be seen in Benegal's films could be found in Patna too, of course, but those were already familiar to him and he wanted to explore their richness elsewhere.

A part of the reason he wanted to leave Patna was that he wanted some distance from the ever present distress. He was wary of pain and although he did very much want to find and expose tragedy, he had perhaps concluded that he would find the task manageable only by reducing it to a formal arrangement of sentences in a well-ordered paragraph. In his hurry to get away from his past, Binod hadn't noticed that he had exchanged the real life around him for the life presented in films and books. He had become an aesthete.

There had been too many deaths around him when he had lived in Patna. Each morning on his way to school during his boyhood he would pass the burning ghat; he had become used to the sight of fathers carrying babies wrapped in white cloth to the river's edge. It was less painful to confront this death in art: in a gallery in Delhi he had seen an installation about a girl whose eyes had been sold for money. The artist had taken the newspaper photograph of the little eyeless girl and blown it up and painted over it. Binod liked that and wanted to do the same with words. He wanted to make a statement about society; he didn't want to go on merely experiencing those things any more. He had made a firm decision that prose was going to be his medium. The romance of writing poetry had appealed to him for a while, but it felt unnatural, as if he were walking around with a flower tucked into his buttonhole.

Orwell had enumerated "four great motives for writing, at any rate for writing prose": "sheer egoism," "esthetic enthusiasm," "historical impulse," and "political purpose." Binod accepted as a formula the list that Orwell had offered, and in order to ensure success he told himself that he could not ignore any one of those reasons in anything he ever wrote.

With Lalji dead, it was suggested by Baba and others that if Binod was going to leave for Delhi he might as well take Rabinder with him to study law. But after a few months in Delhi, Rabinder had returned to Patna and from there he went to Dibrugarh and acquired a contract for felling timber. Binod was earning only a little from the desultory work he had been doing for a small news agency: a piece on the effects on the Taj Mahal of the pollution from the oil refinery; a brief uninspired report, no different from a dozen others published in the city, on the production of the play Tughlaq by the National School of Drama; another piece on the dharna outside the Supreme Court by the protesting Bhopal victims. He had sent his poems and one story to a few publications but—apart from a postcard from the writer Khushwant Singh encouraging him to "keep it up and write more"—he had done nothing to justify his ambitions. It was easy to give up and go back to college. He enrolled as a master's student in linguistics; the subject was suggested to him because it didn't have a heavy enrollment and there was a good chance that he would be given a room in the university hostel.

Binod returned to the safety of academia: in a sense, like Rabinder when he left Delhi, he had given up and gone back home. He took shelter in the idea of acquiring a degree. He was going to be safe for two years, protected from the demands of the world. He was aware of this at some level and, even though he was still young, he began to feel that life was passing him by. In the college canteen each morning, he would eat his breakfast of toast and a thin, oily omelet, and then he would remain undecided about going to class. On occasion he would make the trip down the dusty corridors, the walls lined with torn posters, and sit down in the lecture room. The students as well as the teacher sometimes looked upon him as a stranger. When he returned from these classes, he was invariably exhausted although he had done nothing.

Rabinder came back to Delhi a few times, always brimming with energy. It wasn't only Rabinder. Everyone else too, it seemed, had discovered ambition and was busy defining a niche in the world. Binod read in the papers of a man called Arvind Pandya who had traveled from India to America and run backward all the way, over the course of 107 days, from Los Angeles to New York City. Pandya found entry into the *Guinness Book of World Records*. The news stories that reported this success also mentioned a man in one of the Delhi jails whose moustache was almost eight feet long. The prisoner rubbed butter on it to make the hair grow longer and more luxuriantly. There was another man in Tamil Nadu who had written a page from the Ramayana on a grain of rice and presented it to the prime minister. The papers said that one-tenth of the letters received at the headquarters of the *Guinness Book* came from India.

....

A year had passed in Delhi.

Binod was standing near Jantar Mantar looking at the men who had gathered in front of a bearded fellow who held in one hand a small bottle and in the other what appeared to be like a stuffed chameleon. A hand fell on his shoulder. It was Neeraj Dubey, grinning. Binod was a little embarrassed. He smiled and said, "If I ever get the chance to go abroad, all that I will want to find out is whether men stand around like this in other parts of the world—listening to some fool selling lizard shit as an aphrodisiac."

Dubey said he had begun working on a television serial. He was late for a meeting and was in a hurry. They decided to look each other up but a couple of years were to pass before they would meet again. Rabinder called from Patna and said that Dubey was getting married; Binod was to buy a set of music cassettes from Palika Bazaar and take them as a gift. The marriage lasted only a year, but Binod didn't hear about the divorce till much later when his own marriage was about to end.

Binod was the first in his family, or even among his friends, to get a divorce. He had read an article just that year in *Time* on what the writer called "Marriage Meltdown." In Singapore the divorce rate was up one-third since 1990, and it had nearly doubled in Thailand. In China, it had doubled in the past twenty years. In Taiwan, it had tripled. And the divorce rate in South Korea now exceeded that of many countries in the West. The article said, "Even in India—where a wife was once considered so immutably tied to her husband that she was thrown on the funeral pyre if he died before she did—sociologists estimate that the divorce rate is 11 per 1,000, up from 7.41 per 1,000 in 1991."

He must have been a part of the 0.741 percent, barely even whole. Still, in a country as populous as India, he was a part of the millions who must have untied the marriage knot that year. But it didn't feel like a large number then. He had felt that he was alone in doing something wrong, and who can say, it is entirely possible that he was.

Arpana was a student of his mother's and he had often joked about her with Ma, not only because she was beautiful, but also because she was of a different caste. Binod was only teasing his mother, testing what she called her "open-minded nature." He had been drawn by Arpana's reserve, which implied intelligence, and during the few, short conversations he had had with her, her silence allowed him to weave vague but sweet fantasies of love and caring. Did Arpana know how he felt about her?

Once Neelu had told him that the brother of one of her classmates had fallen in love with a girl who was a neighbor. The youth had never spoken to the girl, but he had often seen her on her roof hanging clothes. She would be up there in the evenings standing quietly by the parapet with her friends. It wasn't easy for young women in Patna to be out on the streets. One bright afternoon the girl was shaking a wet sari, getting rid of the excess water before hanging it on the line, and the boy saw that she had looked at him. He decided that they were in love. In the weeks that followed he had made his sister go over and talk to the girl about him. The girl had laughed and said flatly that she paid no attention to men who stood around and gawked at her. When the sister came back and told him what the girl had said, the young man became furious.

Had the disappointed fellow thrown a light bulb filled with acid on the girl's face? Neelu said no to Binod's question. The young man's rage had given way to a dark depression and he had committed suicide by hanging himself. He had used the clothes line from the girl's rooftop. So little had been said, and so much was presumed. Misplaced sentimentality was every Indian's birthright! Sad melodrama was a way of appealing for conversation—although in the end it felt more like an assault than an appeal. Binod understood all this and of course he was no different from everyone else whom he had known in Patna. Even before he had spoken to Arpana, he had told himself stories about her, and when he read novels in which men and women acted outside social conventions, he often found himself thinking of her.

. . . .

In June 1990, Binod was visiting Patna to write a report on student riots. Ma told him that she had said yes to Arpana about attending a film screening at the Cine Society. She wanted to know if Binod would go instead. Ma wasn't feeling very well, and she didn't want Arpana to have to watch the film alone. His heart leaped but he tried not to show it and he asked Ma the name of the film. She said it was a "foreign film" and he smiled at his mother. The thought crossed his mind that if it was not a Hindi film, it would probably have sex in it, and this made him happy too. He showered and chose a light blue shirt. Before he came out of the bathroom, he looked at himself carefully in the mirror.

At the entrance of the building there was a small poster for *Kiss of the Spider Woman*. Arpana was standing inside.

Binod said, "I'm here to tell you that Ma is unwell."

Her face showed alarm and she asked what was wrong. He said, "Something small," and waited. She said nothing after that and he felt his mouth drying. He said, a little rushed, "But if you are still going to see the movie, I'll be more than happy to give you company."

"Yes, I have two of these." She held out two passes.

He told himself that he was nearly thirty years old; it should not be impossible for him to be at ease with a woman. He felt happy to be standing next to Arpana in the foyer of the building, waiting with his eyes turned toward the open expanse of Gandhi Maidan. There were many teams playing cricket on little makeshift pitches. Less than twenty people stood in the hallway. Most of them, he suspected, were from Patna University. No refreshments could be bought there, but Binod felt the need to drink coffee and then with sudden hope he said to himself maybe later.

The film was set in Latin America and the names of the cast were provided on a yellow sheet of paper. While they were watching the film, Binod decided that he was going to ask Arpana to marry him. He didn't. He only told his mother about it and she began to smile as if a plan she had devised had been successful. Arpana's father had been a doctor—he had died of cancer before he was even fifty—and she lived with her mother and younger brother in a portion of their large house in Rajendra Nagar. The rent that came from tenants who occupied the rest of the house provided for the needs of the household and the education of the two siblings. Just before dinner, Binod heard Ma on the telephone. She was asking Arpana's mother if she could come to Rajendra Nagar the next day.

The next morning, Ma bought a kilo of the most expensive mithai from Punjab Sweet House. She had also put in her purse a gold necklace with a fake emerald pendant that she was going to give to Arpana if her mother said yes to the marriage proposal. Arpana's mother was what Ma would later call, using the English words, "worldly wise." The marriage proposal was welcomed despite the differences in caste, but there was also a great deal of hesitation. As their conversation proceeded over tea, Ma heard Arpana's mother telling her that it was very important for the horoscopes to be shown first to an astrologer. Then there was also the business of the proposals that had come from two or three other families. It would not be easy to say no to anyone, and she was going to discuss the matter with the elders in the family. She said, "In the absence of the father, we have to give proper respect to everyone else who is older than us."

The gold necklace remained in the bag.

But Ma's act had inspired Binod and he asked Arpana to meet him at a new restaurant called Amrapali. His resolve gave him reason to be bold. He went to a jeweler's in Mohun Palace with the necklace that his mother had chosen. After showing him some dull items with artificial rubies set in gold, the jeweler showed him half a dozen kundan pieces. Binod liked one of them, which was small but ornate, with semi-precious stones set in gold and lac; it was a beautiful jewel with a deep red color and shiny inlaid work.

The owner of the shop refused to bargain. He was a young man in a cream silk kurta, his long hair falling to his shoulders. Binod was buying beyond his means and was prepared to haggle so that he could feel better about spending so much money. When he asked again if he could get a better rate, the owner tucked his hair behind his ear and said, "I should perhaps just put the price a few hundred rupees above what is the correct price. Then I can lower it every time you ask me for a discount and you'll be happy."

The humiliation that Binod felt made him want to leave, but he had set his heart on the tiny jewel. Three thousand three hundred rupees. He didn't even have the money to spend like this. Half an hour later, he was back with the cash from the State Bank office. Before leaving the shop, he slipped out the pendant with the artificial stone that Ma had put on the gold chain and replaced it with the kundan piece. The jeweler wrapped the ornament in red tissue and said in a kindly tone, "The purchase you have made is a good one." Binod felt a great sense of well-being. He began telling himself that the piece was going to look beautiful on Arpana. Just giving her this gift was going to make him happy, and it didn't matter whether she said yes or no.

Then he went to the Amrapali restaurant.

....

During those days, Rabinder had taken hold of someone's Jeep that, he claimed, was good for hunting expeditions in the forests near Valmiki Nagar. Binod had borrowed the jeep for his trip to the restaurant. The place looked gloomy; there was no one else there and the manager himself came over to take their order. Rabinder had said to Binod, "Bhaiya, the arrow is already on its way. Let it find its mark." But it wasn't easy to be direct. Binod looked into Arpana's eyes momentarily and said, "There are rumors in the city that many marriage proposals are coming your way."

She smiled lightly. "I think I like only one among them."

A wave passed over him. He thought that he had never been as whole or complete as he was then, sitting in front of this woman in a pale turquoise chikan kurta who looked unbearably beautiful.

He said, "I understand that your mother wants you to marry a doctor." She laughed this time and said, "I don't like seeing doctors even when I'm sick." The coffee that came was of the instant variety and was curiously lukewarm. Binod ordered tea. Then he called the waiter back and also asked for a chicken cutlet. Arpana gave in to his urging and said that she would like some ice cream. The waiter returned almost immediately with a thick slab of vanilla and waited for Arpana to express her approval. The cutlet was to take longer.

Binod began to talk about the film they had seen. Arpana made a face and asked him if the communist was also gay, and the question disappointed him, but only for a moment. He said that he found Sonia Braga gorgeous. He wanted to be seen as someone who was appreciative of women's beauty.

When the tea came, he took a sip as if it were whiskey and, thus fortified, proceeded to awkwardly extract from his pocket the gift that he had brought. As he unwrapped the heart-shaped kundan piece under the table, the tissue paper crackled. To Arpana it must have appeared as if he was taking out a piece of gum or maybe fumbling with his wallet. Even if only for a moment, he toyed with the idea of saying in English, "Will you marry me?" But in the English novels, men asked this question only when they had a diamond ring in their pocket. Binod said, "In principal, you are not opposed to marriage?" Arpana shook her head. And it seemed to him that the matter had now been decided. There could be no doubt about it. He took a couple more sips of the tea and found its taste unusual but welcome and satisfying. He thought he should ask Arpana what she wanted to do over the next few years. Ma had told Binod some time back that she had spoken about going into advertising. But this was another discussion that he thought he could not begin. He watched his future wife eating ice cream in an empty, dimly lit Patna restaurant and told himself that he wanted this sweetness to last forever.

He said, "Arpana, tell me something about yourself . . . what do you like?"

She said, "I like ice cream."

Her laughter excited him and he spoke breathlessly. "Do you like the flowers of gulmohar? I like gulmohar. I like the red gulmohar on the trees after a rain shower."

She was probably taken aback but said, "That is nice. I didn't know that you were a poet."

Binod beamed with satisfaction. Then he brought up his hand and placed the ornament, in its small nest of red, crumpled tissue paper, on the table between them. It sat on the white tablecloth at equal distance from his hands and hers. He said, "This is a small gift . . . for a spider woman."

Before the week ended, it was decided that the wedding would take place a month later. Ma said, "Maybe it will be cooler in July, if the monsoons arrive on time."

Binod didn't write the story on the student riots that he had come to Patna to investigate. Instead, he appeased his editor by sending him a piece on the first anniversary of the Tiananmen Square massacre. Sitting at his mother's desk at night, writing in longhand under the hot table lamp, he found it very easy to see in the heroic but chaotic actions of the Chinese students a deeply romantic and meaningful striving for love among human beings.

14

During that long, hot month of preparations, Binod was alone in Delhi. There was no point in even trying to get leave from work—the newspaper gave only seven days of annual earned leave and he wanted to save all the time he could get off for the wedding. It never bothered him during that month, or to be more precise, during the twenty-six days while he remained away from Patna, that he hardly knew Arpana.

They talked nearly every night when the phone rates went down: he would go to the phone booth close to his barsaati in Lajpat Nagar and stand in line to wait for his turn. Ordinarily, Binod hated waiting—at train stations, in offices and the tiny parlors of people's houses, waiting for those who had forgotten their appointments, or at post offices, where people often broke the queue, or even outside Mother Dairy booths, where at least the lines were shorter and moved faster. But he liked to wait when calling Arpana. He would be in line behind Bihari chachis, Tamil husbands, Afghan refugees, Assamese students, a Frenchwoman perhaps calling to complain about her railway trips or the dirty toilets but her words sounding to him very much like talk of heartache and loss.

Arpana was always there when he called and he would get long reports on what was happening, on the things their mothers had said or bought, and how a guest list was being drawn up. Binod had found a new zeal for reformist wedding practices. He was conscious that Arpana's mother was a widow and did not have a lot of money to waste. This awareness on his part, which was also being asserted as a demonstration of his humanity and sensitivity, found an enthusiastic response in Arpana. For many days, the two of them battled with their respective mothers. They had decided on a simple ceremony at Patna Sahib Gurdwara because he had heard from a friend whose sister had eloped with her math tutor that you could get married there with a minimum of fuss and also host a small reception.

Arpana asked on the phone, "Can we say that we want no more than a dozen guests from both sides?"

He said, "Of course. And no dowry."

She giggled with excitement, and he felt that he was entering a new life.

Their plan did not work. Ma said that Bua was going to host the reception at the New Patna Club and everything was now out of her hands. Binod told her that guests should be told not to give gifts. Ma replied that she had spent all her life giving gifts to others and, after a while, Binod grew reconciled to failure. But not Arpana.

It seemed as if she wanted to convince him that they shared a common passion and she was going to war for this idea. She witnessed all around her preparations that were so diverse and so extraordinary that they baffled her and, in the end, defeated her. So, for many nights, Binod had to comfort her and absorb the anger and frustration that she was feeling. These were not happy or giddy conversations but they were real to him. Love, or at least the relationship that they were now bound in, did not seem to be an illusion any more.

On that day in June when they had watched *Kiss of the Spider Woman*, there was a moment, just as they were coming out of the auditorium, when his right hand had accidentally brushed Arpana's bare arm. There was such comfort in that contact! It seemed difficult for him to believe this later, but it is true that he often thought of that fleeting touch during those days when he was waiting to get married. He was self-conscious about it. On the phone he said to his mother, "I have only spent a few hours with her. And now I'm going to marry her." Ma said, "I hadn't spoken to Baba till a few hours after our wedding. In fact, I hardly said anything. It was he who did all the talking."

....

Binod was standing on the wooden platform on which two tall chairs of crafted aluminum had been placed. The chairs were designed to resemble regal thrones but they only looked tawdry with their dented metal backs and the seats of maroon velvet. A carpet had been spread on the platform and strings of marigold had been nailed to its sides. Behind the twin thrones, a bamboo frame supported what looked like a large, flat flower with petals made of white pleated cloth. The flower's heart was made of red rose petals and tinsel stitched together.

Arpana stepped out on the lawn in the company of two of her aunts. Neelu walked over to her and took her hand. The guests turned to look at the bride, who was beautiful even under the heavy make-up. It was only when she smiled that Binod saw the familiar Arpana again. He was conscious of the sweat on his face and under his armpits, but she appeared unaffected by the heat. Leaning in his chair toward her, he said that at least half of the people in front of them must be uninvited guests. She didn't raise her gaze. Even from where they were sitting, he could see that the waiters from the catering company were shooing away the boys from the street who had crept close to the table on which the ice cream had been piled.

A smiling middle-aged woman stepped on the platform. She was holding a pink envelope in her hand, and she was followed by a silent, somewhat dour-looking bespectacled man. Binod accepted the envelope with folded hands. The woman said, "I am Sanjay's mother. He always asks about you." Binod didn't know which Sanjay she was talking about. He smiled. Then there was a rush of other people who followed this first couple. Everyone handed them gifts. Shatrughan appeared by his side and started putting all of the envelopes in a red plastic bag that said in curving silver letters *Rajbhog Saris*. The packages were piled on the platform behind them.

After a long time, when the crowd cleared, Shatrughan pointed with his eyes toward Rabinder. He was standing a little distance away among a circle of young men. Rabinder was wearing an orange silk kurta and on his left wrist he had wrapped a string of small chameli flowers that he had snapped from the decorations. Most of the men around him were wearing white or cream-colored kurtas and in some cases uncomfortable warm Western suits with sweaty patches at the armpits. Standing among the guests Rabinder looked more fashionable and indeed more modern.

Binod said to Arpana, "Look at your brother-in-law."

Arpana said, "Look at the man he is talking to."

The short, bearded fellow standing in front of Rabinder had a fresh bandage stuck on his right forehead and ear. When he saw them looking at him, Rabinder waved and then, after saying something to his friends, he walked up to them, smiling broadly.

Binod said, "I was just warning her about my relatives."

Rabinder laughed.

Arpana asked him, "What happened to your friend?"

"Oh, he got into a fight with a fellow who was cheating him of some money."

He looked back in the direction that he had come from. He said, "If you ever want to watch a film first-day first-show, Vishnu is the man for you."

Vishnu was the one with the bandage. Apparently, he had a big share in the black market in cinema tickets sold all over Patna, but sometimes the scalpers tried to hide from him the profits they had made. Rabinder was not much concerned about Vishnu; standing beside the newly married couple, he greeted the people assembled before them—politicians big and small, relatives both rich and poor, women who came with their husbands and those who came with shy daughters-in-law with young, already strained faces.

The gateway to the club had been decorated with ashoka leaves and strings of blinking lights in different colors. Baba stood there with Bua and a couple of upper-caste politicians. They were welcoming the guests as they came inside. An elderly couple came up on the platform and Rabinder stepped aside and whispered in Binod's ear that they were Arpana's maternal uncle and his wife. Binod quickly moved closer to them and touched their feet very respectfully.

....

Two years later, he would be sitting in their house in Deogarh soon after he had asked Arpana to divorce him.

They had been left alone in Deoghar that day, in a room that was on the upper floor. It was a small room, with thick walls that had been whitewashed, and it had a window with an ornate iron grille in its frame. At the end of the nineteenth century, a British soldier had built the house as his retirement home. Their room faced away from the town. Outside the window, a rocky hill arose in the distance. Small cashew trees with twisted branches and whorls of green fruit grew on the land below. It was all quite beautiful.

In the years that followed, however, it was the look of concern on the faces of Arpana's old uncle and aunt, the simple poverty of their large, crumbling house in Deoghar, and the undeniable sense that they occupied an abandoned time—these fragments from a little-visited place in the past—that haunted Binod whenever he thought of his divorce, and about its violence, and how everything in life would always henceforth be experienced as broken or misplaced or missing.

15

After their wedding, they went together to Ranchi. The earlier plan had been that Binod would stay in Patna for four days and then return alone to Delhi; Arpana was going to be with her mother for a week or two and then visit him for a full fortnight. They would travel together to Agra during a weekend. But on the third day after the wedding, Binod got a call from his editor in Delhi. A riot had broken out near Ranchi. One village had been attacked; all of its Muslim inhabitants had been slaughtered. If Binod traveled to Ranchi immediately, his editor said, he could stay a few more days in Bihar because the days of his leave that he spent in Ranchi would be counted as work.

Binod was surprised that no one, not even Ma, objected when he announced that he was leaving for Ranchi with Arpana that afternoon. They were going to a place where curfew had been imposed and yet no one wanted to separate a newly married couple. When he came back from the Bata store with a new pair of keds, he saw that Arpana had packed their clothes in one large suitcase and the gesture surprised and pleased him.

In the early afternoon the train passed through a landscape washed by the rains. They bought peanuts and talked easily, even though the train was crowded. It was almost like a honeymoon.

After a while, he fell asleep. It was Arpana who woke him up. The sun had come down in the sky and the light was golden. He looked where she was pointing. Spreading into the distance for a mile or more were the red flowers of the gulmohar. She looked pleased. He smiled back at her and wanted to taste her mouth. But when he looked around he saw that one of the passengers, a bearded man with a large gold-colored watch shining on his dark skin, was also smiling at them, affected perhaps by their happiness. He turned back to the flowers outside, red petals against the red earth.

They spent three days in Ranchi. For the first two days, accompanied by Arpana, he would go out early in the morning to visit the villages around the city and return by late afternoon. In the early evening, they would begin a round of visits to the houses of the people in town—journalists, riot victims, politicians, activists, even a sanyasi who lived in an ashram. On the second day they went to a small town called Khunti where Muslims had found shelter in a Catholic church. The mob was armed with machetes and had first hacked down the Belgian priest at the door and then everyone hiding in the chapel behind him. The slaughter was supposed to avenge the deaths of Hindus in a riot that had taken place somewhere in Bangladesh.

For the two of them, stumbling from one scene of violence to another, there was no time to rest or to have a quiet moment by themselves till they lay down on their bed in the hotel room. That night after their return from Khunti, Binod was still sitting at the small desk, writing down in short paragraphs his observations about the massacre in the church. Arpana was reading in bed. He had turned to see what she had in her hand: it was a copy of *Three Men in a Boat*. What kind of a book was this for an adult to read? When he was a kid in school, a few pages from that book had been excerpted in his English primer. He didn't even remember anything about it now. Why was his wife reading a book for children?

In those early days of the marriage, everything mattered so much. He found that he was telling himself that their interests and commitments were very different. The last book that he had read was a novel by Saul Bellow . . . Just then the power went out. Arpana said at once that if the hotel staff gave them a candle, at least he could go on with his writing. When she said this, remorse stung him. Why had he dragged her down to this place that afforded her no pleasure? In the dark, he found his way to the bed and without saying anything pulled off her kurta. She was wearing a bra. He would need some light to undo the clasp. She said sorry quietly and moved her hands to help him but he pinned her down and pushed up her bra with his mouth. There were thin hairs around her nipples and this surprised him. He kissed her, and then licked her, something he had never done with Bua. Arpana moved in response and her fingers became entwined in his. When he kissed the hollow at her neck, he thought to himself that this is what the earth smelled like after the first rains. They hadn't made love together before. The drawstring on her churidar was easy enough to pull and when he began to fondle her, Arpana took his penis in her hand and held it as if she did not quite know how to deal with his erection. And then, she asked softly, in English, "Do you want oral?"

He thought of this awkward question again several months later when Geeta Rangarajan and he first kissed each other. Geeta was a fellow reporter working in the same Delhi office as Binod. They had both come out of a bookstore in Daryaganj. He had stepped behind a pillar, with a cigarette between his lips, and was fumbling for a matchbox in his pocket. Geeta had removed his cigarette with two outstretched fingers and kissed him gently on the mouth. He had wanted this and yet he was taken aback. She smiled and said, "Got to grip the cigarette harder."

But he had been happy in Ranchi with Arpana.

They returned to Patna, and then soon he was back in Delhi. Once again, Ma and Arpana had both come to the station to say goodbye, and Binod had bought Britannia fruitcake for everyone, but he was the only one who wanted to eat. When he returned to work, he felt that he had come back a different person, and that a part of him was still in Patna. They wrote letters to each other but mostly they talked on the phone. Instead of staying with his parents, Arpana had decided to go on living with her mother, who would otherwise feel lonely. He made the STD calls at night and Arpana nearly always picked up the phone. The phone was in the living room where the television was, and when her mother or her younger brother was there, she didn't say much. On those occasions, he needed to keep talking. He would prepare for this by writing down on a scrap of paper a list of four or five things that he wanted to tell her. Unless he did this, he was likely to forget something in the booth, watched by all those waiting in the line behind him.

....

When Binod started spending more time with Geeta—the affair lasted only a few months—his calls became less frequent. But Arpana and he talked on the phone even after he had brought up the matter of the divorce, and, although he felt bad doing this, he also called her whenever he felt lonely. He would eat his dinner and then feel he hadn't done the necessary thing, and so he would go out for a walk in the neighborhood and stop at the corner and make a brief phone call. When the affair started, it was summer again, and he would come out of the flat at night because it was pleasant outside. He would feel like calling Arpana and he would enter the phone booth. It was a familiar place by now, the stains on its walls as recognizable as the maps of nations in geography books, and, on the wall to the right, just above the phone, written with a red ballpoint pen "44 Dn reservation 1/20 Kamla Devi 36."

The last time he spoke to Arpana was when he called her not from the booth near his house but from a small town in Haryana where he had gone to do a story about the suicide of a soldier who had been crippled in the Kargil War. He met the wife, freshly widowed, and then the father. The man's brother said that it was okay that the man had died: he was in pain and he was also very depressed after his discharge and ended up mistreating his wife. Binod looked at the widow, who continued to cry quietly.

He had the story; all he needed now was one or two quotes from the army authorities, and if the editor was insistent, a comment from an academic or a psychologist. But all of that could be done in Delhi. That night, after he had eaten at a dhaba, he passed a liquor store with its shutter half-down and a candle burning inside, the owner pretending that the shop was closed because it was past the legal hour. He bought a quart of gin and mixed it with a Limca in the shadow of a paan shop. The gin lifted his spirits immediately and he went back to his room with the bottle of Limca. After he had drunk some more, pillows propped against his back and his mind empty of any worries, he wanted to phone Arpana.

It was much more expensive to make that call from the room but he called her anyway. She answered the phone. He knew she was alone in the room when he called because she surprised him by asking whether she should continue her pills. He was unable to think very clearly. He had felt amorous when he had called but now his defensiveness made him combative. He said, "That's for you to decide."

She said, "I have heard there are side effects from the pill. I don't see why I should be taking them if there isn't any real reason for it."

Such shame. It was Arpana who ended up crying on the phone.

. . . .

Six months after they had become lovers, Geeta and he broke up. He had suspected that she and a colleague at the office were very close to each other; he would bring this up at the worst moments during the few conversations they had about the matter. In the stairway of their office she once snapped at him, "What men like you need to learn is that you don't own the women you fuck." Even when he behaved badly he excused himself by saying that what Geeta had liked in him was probably everything in him that was crude and unformed. He missed her when they stopped seeing each other. Arpana was very dear to his family and he couldn't have imagined Geeta meeting them. When he was going through his break-up with Geeta, Rabinder came to Delhi on business. He saw that Binod was unhappy, but he assumed it was because of what had ended between him and Arpana. Once or twice, Binod was tempted to introduce him to Geeta, but in the end he didn't even mention her to Rabinder. No one in Patna would have been able to understand her. To start with, she had short hair, hardly ever spoke Hindi, and she smoked. There was in her walk something very sexual or at least very open and uninhibited; Binod had often wondered what his mother would say if Geeta and he were about to step out on a street in Patna.

16

Like everyone else, Binod had discovered sex through the movies.

If it had not been for films, who would ever have thought that tears were sexy? He remembered this while working on the story for Dhar. He had watched Mahesh Bhatt's *Arth* soon after entering college. In that film a woman named Pooja Malhotra is married to a filmmaker. His name is Inder and he has an affair with an actress. Inder's and Pooja's marriage of seven years is finished. At the film's end, the husband returns to his wife, but she refuses to take him back. The role of the wife was played with great feeling by Shabana Azmi. In a more formulaic, moralizing touch, the second woman, the actress, was portrayed as a neurotic. Kulbhushan Kharbanda was the conflicted, not very likeable, husband. It was said in the press that Kharbanda's character was based on Bhatt's own life.

Binod was young when he saw the film, he was a virgin, and he was affected most by the film's emotional candor. No one around him talked or behaved in that way. As a boy, he had placed his lips on Bua. But it was something that one could not speak about. He had never heard people in real life talking about these things. There was a scene in *Arth* that showed the illicit lovers on the balcony of a house while the blue dawn was breaking out behind them. The two were talking. Bhatt had cast Smita Patil in the role of the high-strung film actress. In that scene, which Binod never forgot, Smita was holding in her hand a candle inside a round, open-necked bottle. Her lover began to cry, and Smita, loving and intense, wiped his tears with her finger and burst out laughing after tasting it.

Binod was reminded of the tears that Bua shed with such abandon whenever they had sat in the darkness of the theater watching Hindi films. At that time, Lalji was in the asylum, still alive, and Bua's relationship with Parshuram was many years away in the future. In the public space of the dark cinema hall, Bua cried quietly but also as if she were alone. After watching *Arth*, Binod imagined something new. In a modern, fashionable city, where people loved and cheated and talked about it with each other, he would meet a woman who would one day become his wife. He would find her tears incredibly sexy. What would he say to make her cry?

....

When Binod had been a boy, the phrase "love marriage" was uttered in Patna only as a term of scandal. There was a bureaucrat-couple whose marriage had not been conventionally arranged by relatives. The two had met in college and secretly married—they were described as being "modern." That too was a term of scandal. But then things changed. By the time Binod was out of school and ready to leave Patna, it was no longer love marriage but adultery that carried a strong sense of scandal. And he wondered sometimes whether these days it was committing adultery that would make a man or a woman modern in his hometown. People sometimes spoke of the new phenomenon of spouse swapping in Delhi but no one in Patna had left behind those old days.

Did Mala Srivastava tell herself that she was stepping into a new age when she became Surajdeo Tripathi's mistress?

Dhar had told Binod to turn the widow in his story into a woman who was in an unhappy marriage. And in the weeks that followed, Binod had worked on that idea. The woman in the film would make a pilgrimage to Haridwar, to hear the bells ringing in the temples. She hoped to find peace there—and instead she would end up finding love.

In the revised story Binod had written a scene in which the monk discourses on the romance of Shakuntala gazing up at the sky for the rain clouds that were the messengers of love. Kalidasa's lines were about clouds as dark as a pregnant woman's nipples. The first night the monk touches his lover is after their return from Har-ki-pauri, where the woman had watched entranced the flotilla of lights dancing on the pure waters. Their lovemaking has the pace and grandeur of a slow, religious ritual performed with oil lamps and clasped hands. And yet, in the way in which Binod had portrayed their passion there was very little of youthful lust. This is because when Binod thought of Bua and Parshuram, he felt that their love lay in the ease with which they exchanged words. When they conversed, they never appeared like a pair who had been forced to define themselves in terms of a secret loneliness shared against the fury of the world.

When the two had begun to be seen as almost a couple, there was a lot of talk but little opposition because neither of them was cheating on anybody, and everyone was older now. This despite the manner in which the matter came to light for the larger public of Patna. Bua had employed a servant from a village close to the one in which Lalji's family lived. Over a period of some months she noticed that small items kept disappearing from her house. One day, she couldn't find her watch. Instead of calling the police, she gave her servant money for a bus ticket back to Motihari. The fellow was sixteen or seventeen years old; he ended up finding employment at the cold-storage facility run by Manik. The boy belonged to a low caste. The following week a story appeared on the front page of *Dainik Khabar*. It said that a dalit had been dismissed without pay by a political leader who claimed to be working for the masses. The worker was also a minor, the article said, and his employer had stolen the boy's future. The news item ended by quoting the boy, who had said that he had loyally served Bua at home and also at the home of the industries minister Parshuram Singh whenever she spent her nights there.

It was Manik who had been responsible for the smear but Shatrughan found out that there was more to it. Whether acting on Bua's orders or not, the local superintendent of police as well as the revenue officer had in the previous months paid visits to Manik's businesses. It didn't seem likely that Bua wanted to force Manik to hand over the property that was hers. She may have been using her authority only to rattle Manik. Perhaps she had heard what he often said in public about her and she wanted him to know that she could make his life a little bit difficult. Manik had suffered the blow and now bitten back.

But Bua didn't flinch. Her behavior in public remained the same. At most official parties and cultural events, the two of them appeared together. Balding, long-haired Parshuram with his sleepless eyes, always wearing a dhoti and kurta, and beside him Bua, smiling, on occasion dressed in expensive saris, her neck and wrists adorned with elegant jewelry. No one in Patna, not even Ma and Baba, finally cared whether the two got married or not, and, as far as Binod knew, no one had ever spoken with Bua about it. For her, the fact of her love for Parshuram was neither to be hidden nor explained.

So much had changed in Binod's lifetime. And so much also remained the same.

v

❋

News of a

Kidnapping

17

Film City, on the set of *Manto*.

The previous night Binod had signed on a pad held by a courier and opened the envelope to find a check for twenty-five thousand rupees. It was from Dhar. A letter from Dhar's brother explained that Binod would receive another twenty-five thousand after he submitted the complete screenplay. When the film was released, he would get another check of one lakh rupees. Unable to contain his happiness, or his surprise, he had called Dhar.

"Arre bhai, where have you been?" the man demanded.

"Sir, I've been working—and waiting for your call."

Dhar said, "I'm shooting. Come to Film City tomorrow afternoon at four. I want you to tell me—the woman in your story, what does her husband do?"

Binod had now come with an answer for Dhar. And he felt a sense of excitement in his stomach as he waited. But so far he had waited for more than three hours, standing in the company of a mongrel dog chained to a metal chair. The dog was going to be used in the film. He was dark brown in color, with faint thin black stripes on his back. He had been picked up from the street and tied to a metal chair. Only the chain around his neck was new and shiny.

A light rain had begun to fall earlier and Binod stood under a concrete porch. The dog was restless, probably because he was unused to the chain. Every few minutes, he would emit short barks and then appeared to bite his paws.

The field in front was part of the outdoor set in Bombay's Film City. A low hastily built fence stood on the right and beside it was a row of branches and stumps that had been planted in the damp earth. Several months later, on the screen in a theater in Malad, Binod was surprised to see that those dead branches glistened like wet leafless trees.

There was no sign of Dhar but, after a while, an assistant with a ponytail walked out and shouted commands. Although it was still bright outside, three klieg lights were quickly turned on and the landscape lit up with a warm yellow glow. In a while, a boy brought a tray that held tiny glasses of tea. A wet newspaper covered the glasses.

An hour later, the dog was still chained to the chair. He was now licking the last few drops of milk from a bowl that had been put in front of it. A security guard was standing close to the chair and he said to Binod with a smile. "Every dog has his day. This one will be an actor now."

The man nudged the dog's rump with his boot, and the dog, finding himself addressed, thumped his tail lightly.

The guard was speaking to the dog for Binod's benefit. "Hero, if you act well today, in the next birth you will come back as a human being." The man could not have been much more than twenty years old. He was a bhaiyya from a small town like Darbhanga or Jaunpur, probably employed by a private agency that had supplied him with his gray uniform and hat and a black pin-on cotton tie.

When Binod smiled at him, the guard carried on jokingly, still addressing the dog at his feet, "But if you fail and the film flops, in your next life you will be a security guard."

After a while, the boy came by once more with tea for everyone.

And then the door of a cream-colored van parked on the side swung open and Dhar stepped down heavily. He stood in the middle of the set with a mobile phone in his hand and asked that the lights be switched off one by one. An extra was told to stand under a tree. Someone shouted, "Baby on karo." And then, "Four Par, Four Par."

The dog was to move through the empty devastated street, empty except for the scattered intestines of men and bits of women's clothing.

The fence stood only on one side of the set and a technician unrolled a nylon mesh and secured it to the fence and then ran it all around so that it formed a rectangular enclosure. It was decided to leave the chain around the dog's neck. Then, two men took turns chasing him.

The dog trotted in circles, his tongue hanging out.

The camera was mounted on a large trolley. The dog didn't snap at anyone—it would yelp and then would either run or stop when the men raised their stick. After the filming was stopped, the animal came up to the trolley and sniffed one of its front tires. A small video monitor on the side allowed the director to review the shot. There were more takes. It was difficult for Binod to imagine drama being created from such a process, but he immediately thought of his own struggle to write, and all his dissatisfaction with the hours he had wasted that day vanished.

Dhar asked a man to walk slowly while the dog ran down the street. There was some unhappiness among the crew that the animal only ambled past the actor. An assistant with thick glasses complained that they had made a mistake by feeding the dog. A make-up man suggested that a bit of spirit or alcohol could be put on its tail and when the liquid evaporated the dog would run like crazy.

Dhar didn't approve, but the suggestion had touched a nerve.

One of the assistants standing around the camera had a question. If the point of the sequence was to show the atmosphere of the riots, why not tie a cloth to the tail and set it alight?

Dhar pointed to Binod and two other journalists standing nearby. He said with a smile, "We have the media here. Be careful about what you say."

It was decided instead that a small fire would be lit on the side of the road. A rubber tire was thrown on the flames. Two men brought small portable chulhas with hot coals: when a white powder was sprinkled on the embers, ribbons of thick, aromatic smoke rose into the air. The actor and the dog appeared at the far end. The animal's tongue hung out drily; it looked disoriented by the warm carbon lights and the shouting and the smoke. There were several takes of the dog's head close to the fire, drool hanging from its jaws.

Even this last bit took about an hour while Binod and the young security guard and other onlookers stood watching with the lights shining in their eyes.

It was nearly eight at night by the time shooting was over. Binod, sitting with Dhar in the back of his car while he gulped water from a bottle, said, like an actor who had memorized his lines, "The woman's husband deals in pornography. He doesn't love the real woman."

Dhar laughed again. "Sounds good. He is a pornographer. But you have to say that. The viewer must see that."

When Binod gave Dhar this particular answer, he had thought of Rabinder in jail. Ever since his cousin had encouraged him to think of Bua's own life as a part of his story, bits and pieces of Rabinder's past had also begun to appear more and more naturally a part of the narrative he was writing. Nevertheless, especially after hearing Dhar's enthusiastic response, he felt that he had taken his first step toward producing what was now going to be a B-grade film. He was disappointed with himself, because he saw that he had become desperate and didn't want Dhar to lose interest in him.

Worse, he was not confident of success. The truth was that he could not describe himself as a connoisseur of porn.

....

The only piece of porn that Binod had bought in his life was the cheap, pirated version of the Starr Report. He was working in Delhi then and had read excerpts of the report in *Mid-Day* the day after it was released in America. It was winter and it had turned dark early but when the bus crossed Tilak Marg two young men came aboard and began hawking pirated copies of the report. The document they were selling was in English and cost a hundred rupees each. But across the Yamuna bridge, right around Anand Vihar, another group of young men clambered on to the bus; they were selling the Hindi version for only ten rupees and he quickly bought a copy. The document was about sixty pages long and had been printed on rough brown paper. *America ke Rashtrapati Bill Clinton-Monica Sex-sambandh*—America's President Bill Clinton and Monica's Sexual Relationship. That was the title. On the cover was a picture of the two principal protagonists, but above them was a keyhole and visible inside it was the picture of a muscular white man, his upper body bare, kissing a partially clothed woman on her breast. The text contained a two-page prologue whose first line read "In the more than two-hundred-year-long history of the United States of America, there have been not one but many pleasure-loving presidents."

It was not till page 9 that there was any graphic mention of sex. Monica and Bill, the report said, had engaged in sexual acts on ten occasions. Binod noticed that the words "oral sex" had not been translated into Hindi. There was a detailed accounting of the gifts that were exchanged between the lovers. At the end of that section there was an ad for a publication that would help in increasing one's height.

In the pages that followed, the booklet carried a report on Monica's first relationship, with her schoolteacher who had a three-year-old son, and then a more mysterious story about her sexual relations with a senior military officer as well as a graduate student at UCLA. There were two chapters on Monica's family life and her ambitions. Was all of it a part of the official Starr Report, or was it instead the work of a young man in Timarpur?

The sexual lives of Indian leaders had escaped legal scrutiny and one could make the mistake of suspecting that they never had sex. The nation had never had to participate in a deep examination of the bedroom habits of its rulers. Gandhi slept naked next to his own nieces, but his was an experiment in abstinence. The public interest in Clinton was very different. The Starr Report brought the man who risked impeachment closer to the ordinary Indian and that is why, when at the end of his presidency Clinton traveled to India, even the distinguished Indian representatives jumped over their desks into the well of the Parliament to get a chance to shake his hand.

On page 34, Monica's testimony got underway and, on page 44, it was followed by Clinton's deposition. The well-known details about the episode with the cigar or the navy blue dress were transparent enough, but Binod couldn't help wondering about the terms in Hindi that referred to body parts. These were not common words. Instead, they were abstract and literary. On the night of March 29, 1997, Lewinsky saw Clinton at the White House. The president was using crutches at that time because he had hurt his knee. From the description of that meeting, it was unclear to Binod, because of the language used, whether what Clinton placed on Monica's thigh was his cock or his crutch. He turned the pages quickly and came to the last section that listed the names and brief bios of all of Clinton's lovers. Eight pages of advertisements followed. Ads for romantic love stories, health-restoring herbs, a booklet to help breast enlargement, a guidebook to a better sex life, a ring with a stone that had magical powers, clinics that offered cures for sexually transmitted diseases, a medicine book for women, and a toy revolver with a free gift of a wristwatch.

....

The arrival of Rabinder's InTouch cybercafe had opened a new and more glamorous world of porn for a few middle-class youth in Patna. Each computer was placed in a private booth that could be secured from inside with a small latch. There were two cushioned chairs facing each computer and enough space for the keyboard to sit on a shelf that could be pulled out. Often small groups of youth crowded into the tiny booths. There was also a steady stream of young couples who shut themselves inside for an hour or longer and came out with the look of those emerging from another, more intimate world. Shatrughan told Binod that plain-looking Patna girls with notebooks in their hands, pretending to do research on the Web, would spend hours online posting anonymous pornographic messages to friends and strangers.

The bad news was that the business didn't flourish. Despite the expensive equipment, the electricity supply was erratic and Rabinder had to rely on two Japanese generators that often ran for hours. After the initial months, there were very few new faces; the clientele was largely limited to a loyal but small circle of customers. It was becoming obvious to Rabinder that he needed to revise his business plan.

Just about then, the Tehelka scandal broke. For eight months, two reporters from the Internet news site had posed as arms dealers for a fake company called West End International. They used a hidden camera to shoot footage of politicians and people in the army accepting bribes. These tapes were broadcast on national television and caused a scandal that left the government badly shaken. There was a lot of discussion in the media about the rot in the system. Binod wrote an editorial on the importance of fiction in truth.

Rabinder had his own, more vigorous take on the Tehelka scandal. His first declaration was that the sudden fame of a website was proof that he had made a solid investment by setting up InTouch. Everything from now on, even in a backward country like India, was going to be determined by the information you got on the Web. But there was also a hidden lesson that Rabinder drew from the whole drama. The bribes that had been paid by the two reporters were not huge. The president of the ruling party was seen accepting one lakh rupees. A major general in charge of ordnance and supply to the army had said to the two men that they could not come to his home without a bottle of Johnnie Walker Blue Label. If they had more money, the reporters boasted, they would have gone further with their investigations. Rabinder had begun to think that he too could be a player in the corridors of power if he used his technology and his cash with greater enterprise.

He installed tiny cameras on the computer monitors in his shop. There were also two cameras looking down from above, their lenses hidden in the holes bored into the false wooden ceiling. InTouch began to film young couples as well as lone individuals who came to the booths to download Internet porn. In some cases, the young men and women, ignorant about computers but also much else, had come to the cybercafe just to have the privacy to put their arms around each other and kiss. Rabinder decided that he couldn't ask kids to fork out money. They wouldn't have had much to give even if he threatened to make the tapes public. Of course, he tried with a couple of them and was rewarded with a lot of tears and even a threat of suicide. The footage that had been collected served its primary purpose. It was edited by a boy in Pataliputra Colony and turned into a low-budget porn film. Rabinder had hoped to make tens of lakhs from the sale of this film, but, again according to Shatrughan, he got only fifteen thousand from a distributor in Jalandhar and gave away most of his own copies to his friends for free.

It was this tape as well as the evidence of illegal filming being done at InTouch that the police furnished as the causes for Rabinder's arrest. But as always with Rabinder the truth was more mixed up and devious. The charge of pornography was only a ruse on the part of the police.

....

Binod had found out about Rabinder's arrest when he got a text message on his phone from Neelu. He called her back, but she didn't answer. While waiting for Neelu to call him, he read about the arrest by chance on the UNI wire. He came across the phrase "Internet brothel" for the first time in his life. It was not clear from the dispatch whether it was Rabinder who was involved in porn or the customers at his cybercafe. Binod called home from the office—while the news about Rabinder remained stuck on his computer screen—and Baba answered the phone. He confirmed that Rabinder was in prison and said that it was the result of a misunderstanding. Binod asked him to explain, but Baba remained vague in his answer. Was Rabinder going to be released soon? Baba said that he did not know. He was being evasive in his answers and Binod felt that he just wanted him to get off the phone. He reluctantly ended the conversation.

Ten minutes later, the phone rang. It was Baba on the line. He said he was calling from a phone booth close to their house. He feared that the police were tapping his phone and he couldn't speak about Rabinder. This sudden disclosure made Binod's head whirl. He asked what it was that Rabinder had done. The name of Romola Banerjee came to his tongue, but he could not mention it to Baba. His father's reply was characteristically precise but utterly unhelpful. He said, "A case was registered by the police against Rabinder at 11 a.m. yesterday under sections 292 and 294 of the Indian Penal Code and section 67 of the IT Act."

Binod asked what these accusations meant.

"They mean nothing," Baba said. Then he said, "It means that he is being charged with the sale of obscene materials and there are new laws about the use of computers. But this is a front. It is only an excuse."

So, it was indeed Romola Banerjee then.

There was a pause and Binod wondered whether Baba was hesitating to say what he had found out about Rabinder's relationship with a married woman. He waited and then he heard his father say, "The police believe that they have evidence that Rabinder is involved in the kidnapping of various persons in Patna. They have traced phone calls to his mobile phone. That is why we are afraid that our phones are being tapped."

And Baba had been right. The real reason for Rabinder's arrest was his involvement in extortion. He was running a gang that demanded ransom from the families of kidnapped businessmen and officers. No one was certain how much Bua also knew about this. Shatrughan had learned from one of his political patrons that Rabinder's activities had encroached upon the territory of one of Bua's rivals in her party. He was a legislator who ran his own extortion ring. The arrest had to do with the battle for turf.

．．．．．．．．．．．．．．．．．．．．

The immediate cause of the arrest was a mystery till Shatrughan returned with a story that he no doubt had spiced up a bit. The previous day an employee of Rabinder's at InTouch named Kareem had picked up an income tax inspector at gunpoint. The inspector was notorious for his corruption. Kareem was with two other accomplices. The men had taken the officer in a car to a house in Hathwa. Even though the man was offering no resistance, Kareem had taken out his handmade gun as a precaution. On the staircase of the empty house in Hathwa, there was a scuffle and Kareem's foot slipped and when he fell the gun went off. The bullet entered his left hand and then tore through his chin and front teeth. Despite his blindfold, the prisoner managed to turn back on the stairs and step out of the open door.

As it was night, there was no one in the dark alley. The man must have looked a bit ridiculous, a somewhat stereotypical fat man in a stereotypical safari suit, stumbling in the dark. He fell down and felt someone grab, but a wild energy had been unleashed in him. He slipped free. His shoulder hit the wall of a house bordering the alley, but he straightened himself. He was breathing hard and perhaps because of his weight he was able to lurch away. He did not know this, but the alley was connected to a road that was only fifteen feet away. The man had heard the sound of an approaching truck and he ran in that direction.

He had just appeared on the road, blindly rushing out, when he was hit by the truck. The impact made him spin around and as the vehicle turned away from him a piece of metal on its side sliced open the back of his head. The truck drove away without stopping.

On this particular night the district magistrate was returning from a late-night meeting in Patna where the railway minister visiting from Delhi had been the chief guest. The body was still on the road; the accident had taken place only a few minutes earlier. The district magistrate's Ambassador, and following closely behind it the jeep carrying the police escort, stopped at the side of the road.

The driver of the Ambassador had seen one man running away into the alley. They didn't find that man, but they found Kareem easily enough, slumped at the bottom of the staircase in an empty house, howling in pain. Before morning, a non-bailable warrant of arrest had been issued in Rabinder's name. The police made no mention of kidnapping in the warrant because there were at least half a dozen other cases of extortion still in negotiation all over Bihar, and they wanted to make sure that nothing would complicate their work elsewhere.

When the police found Rabinder, he had been expecting them. He had checked himself into a clinic that belonged to an old friend of his. When the police arrived there, the records showed that Rabinder had been at the clinic for the past three days. He had complained of chest pains. The young officer assured him that his chest pains would really begin only in the police station.

Rabinder's friend, the doctor, protested. He was wearing a white lab coat for the occasion. The officer said in English, "One minute," and invited him to step out of the room. In the doctor's office, the policeman switched back to Hindi. He said, "We know one thing. You have not been preparing the correct paperwork for the men who have been coming here with gunshot wounds. We have proof. If you give me trouble, I can have your clinic shut down." The doctor found this funny. A smile spread like a taunt on his full lips. He had the "backing" of enough politicians. The clinic treated all their men when they got hurt during elections, riots, or in kidnapping raids. He had nothing to fear and he said to the policeman, "Do you want to get your blood pressure examined? Because what I'm going to tell you now is going to raise it sky high." But the officer didn't wait to finish the conversation. He quickly stepped out of the room, grabbed Rabinder by the arm, and started dragging him to his jeep. Rabinder allowed himself to be led like that. He only stiffened when instead of making him sit in the front, the officer pushed him roughly into the back of the jeep.

18

The previous summer, Binod had gone to Patna to write about a doctor who had been kidnapped. The doctor's name was Ramesh Chandra. He was a well-known neurosurgeon and his kidnapping had led the state's doctors to threaten a strike that would shut down the hospitals.

Dr. Chandra was driving back from dinner when a red Maruti came to a stop right in front of his car and four men jumped out. The doctor's driver was on leave. The Indica that he was driving was also new; he wasn't familiar with the controls, and when the men appeared beside his door, he tried to lock the car but couldn't. The men had pistols. They got inside the car and one of them began to drive. The young man sitting next to Dr. Chandra said that he and his friends had just committed a crime and were going to use his car to make their escape. He asked the doctor to sit quietly. The car passed the Patna airport and then Phulwari. The men had taken away the doctor's mobile phone. One man made a call on that phone. Dr. Chandra's heart sank when he heard the man say, "Okay. We have got him."

....

Binod had been thinking of Dr. Chandra ever since Baba told him that Rabinder was probably involved in kidnapping and extortion. When he was able at last to get Neelu on the phone he asked her whether she had been able to find out anything yet. She hadn't but she said, "It is possible that he is involved." And then she said, "Anything is possible with Rabinder." Three hours later, Shatrughan called with the first few details he had been able to extract from his politician friends. For a while, despite what they had learned about the charges against Rabinder, there had been hopes that he would be released soon. But that hope vanished as the days turned into weeks. When Binod called Bua, she didn't seem optimistic. She sighed and said, "It is all political."

....

Months later, Rabinder was still in prison when Romola Banerjee was killed. Neelu was among those who believed that Roma's death had something to do with Rabinder. Binod had just heard the news from Shatrughan and was finding it difficult to be coherent in that conversation, but he suggested that Patna faced no shortage of causes for homicide. Rabinder was only one name on a long list. Neelu was unmoved. She found it easier to blame their cousin than their city. Her judgment on the matter was that a thin, unbroken line separated Patna from hell. But while people did violence to each other in the worst ways, there were no unmotivated killings. She believed that there was justice amid all the depravity. In the trial that was played out in her mind, Rabinder lost, and Patna won.

There was no fairness in Roma's death.

The killers had put her body in a gunnysack and thrown it in the bushes near the railway track close to the Patna airport. Stray dogs seemed to have bitten into the sack through the night. At nine that morning, the train from Calcutta bound for Amritsar passed by. Much before that happened, vultures had gathered there. The sack must have been torn apart by then, and the birds gorged on the corpse. They had fed well because not much was recovered; only the portion above the torso had remained completely intact. The eyes had been plucked out by the crows and the left part of the face torn away probably by dogs. The police would ordinarily have been looking for a sari to match the color provided in the missing persons case, but the recognizable proof in this instance came from Roma's right arm, the hand still whole but with the flesh swollen around the gold ring and bangle, discovered nearly fifty feet away beside a concrete wall that had been built and left incomplete by the railway authorities.

The people who lived in the huts only four or five hundred yards to the east on the other side of the tracks said that they had seen the vultures but imagined that an animal had been killed by a train. It had happened before. A few months earlier, a cow had got its hoof caught in the siding. On this occasion, two or three people at different times tried to look, but there was little that was visible in the bushes. The murderers had hacked the body into smaller parts in order to fit it into the sack. Dogs and then the birds had scattered the parts of the corpse and it was impossible for anyone who looked in that direction to guess that what they were looking at was once a human body.

The vultures had fed heavily and several of them were sitting on the tracks when the train from Calcutta came. The driver of the train had seen the birds but expected them to fly away when the train neared them.

The birds had just fed and were heavy. There were some that tried to amble away but the metal fender of the train, which resembled an above-ground plough, caught many of them and sent bits of the birds soaring into the air. First one, and then another, huge headless vulture landed inside the fence of the adjoining house.

The house was occupied by Bihar's finance commissioner. It was one in a long line of official bungalows. The birds fell in the garden after having cleared the embankment and the five-foot-high fence. But there was enough life left in them to carry on a macabre death dance. It was the sight of the headless vultures dancing in his garden at nine in the morning that made the finance commissioner, Mr. Ranjit Dua, call up a deputy inspector general in the police department who used to take part with him in the Sai Baba Satsang on weekends. An hour later, Roma's body had been found. Her identity, however, was not established till four in the afternoon. Her husband said that he had begun to suspect that Roma had been kidnapped: he was waiting for a ransom call when the police arrived.

....

Binod's mobile phone was new at that time and when it rang that night he was already asleep and didn't respond at first. It was Shatrughan. Binod looked at the tiny time display on the phone. Shatrughan said that he had gone to Hajipur Jail in the evening to give the news to Rabinder. It was past midnight when Shatrughan had called him, however, and Binod suspected that his brother-in-law had been drinking. Shatrughan said that Rabinder had asked on seeing him, "Have you brought a special dinner for me?" Then he had seen Shatrughan's face and asked him to sit down and waited to hear what the other man did not want to say.

Rabinder had thought it extremely unlikely that Roma's husband was the one who had engineered the murder. Banerjee just didn't have it in him. He was certain that the same people who had got him thrown into jail were also behind this murder. Rabinder had surprised Shatrughan by mentioning the name not only of the politician who was Bua's rival, but also of the man who was one of his major financiers, Manik. Rabinder had said that when he was out, before he did anything else, he would have to deal with his cousin Manik.

Shatrughan had a ready analysis of the relationship between Manik and Rabinder. He said, "Ek mayaan, do talwaar." They are like two swords, and there is only one scabbard. Was Manik also having an affair with Roma?

Shatrughan laughed. He said, "No, no. That would have been different. Why are you dragging that poor girl into this? This is a game at a higher level."

Roma's murder had been a warning to Rabinder. The kidnapped person was called an "item" and Manik's job was to provide muscle to keep the "item" safe. The politician to whom he had given the AK-47 was also interested in promoting Manik in state politics. Shatrughan believed that Manik had already gotten Bua's property. What he was also making certain was that Rabinder didn't inherit Bua's political capital. The ticket for the home constituency would be Manik's and never go to Bua's son. Shatrughan said, "By killing Roma they are saying to him you're safer in jail. You come out and we'll chop your body into a hundred pieces."

....

Binod slept very little that night. The next morning, after spending half an hour at the office, he went out for a walk. There was a small pond nearby and he sat down in the shadow of a wall. At different times of the day, depending on the light, the color of the water in the pond changed from a slimy green to black. He sat staring into the pond. The reflection of an airplane appeared to fly silently through a darkening sky of water and moss.

The papers had given a few paragraphs to Romola Banerjee of Patna. It was difficult to predict whether there would be more in the days to follow. There would certainly have been more if the police had hinted at the possibility of extramarital relations; but they had been kept on a leash. As a result, there was only the excitement of the murder itself, which would disappear in a day or two. If Roma hadn't been the wife of an official, and a poor woman, her case would have merited a statement of outrage from a human rights or women's group. That would have meant an extra day's presence in the papers but also ensured a permanent burial of the news.

Just a few months earlier, in Bikram near Patna, a fourteen-year-old girl had died by the roadside. She had been living on the street, and the shopkeepers, beggars, and even the police said that the girl was mentally disturbed. However, the girl was able to tell people that her name was Kusum. She had been brought to Bikram by some truck drivers who had abducted her from her home, raped her, and then left her by the wayside. A local officer called Anjar Mian had taken pity on her and given her shelter, but he couldn't keep her in his small house for a long period.

Kusum had ended up back on the street. It is possible that she was gang-raped a second time. A few laborers had taken the girl—her clothes were soaked with blood—to a hospital nearby. But they were turned away and so Kusum was abandoned by the river, where she died two days later.

A colleague of Binod's named Varghese from the Patna office had gone to Bikram to talk to people there. He met a schoolteacher named Chandrabhushan who said that Kusum "had muttered names like D. K. Singh, Feroze, and Kishen gang." She asked for her mother. The schoolteacher told Varghese, "When I asked what troubled her, she repeatedly pointed to her abdomen."

Later, when he was writing about Mala Srivastava, Binod had only thought about Bua. He had buried Roma somewhere deep in his heart and tried to forget her. But sitting by the pond in Bombay that day, on the morning after he had received news of her murder, Binod wanted to have met Roma before she died. If he had known her while she was alive and happy in Patna, he would have found out from her who she was and what she wanted to live for. But even if he had met her only when she was dying, he had the selfish desire to put his ear close to her mouth so that she could whisper names and he could be satisfied that all of them would have been as meaningless to him as the ones that had come out of Kusum's lips.

19

On the phone, Rabinder would only talk about making films and it was Ma one night who gave Binod the good news when he called. A new police officer, a Muslim man whose name was Qamar or maybe Qaiser, had been appointed to the precinct in which Bua's house was located; the man was helpful and had, in exchange for what amounted to a flat in a new high-rise building, agreed to change a couple of details in the record books in his office. Rabinder would be released sometime in October.

Binod was going to Patna for the Dussehra holidays and he began to hope that Rabinder would be out by then. Baba had been given a positive report by the doctors. It was likely that he had beaten the cancer. He certainly seemed in good spirits on the phone. The U.S. government report had just been released. Saddam Hussein didn't have any weapons of mass destruction. Baba felt strong enough to call Binod to tell him about the BBC story he had just heard on the investigation. "We were almost all wrong," the investigator appointed by Bush had told the Senate.

Binod told him during the same conversation that he was writing a screenplay for Vikas Dhar.

Baba asked, "What is the conflict in the film?"

The question left him struggling for the right word. He wanted to say desire—the struggle of desire against—what exactly?—and then he quickly said, "It's about old age. People getting old. But wanting more from life."

He heard the chuckle at the other end. Baba was unconvinced that Binod knew anything about getting old, Binod was sure of that, but he enjoyed the sound of his father's laughter. So it was more of a shock when the call came that he had contracted pneumonia and had been taken to the hospital.

The Dussehra holidays were nearly a fortnight away. Binod told Bua that he would call the next day and tell them how much sooner he would be coming to Patna. But that night, a second call came. Neelu was on the phone telling him that the doctors had said that the situation was more serious than they had first thought.

In the morning, Binod took a Sahara flight to Delhi and then waited at Palam for a plane that would take him to Patna. Planes were leaving for nearly every city in the country, but no one was going where he had to go. After three hours, an announcement indicated that the flight to Patna had been delayed for another hour. Then, Rabinder called on Binod's mobile phone to tell him that in Patna the hospital was in disarray. The doctors were on strike there because of the kidnapping and murder of a surgeon.

Despair, or maybe it was just sorrow dressed differently, came and sat down in the seat next to him. But the rest of the people in the airport were going about their business with great energy. The airline staff, busy in blue skirts, spoke into their walkie-talkies and loudly called out the names of cities. "Guwahati, Bangalore, Chennai, Jammu, Jammu, any passengers for Jammu. . . ." Those traveling to Patna were being asked to pick up a voucher for a meal in the café. Away from him, a couple of kids ran shrieking around a rotating plastic model of a mobile phone, and on the large screen at the end of the hall was a clip from a Hollywood film starring Christopher Reeve. Reeve had died while lying in coma in New York City. At least Superman didn't have to contend with missing doctors. Binod imagined his father, grotesquely, with ice in his lungs. And there, in the noisy airport lounge, he began to wish, childishly, selfishly, that Baba would not die yet, that he please live long enough to watch the film that was going to be made from the story that he was adapting for Vikas Dhar.

....

Baba was sleeping on a white sheet that had a large inkblot on the side. The latest Frontline lay open on a small table to an article by Amartya Sen, who was wearing a suit and a red tie in the photo. Baba was in a faded white kurta so creased that it seemed to hide a story. His skin had turned darker but his gray hair had just begun to grow back. Yet he was barely enough there. Binod put his hands on the old metal headstand and stood beside the bed not saying anything.

"He's sleeping," Shatrughan said. "You stay here. I'll get tea from downstairs."

Suddenly alone with his father, Binod moved closer and sat down on the bed. There was a window on the other side of the bed. The Ganges was visible in the distance, a solitary boat with bare masts slowly floating past.

Before he fell ill, it was Baba's habit to come to the railway station whenever Binod returned home from Delhi or Bombay. His father wanted to have him for himself for the half hour before they would reach home and see the others. Binod would step off the train and Baba would be there, waving his thin arm, and then he would turn around to lead him to the Hanuman Mandir. There was such a lack of vanity in his love, such an absence of demand.

Ma and Neelu arrived with some food from home and they gently woke Baba up. Binod touched his feet and his father said something that was slurred. Ma opened the tiffin and asked Binod if he was hungry, but he said he would just go downstairs and have tea.

The yellow building next door had a sign on it saying Skin and Venereal Diseases Research Institute. In the open verandah of the building, a vendor had set up shop with a small paraffin stove and a couple of jars, and several upturned glasses placed on a pile of bricks in the corner.

"I would happily pay money for a bit of a breeze," Shatrughan said. And then, "You should have brought a doctor with you from Bombay."

....

Late in the afternoon, an intern with a clipboard in her hand stopped by. She put her fingers on Baba's wrist and then listened to his breathing with her stethoscope placed on his chest. Before she left, she turned to Shatrughan and said, "You will have to stay on alert."

The next day, the same woman was back at the same time, this time looking different because she was wearing pants instead of a churidar kurta. She said Baba needed additional medicines and then, almost casually, she said that he would be shifted into the intensive care unit. His lungs needed constant examination.

The new wing was quieter. It was also air conditioned and this was a relief. But the glass in the windows had been painted white and you couldn't look outside. That night Binod dozed on the cot that had been placed beside Baba's bed. His father slept an undisturbed sleep, wheezing faintly but otherwise at peace. More than once Binod was woken up because he could hear repeated laughter through the walls. He dreamed that he had sat down on the floor to eat his meal, but just as he was about to begin a lizard fell down on his plate. He couldn't eat and Neelu had run out of the room weeping.

Late in the night, he woke up with a feeling of dryness in his throat. When he stepped out Binod saw that the door of the room next to theirs had been left ajar: he caught a glimpse of a young, fully dressed man sitting on a chair watching the television that was placed on the bed. He had the feeling in the morning that he had heard Baba murmuring something, but it is possible that it was only the television next door.

Just before eight o'clock, he fetched a cup of tea and a newspaper. He was reading the *Jansatta* with his feet propped up on the bed when he saw that his father wanted to cough even though he appeared to be in his sleep. Baba tried to dislodge the phlegm in his throat a few times and when he didn't succeed he woke up breathless. Binod went out to call the nurse from her desk at the far end of the corridor. The nurse was a youngish woman from Cochin or Kottayam or some such place in the south. She was thin, dark, and pink-lipped. She said in an accented Hindi, "Ab bahut time nahin hai." There was very little time left.

That was all.

....

The thing that disturbed Binod most about Baba's death was the worry that he had been trying to say something to him when he had coughed. When Binod had looked at him, it seemed a light had come into his eyes. But Binod had panicked and not said anything at all; instead of running off to fetch the nurse, he ought to have spoken to his father, he should have comforted him by saying something reassuring. In English films, people said "I love you." But his father had always been formal with Binod and Neelu. Even when he called he would mostly talk about what work Binod was doing and then allow himself a question about his health.

In the jeep later on, when the body was being taken to the cremation ghat, Binod considered the different possibilities. What could he have said? "Baba, I am here." "Do not exert yourself, Baba." "Baba, would you like some water?"

Bua brought Ma to the hospital in her white Ambassador. Ma stepped into the ward and stood for a moment, looking around helplessly, like a bird whose wings had been clipped. She didn't break down, as Binod had expected her to do, and when she saw him she spoke as if they were resuming an interrupted conversation. She said, "You must take Baba's remains to Benares." The matter had never been discussed before, but again, they had never discussed anything related to death. Binod said that it wasn't a good idea to delay the cremation. Ma said, "Okay. But take the ashes, take the ashes. Put them in the water in Benares."

She sat down next to Baba. But when the ambulance arrived to take the body to the house, Ma began saying in a soft voice that they shouldn't use the ugly blue van from the hospital. This was no way to take Baba home. Her voice was like a girl's. "Binod, Binod," she said, "We can't do that. Locking a body in the ambulance would be like putting him in a coffin. We shouldn't act like Christians."

Binod had never heard his mother speak like this before. He turned to look at Bua and she said that she would arrange for a jeep.

When the jeep arrived half an hour later, Ma and Bua got into the Ambassador while Binod and Shatrughan accompanied Baba's body. When they came out of the hospital, Shatrughan said that they should buy flowers and directed the driver to take the inside road past the Patna Museum. Binod sat silently while outside Shatrughan haggled over the price of the marigolds. He noticed that the white kurta Baba was wearing had a note in its pocket. This is what his father was trying to tell him when he died! His mind had seized that thought, as a drowning man might clutch air. It was a piece of paper folded twice and Binod was still looking at it, unable to read it, when Shatrughan returned with an armful of marigold garlands that he placed gingerly in a heap at Baba's feet.

Binod stayed silent. He realized that his heart was beating fast, perhaps because he was keeping a secret from Shatrughan, feeling like a schoolboy hiding a prank in class. When they were close to home, Binod smoothed the paper out. He saw Baba's handwriting, looking a bit more crooked than usual, perhaps because he had written the note while lying down.

Dictionary

"I have studied it often, but I could never discover the plot."

Mark Twain

Had he copied it down from a newspaper or a magazine? Binod folded the paper back into its original shape and put it in his shirt pocket.

....

Ma asked, "Will Rabinder be able to come?"

When nobody responded to his mother's question, she repeated it without any change in wording or inflection. For over an hour, Ma would direct the same question to anyone who entered the room where she was sitting. Each face looked stricken on her account, but still no one knew what to say to her.

Binod saw his mother gazing emptily at each person as they hurried about making preparations for the cremation. Her hair was spread open, she had wiped away the red sindoor from the parting in her hair, and her arms looked bare without her bangles. The voice in which she repeated her question about Rabinder was unnatural. It occurred to Binod that his mother was trying hard to retain the calm in her voice. She wanted to sound rational and therefore kept making what she felt was a reasonable appeal.

Shatrughan had found a priest through an advertisement in the *Times of India*. His name was Ratan Raj and, they soon discovered, he had been born in Guyana. He was in Patna because he was doing research on the traditions that were particular to Bihar and that could even today be found in the Caribbean. Ratan Raj was still young. He was wearing a white kurta and a rope of beads around his neck. When they were ready to leave for the cremation ghat, Shatrughan said to the priest, "Panditji, ready?"

With great solemnity, and a voice that was deep and sonorous, Ratan Raj began to recite Sanskrit shlokas that must have been familiar to people in the family because immediately the women broke into loud wailing.

....

Baba's body had been washed and laid out on a wooden pallet fashioned out of a bamboo ladder and white cotton sheets. A bright yellow cloth with the name of Lord Ram printed in red all over covered the body and Binod was touched that the servant had made a small pillow of the same material and put it under Baba's head. He did not look at Ma or Neelu, and didn't even know whether they were watching when Baba's body was put in the jeep; it was humid outside and he wanted a glass of cold water and the chance to sit alone on a chair in a dark room for a minute.

When they began to move, there were shouts. Shatrughan had arranged for coins to be thrown on the road as they came out of the gate; little urchins were already scrambling in the dust behind them. He held up his hand for the driver to stop. He wanted to look out of the window to make sure that his instructions were being followed.

Ma would have said that Baba's soul would not find salvation if he was not cremated on a wooden pyre that had been lit by his only son. But instead they took Baba's body to the electric crematorium that stood alongside the burning ghat. Binod was certain in his heart that this is what

Baba would have wanted—he could almost hear his father producing some arcane piece of statistic or a piece of graphic evidence demonstrating that 25 percent of the bodies on wood pyres remained only partially burned and polluted the rivers into which they were thrown. He knew that this was the right thing to do.

When they neared the ghat, the driver of the jeep spoke for the first time. He said that the electricity bills for the crematorium had not been paid and as a punishment the government had cut the supply even though the crematorium was owned by the state. This piece of information was unsettling, and for the first time that day Binod felt emotion rise from deep inside him. Except it didn't seem to have to do anything with grief; it was more a species of rage or even irritation. Shatrughan quickly said that there was always enough wood available at the ghat for cremations, and the priest said gravely, "That is correct. The difference is only in price, it will cost about one thousand rupees more. And of course, time . . . instead of two hours, it will take four."

Binod didn't know that it took that long, even in the electric crematorium—two hours! But that is exactly how long it took for Baba's body to be reduced to a small heap of white ash and dust.

When they had reached the ghat, they found out that thanks to a makeshift arrangement the crematorium was in operation. There wasn't even any paperwork to be done. They were told to wait for fifteen minutes; the fifteen minutes became forty.

. . . .

Ratan Raj brought his palms together and begun to intone a prayer. On a stainless steel plate he arranged various items for a puja. Binod was to pour gangajal near Baba's head and then place fresh hibiscus flowers at his feet, which looked like the feet of a dead man. A small object wrapped in black cloth was Yamaraj, the god of death, and Binod put some rice and money in front of the idol. Ratan Raj demanded wet clay from the attendant at the crematorium. He patted the lump into tiny discs and stuck into them sticks of incense that smoked with an overpowering fragrance. The clay got fired in the oven and turned into what appeared at first to be spinal discs. But that was hours later. Before that could happen, the attendant needed to lower a metal rod protruding from the wall and then with a macabre clang the tray on which the corpse had been put began to move. Baba's head, the small white hairs on his scalp looking yellow and damp, was the last thing Binod saw disappear inside.

They were advised to wait out in the yard. Black smoke rose from the metal chimney and then became thin after twenty minutes. Binod was told that a Marwari businessman who had a store nearby for selling oil had rigged up an illegal connection to the crematorium. It was he who had now begun providing the electricity; he did this on a case-by-case basis and charged four hundred rupees. He was a heavy man with tiny moles clinging like miniscule orchids to the folds of his neck. When they were paying him, Shatrughan said to the man, "If you are successful, there will be no more need for this wretched government."

The man looked down at the wooden box where his money was kept. He said, "It is just a service for the dead."

When they were back in the jeep, Shatrughan said, "The attendant probably receives his cut too."

The driver nodded. He said, "Eighty rupees for every corpse."

20

When the train arrived in Benares, Binod stood looking for a moment at the imitation temple domes on the roof of the railway station.

Thirteen days would need to pass before the shraddh ceremony; to bring peace to the departed soul, a fresh puja would be held and Brahmins as well as the neighborhood poor would need to be fed. But Binod could not wait in Patna that long. If his job had still been in Delhi, he could have gone and come back in time. The only acceptable plan was that he would go first to Benares, and then he would make his way to Bombay via Delhi.

The toilet in the train had been covered with excreta and he walked over to a wall outside the station. Above him were posters showing Amitabh Bachchan's face with the appeal that small children be given the polio vaccine. On the right was a different poster, showing the outlines of a woman's exposed breasts, for a film called *Korean Kama Sutra*. And there, in the distance, were all those fake temple domes above the pink walls of the railway station.

A few minutes later, Binod hired a three-wheeler and asked the driver to take him to Manikarnika Ghat. Beneath the rickshaw's rearview mirror were painted two rhymed sentences: "Mitti bhi jahan ki paaras hai. Uss shehar ka naam Benares hai" (Even the earth of which is blessed, the city named Benares).

The steps leading down to the ghat were barely visible in the half-light of the shops that he had left behind him. The bag with Baba's ashes hung from his shoulder. In his hand, he was carrying a suitcase. A priest standing in the doorway of a small, illuminated temple was looking at him and Binod asked if he could take the ashes down to the water and scatter them there. A painted sign in Hindi on the wall said Shri Harishchandra Temple. The priest had a bright yellow flower tucked behind his ear. Except for this small adornment he could have been mistaken for the electrician called to repair a faulty wire connection. He said, "You offer prayers here first. You can put some flowers here, and depending on your devotion, any money. Whatever you can give. We can take care of other business after that."

When he started to move away, the priest said loudly, "You have come a long distance. Do everything right." But Binod didn't want to begin bargaining. He wanted peace and he made his way down to the water.

Five pyres burned in the evening dark. He stood and waited to see what he should be doing. A handful of people, relatives of the dead, moved around slowly. The driver of the rickshaw had said that the electric crematorium, built ten years earlier, had never really been used. Its brick hulk and a metal chimney loomed behind him now, the outlines framed in the glow behind it of the city's lights. Once or twice a column of sparks would rise from a pyre when a skull or a body part exploded in the heat.

In Patna, when he had taken Baba's body to the crematorium, there had been others with him. Here he was aware only of a profound solitude. He felt he was now alone with his father, and he didn't want to let him go in the dark. The heat of the flames from the funeral pyres lit his face and he turned away from the fire and also the emotion that had caught him unawares. He told himself that he would return in the morning.

....

The room that he was given in the Parvati Guesthouse was small but comfortable; its cemented floor had turned dark from use and tilted toward the window. The room was on the second floor and when Binod looked out he saw a well-lit medical store below. The store's name was printed in large letters and beside it was the picture of a man in profile: a red liquid, perhaps a cough syrup, filled his mouth and flowed down the gullet that had been painted a bright pink. The lungs were outlined in black and had been left an empty white. Binod thought of Baba coughing before he died.

He must have fallen asleep soon after he lay down in bed. During the night he was woken by the sound of chanting, which came closer. "Shree Ram . . . naam satya hai." Midnight mourners were on their way to the ghat. In the corner of the room was a wooden stool where Binod had placed the pot with the ashes. He wondered whether Baba during the final days of his illness had imagined that at the end Binod would be making this journey to Benares.

He couldn't return to sleep. In that dark room in the guesthouse, Binod's thoughts wandered and returned to his childhood. He thought of Ma, who used to come to Benares for vacations when she was a girl.

The meaning that this place had in Ma's life as a child had remained intact all through her life. This sense of continuity tethered Ma's attitude to the world; her conduct was not likely to change as long as she lived. Binod couldn't quite say the same about Rabinder. It sometimes seemed that he had made a mistake and each mistake had led to another and his life had now achieved its own untidy coherence and it spelled his doom.

However, the odd thing was that Rabinder was most hopeful about the future. Unlike Binod, who always felt that he didn't know or understand the changes that had taken place in Patna, Rabinder behaved as if he was at the heart of those changes. This gave him a place in that city. It even gave him reason to believe that he could reach out and touch Bombay.

Dawn was already filling the window with a blue-gray light when Binod began thinking of his own life. He felt that he had taken wrong turns on the road in the past, but in the future things would be better. That was his hope now. He had left Patna, he had a job in Bombay. He had ideas that he wanted to put down on paper.

Inside the guesthouse, someone was clearing his throat with loud, hawking noises. Binod lay in bed hoping for silence but other sounds had formed a chorus—a clamor of coughing and men calling out to other men and children.

. . . .

Binod had put a fresh kurta in the khadi bag along with the red pot holding Baba's ashes. A little to the west of where he had spent the night was Assi Ghat where centuries ago Kabir and Tulsi had composed lines that were no doubt being chanted on the riverbank and in temples around Binod even as his rickshaw passed through a crowded vegetable market. On reaching the ghat, he saw a tall white man meditating near the river; the man wore a blue cotton tunic and his matted hair was tied at the top of his head like a sadhu's. Assi Ghat was a small tourist site now with smart riverside hotels and signs advertising tutors who gave lessons in classical Indian music. There was even a small bookstore with books in English, and Binod stood for a moment looking at its glass wall covered with glossy posters from National Geographic.

The water felt cold only for a moment. Binod took a few quick dips and to keep his mind occupied recited the Gayatri mantra and bowed in the direction of the rising sun. With his hands, he stirred the water, as if to clear it of any debris. Some portions of the human body, men's lower backs and in the case of women their hips, are slower to burn, and are often thrown into the water along with the ashes. Binod had walked up to Assi because Manikarnika was downstream from him. By bathing there he was hoping that he had performed his duty but also come out cleaner than when he stepped into the water.

While he was changing back into dry clothes with a towel wrapped around him, a young man came up. He said that he had a boat and would row Binod downstream for a hundred rupees. Binod offered sixty. The youth said it was the first business in the morning and he would like to start right; Binod added five more. The boat was painted a light blue and white and it had an advertisement for the Hindi newspaper *Jansatta* painted on its side. Balanced on the stern, the youth used a pole to push them into the current and soon, with the sound of the boat's creaking spreading like ripples in the cool morning air, they were sliding away from land.

The river smelled dank but it also seemed as if what was filling his nostrils was the smell of the night. This smell would evaporate with the sun and indeed in the distance a pale cover of mist seemed to rise from the river, partially hiding, on the right, the small islands of sand. On the left were the ghats, stone steps leading the eye away from the water, and above them the tall buildings, most of them old and decaying but striking to look at because of their elegant canopies and ornate balustrades.

The evidence of death wasn't to be found only in the smoke rising from the pyres downstream; it was there in the thin bodies scrubbing themselves on the banks and the rotting walls that loomed behind them.

Grimy, inflated polythene packets, with flowers and other offerings trapped inside, floated on the water. Binod was looking at the striped stone tigers mounted on the two ends of a balcony in the distance when he heard the boatman say, "It's a cow." And there, close to them in the same direction that he had been looking, floating like a dark shadow in the water, was the barely recognizable carcass of a cow. Flies were clustered on the part of the animal's side that stuck out of the water.

The sun was still very low in the sky but it was bright. Bells rang out from the temples on the bank. The young boatman had lank, oily hair covering a head that was too large for the short body and which pressed down into a foreshortened neck. He seemed to know why Binod had come to Benares. He said, "If you want to put the ashes in the water, this is a good place." Binod untied the red cloth that covered the mouth of the clay pot, and regretted that he had not brought any flowers, particularly marigolds, which he would have liked to have strewn on the water. He had seen the flowers floating on the river after a funeral in so many Hindi films.

Leaning over the side of the boat, a little unsure of himself, he overturned the pot. The ash was dark but it sank into the water with a silvery dazzle. Then he scooped some water in his cupped palm and threw it back over his head. When he stared into the water as the ash disappeared, he tried to say in his mind, "Baba."

The pyres of Manikarnika were visible from there. The boatman had let the oars trail in the water, but Binod told him that he would like to return to the bank. The young man nodded and shifted the angle of the boat. He was also conscious perhaps that he would be paid soon, and so he slipped into the role of a tourist guide. He said that music concerts were often held at the ghat they were crossing; Binod could see the concrete steps and a balcony built on a ledge above the water. The audience filled the steps while the musicians sang till the early hours of the morning. The previous week Pandit Bhimsen Joshi had performed there. But on this morning there was hardly anyone around, just a group of skinny boys running on the steps, one of them holding in his hand the string of a purple kite.

At Manikarnika, the small temple was once again open and the priest whom Binod had seen the previous night was still there. Binod folded his hands in front of the idol. Then, further down, closer to the riverbank, he saw the shrine of the lord of the burning ghat. A small metal stairway led up to the temple: it had a corrugated tin roof and was open on all sides. From the river, a slight breeze wafted in, touching his face. Binod stood in front of the brass shiva-linga and remembered his father's voice reciting Sanskrit shlokas in the early morning prayers during Dussehra. Small bells hanging from the perimeter of the roof tinkled in the breeze.

In Patna, Binod had decided that he would wait till he was in Benares to get his head shaved. The barber that was pointed out to him at Manikarnika was lazily brushing his teeth with a twig. He asked Binod to wait on the steps. After a while, the man walked over with a lota filled with water. Unfolding a frayed white cotton towel, he chose a razor from the three that lay hidden inside.

The razor was cold and it scraped the scalp. The barber sat on an upturned brick and Binod, sitting below him on a step, kept his eyes on the torn piece of an old newspaper on which fell small, sticky clumps of wet hair.

When he had paid, he looked up at the others who stood around the burning pyres. No one was crying or laughing; people were soberly doing only what needed to be done. He felt his work in Benares was complete. He felt lighter and clean.

....

The train from Benares took him to Delhi and from there he needed to catch another train to take him south to Bombay. He had not made any plans for Delhi because he didn't know whether the train would be on time. It turned out he had to wait for five hours, and during that time he sat under a fan on platform number three at the New Delhi railway station, idly observing the arrival and departure of trains and passengers. It was a little bit like sitting beside the river in Benares. The rush of human bodies ebbed and flowed; the movement of the trains seemed eternal. A man rushed up to greet a passenger amid smiles and laughter, and a quarter of an hour later, one would think it was the same person saying goodbye accompanied by tears.

At a small nondescript station called Pasi, Binod bought some spicy pakoras. The tea that he got smelled of the kerosene that had been used to heat it. Just as the train was pulling out, he tossed the clay cup out of the window. He saw it shatter on the platform, and he was back in Benares watching mourners breaking small earthen pots on the road while they followed corpses being taken to the ghat. In Bombay, a city of countless millions, he had rarely seen people carrying a corpse. They perhaps used ambulances or a taxi. He had certainly never seen anyone breaking clay pots on the road.

The moon rode with the train through the darkness of the night. Binod woke up in the morning when the train was maybe an hour away from Bombay Central. Tiny houses patched together with corrugated tin and blue plastic sheets on their roofs gave way to the waiting crowds of Borivali and Malad. Right beneath the huge billboard for Sahara Lake City were four men squatting, their buttocks almost touching the ground. A young man sat with a Pepsi bottle filled with water and the others had small tins beside them. One of them was talking on a mobile phone. This was Bombay.

VI

Nobody Does

the Right Thing

21

The first night that he was back in his flat in Bombay, Binod fell asleep and found that he was with Baba. They were on a train headed to Patna after a visit to Benares—it seemed that they had gone there to put someone's ashes in the Ganges. A few young men came into the train at the Mughalsarai station and began to throw red color on all the passengers. It was still morning, but it was quite warm inside the train and the colored water felt good on his skin. The men were shouting and laughing, and so too were the others around them. It had slipped Binod's mind that it was Holi. He shouldn't have forgotten this. It was because of the festival that there were fewer travelers on the train and it was possible for Baba and him to find seats.

The men had probably drunk too much bhang. They stopped when they saw Binod and his father, with their freshly shaven heads, the only two of the passengers who were not participating in the revelry. But one of them, a bearded fellow in his early twenties, came close to them and, all the while laughing, rubbed what must have been black grease on Binod's scalp.

Binod didn't say anything because he didn't want his father to get upset. The young man was still laughing when he touched Baba. Strangely enough, the bearded fellow seemed to know that Baba's eyesight was poor. He gently touched Baba's face. At first, Baba didn't react at all. Then he got up and placing his left arm lightly on the man's shoulder slapped the fellow hard with his right hand.

The youth fell down into Binod's lap. Almost at the same time, one of his companions leaped forward and hit Baba's nose with the palm of his hand. The blood on his father's face and shirt looked brighter than the colored water on him. Binod struggled to say something, but the young man had fallen on him and he was unable to breathe. Baba was screaming in pain or perhaps in rage. He called the men dogs and said that they had disgraced the memory of the person whom he had just cremated. He said, "All of you are no better than worms that feed on corpses."

The mention of death made everyone silent. Binod wanted to take Baba's hand and make him sit down, but he was unable to move. He noticed that his father was blind. He had forgotten that Baba had always been blind.

Then Binod became aware that Baba wasn't there anymore and the train was strangely empty. He had begun to wonder who it was that they had cremated and whose death they were mourning. Just then, a sweet-looking young man came down the aisle with a large peacock in his arms, the bird's beautiful, resplendent feathers trailing behind on the floor. A light fragrance had entered the train carriage. Binod saw that the peacock's feathers were filled with large sad eyes and he doubled up in pain and began to weep with what felt like inexhaustible sadness.

....

Binod was returning to college one summer from Patna. The train, which was running three hours late, stopped at Aligarh. Binod looked up from his reading when an old man began to claim in a loud voice that he was Jawaharlal Nehru. It was very hot outside. The train began to move. There were many new passengers on the train now, daily commuters with their bags and loads of merchandise. Plastics, metal products, slippers, saris wrapped in polythene. The Aligarh passengers sitting near Binod—all men—settled down to a game of cards. They asked the old man a question or two and then began to tease him. Like many others in the compartment, Binod was amused by this teasing. The old man, sensing that he was being mocked, began to shout louder till one of the men sitting on the upper berth bent down and slapped him.

The old man was wearing a white cotton cap, as Nehru did in photographs. At some point, a hand knocked the cap from the old man's head. He picked it up and turned on his tormentors with filthy abuses. This was all the provocation that the men needed. All along the narrow pathway between the berths, violent blows rained down on the old man. He swore and spit on the men closest to him. Another blow and his head began to bleed. One man gave his rubber slippers to the old man and asked him to use them to sweep the floor. "Do that, Jawaharlal," he said. When the old man tried to use the slippers to hit back, he pulled the old man's dhoti, leaving him naked from the waist down.

Binod's fellow passengers, many of whom had been sitting quietly till then, crowded around the old man and tore off his shirt. They kicked his genitals. Someone on a nearby berth asked that this be stopped, but this appeal had no effect. There was a stink coming from the corner in which the old man had been pushed. The landscape outside was burning in the heat, and even inside the train it was hot and stuffy. Binod did not want to move. He thought of the old man when he got to the hostel and was preparing to sleep, and although he had not thought of him for any length of time ever again, he felt that the dream about his father being assaulted in the train back from Benares had more than a little to do with that old memory.

That memory of derangement and violence was evoked possibly by Baba's death and the long train journey that Binod has undertaken to get to Bombay, but who's to guess what triggers into consciousness the sense of claustrophobia of closed, middle-class lives, or slips into recall a sour taste in the mouth and then the sudden shame of collective nakedness ringing with abuse.

22

Bua used Baba's death to have Rabinder's release date moved up by a
week.

On Dussehra, Binod had just finished interviewing an Adlabs executive
in Powai when his phone rang. Bua said, "Binod, I have someone here who
wants to talk to you." It was Rabinder. He said he wanted to come to Bombay, but first he must deal with business in Patna. Binod thought Rabinder
was talking about his cybercafe. A week was to pass before Shatrughan
would tell Binod that Rabinder had, upon his release, filed a case against
the government on grounds of wrongful confinement and bodily harm.
But at the end of that first conversation, Bua had taken the phone from Rabinder and her voice was more somber. She said, "He is out now and will
take care of the shraddh. You need not worry about anything anymore."

A conch was being blown behind him. Binod turned around and saw
the canopy under which rose a flower-bedecked idol of Durga astride a
lion: the animal's paw, bloody claw unsheathed, rested on the demon,
who looked like Osama Bin Laden. Stalls selling sweets and fruit lined
both sides of the road for fifty yards. There were families walking on the
street, the women in bright new saris and the children in clothes that still
had their creases intact. A small truck passed him carrying goats whose
hides had been painted with brilliant red stripes.

"Bua," Binod said, "Ma might need money—"

"You don't worry about anything," Bua said, and then added, "Rabinder
wants you to write a script for him, just as you are doing for Vikas Dhar.
He will produce a film. Neeraj Dubey has promised to act in it."

Months ago, Rabinder had advised Binod to turn bits of Mala Srivastava's life into a love story. He carefully considered the fact that Vikas
Dhar had wanted a story about a murdered girl and had decided that it
wouldn't be a bad idea to also make a film about another recent death.
This one too had its moment in the media. A young Bihari named Satyendra Dubey had been killed toward the end of last year in Gaya. He was a
civil engineer and it was believed that he had been murdered. Rabinder

wanted to portray on film the idealism of the young man as well as the conspiracy that had destroyed him.

The newspapers said that Satyendra Dubey had sent a confidential letter to the prime minister. He had provided names of those who were siphoning off funds from the project to build highways across India. He had called the project a loot of public money. Although he had appealed for secrecy, the prime minister's office had been callous: his cover was blown and now the young man was dead. Idealism was as scarce as ambition: it bloomed briefly in the wilderness and then someone quickly came along to pluck it.

Binod had borrowed from Chekhov's story and now it seemed that Rabinder was borrowing from his editorial. Binod didn't blame him. Everyone was in the borrowing business. Vikas Dhar did it too and proudly proclaimed it. He had recently said that genius all too often was only a difference of degrees, and not of kind, even in the most successful kind of filmmaking. He had said that there would be no Bollywood without Hollywood.

What bothered Binod more was that after the check, Dhar hadn't even returned his calls. In his anxiety, Binod had taken an appointment with Neeraj Dubey to see if he had any advice. At the actor's flat, he had begun to tell him about his worry, but Dubey was watching cricket on television. He was probably not listening to what Binod was saying because after a while he had apologized. "I get very caught up in the game," he said. "I'm very excited right now. But don't mind me. Go on."

India was playing Australia at Chepauk. Virender Sehwag was at the crease. Just the mention of his name sent a wave through the blood. The previous year, Sehwag had been batting at 195 in Melbourne and had dared to hit a six to get to the double-century mark. He had been caught but didn't seem to care. His fans loved his aggression. Dubey was sitting wearing only a lungi; he had an exfoliant mask on his face because he was going to a shoot that evening. He was smoking nervously. Sehwag was on 92 and had lofted McGrath to mid-off and one of the fielders had almost got his hand to it. Then the umpires had signaled the drinks break.

Dubey began quoting the *Time* magazine article about Asian heroes that Binod had also seen. "To India's impoverished youth, Sehwag is the man of clay astride the mountain of the gods," Dubey said, smiling, "His parents still have a buffalo in their yard."

They turned back to the television when the drinks break was over and were soon rewarded. Sehwag reached his hundred by cover-driving the Australians for four. Dubey and Binod shook hands. Fresh cigarettes were lit.

The mask had dried on Dubey's cheeks and there were tiny cracks on its surface. He clasped his hands behind his head, showing off his muscles, and paid tribute to Sehwag. "His English has now improved. He can talk to anyone. But in his press conferences, he insists on speaking in Hindi, so that he can be understood by all his friends back home in Najafgarh."

Sehwag was stocky and because of the pads and the helmet his body appeared all the more compact, like a small sack filled with bombs. They watched him for another half hour, excited by his hunger and by his skill. He was stroking the ball with abandon. His success made Binod optimistic. When Dubey asked his servant to bring more tea and had taken a sip, Binod took his chance and said that Vikas Dhar had offered him some signing money but after that hadn't contacted him again. Weeks had now passed. Dubey gave a short laugh and said in English, "Welcome to the Bombay film industry."

....

Each day Rabinder had a new idea for a film.

One day he told Binod that the long stay in prison was an experience he didn't even wish on his enemies. Binod asked him if he had enemies: he was thinking of Roma's killers. Rabinder said, "We are talking on the mobile phone. Let's discuss other things." But Binod had nothing else to say. After a while, Rabinder said with some bravado, "You know, bhaiya, Dhirubhai Ambani used to say that when he had to deal with enemies, rather than wasting time engaging with them, he would shift his orbit. You take the eastern route to the sun, I myself will turn to the west . . . That is how I am going to respond to those figures whom you were calling my enemies."

"There's an idea," Binod said. "Forget Satyendra Dubey. Make a film on Dhirubhai."

He heard Rabinder suck on his teeth at the other end.

By the time of his death two years earlier, Dhirubhai Ambani had erected a business empire that was valued at U.S.$12.5 billion. Reliance, his company, had been built from scratch. This was what made Dhirubhai a legend. He had started life as a gas station attendant in Aden. He earned the equivalent of three hundred rupees for that work. When he began work in Bombay, he lived with his family in a cramped chawl. Dhirubhai's first major profits came from the marketing of polyester; he built a textile factory to meet the rising demand for that fabric. At the same time, Ambani had been open to other opportunities. He had sold dirt to an Arab sheikh who wanted to grow roses in the desert.

Binod said to Rabinder, "People want to see people in films making money."

Rabinder said, "Yes."

Binod said, "But I don't know enough about Dhirubhai. What were his gambles in life? How did he deal with losses?"

Rabinder made a humming noise that meant he didn't know.

Binod said, "Here's a question for you: did Dhirubhai ever buy off a person like Satyendra Dubey?"

Rabinder asked, "Aren't there reports in the press about all this?"

"There might be. I don't know about them. Also, I have learned that you can't make stories out of newspaper reports. You have to create characters . . . Who will you treat as a character here? Dhirubhai himself? Then you turn your film into biography. Who wants to watch a film like that?"

Rabinder paused. He said, "How about the character of a journalist like you? Someone who is trying to find out about a matter that is of interest to him. Because it's his job. Or because he's a writer. He is finding out about Satyendra Dubey, or about Dhirubhai, or about someone who is a nobody."

It was now Binod's turn to make humming noises to suggest that he was thinking this over.

That is where their conversation ended. Binod was preparing to attend the film festival in Goa. When he had time, he looked at the files in the office, reading about Satyendra Dubey and once or twice even about Dhirubhai. When he had been a student in Delhi, a popular film in the leftist circles had been Costa Gavras's Z. But a political thriller was hardly a popular genre in Hindi cinema. His own heart leaned toward films that dealt with ordinary human conflict. No one had made films like *Do Bigha Zameen* or *Garm Hawa* during the past two decades. The first was about a landless peasant who ends up as a rickshawala in Calcutta racing against horses and the second about the trials of a Muslim family in Agra immediately after Partition. He thought about what he had done with Chekhov's story. Had Vikas Dhar read his story carefully and decided that there was nothing to be done with it?

....

Instead of Dhar, it was once again Rabinder who called to discuss stories for films. Early one afternoon, while Binod was waiting in a builder's office, his phone rang. He could hear cricket commentary in the background when he answered. It was the second or third day of play in the Eden Gardens. India versus South Africa. On the other end, Rabinder said, "Have you thought more about my idea of using the character of a journalist?"

Binod said, "What is happening in the match?"

South Africa had scored a bit over 300, and India was 86 for the loss of one. Rabinder stopped speaking for a second. Sehwag had just hit a four and then a six. Binod took his shoes off and asked his cousin to put the phone close to the TV. Rabinder said something and then Binod heard the roar. Another four. Binod was shouting for Rabinder, and he was back soon, saying, "He has hit another four." Rabinder began to laugh again, but it was only because on the last ball of the over, Sehwag had cracked another boundary. The whole stadium had gone wild.

Binod stepped out of the office and stood on the steps that led down to the street. He heard Rabinder say, "I called because I was thinking of all this madness about cricket. How did the journalist who broke the news a few years ago about match fixing—how did he find out all this?"

Binod wasn't sure. He thought it was a former Indian player who had come up with the allegations. The journalists hadn't done much at all. It was only later that they put a wire on that player, Manoj Prabhakar, and had him interview his pals. People mentioned names, often the same names, and an intelligence inquiry was instituted. Earlier, a retired chief justice had submitted a report to the cricket board in which he had called Prabhakar a failed player and a frustrated politician. There was a story there, perhaps, of a youth from a low-income family making it to the national team, but wanting more—and, on not getting it, going a little bit crazy in anger and despair. But you couldn't make a popular film about the dissolution of a hard-working and unlikeable guy.

But what was the use of going into all this with Rabinder? Binod was feeling a bit irritated at his situation. He had wanted Vikas Dhar and instead he got Rabinder.

He became cruel to his cousin. He said, "From what I can understand, all the major parties were interested in telling a story, stories that were true or false, so that they could become rich. In some instances, as in Prabhakar's case, and also one or two journalists, these people came off looking worse than before. This is a danger that you too should consider."

Rabinder was unfazed. He asked innocently, "You are talking of the character's motivation inside the story?"

Binod felt like laughing. This jargon from the film studios was actually coming to him from a man who had till recently been locked in a prison cell in Bihar. He said, "Yes. That is what I am saying. Why are you telling the story? To tell the truth? Because of some bullshit you believe in about exposing the rot?"

Rabinder ignored the questions. He said, "Think of it this way. You are a successful cricketer. Successful beyond your dreams. People love you because of the way you play and what you stand for. But you're greedy. You have made so much money, and so quickly, that you think you can do anything. What is your motivation in fixing matches?"

"Yes," Binod said, half against himself.

Rabinder went on, "You are a good person. Your parents are good people. They still live in an ordinary small town, but you are building them a mansion at the end of street where they have always lived. You have changed, of course. How could you not? At parties, when you're not playing matches, you meet people who convince you that they're the movers and shakers. They are the ones running the country. You want to be like them; you want their confidence. Their girlfriends. You want imported cars, and houses in Bombay and Delhi, and you want the most expensive suits and watches. You're not afraid to gamble. In fact, you gamble because you are good."

"Okay . . ." The thought crossed Binod's mind that Rabinder was describing himself. But that was unlikely. Perhaps Rabinder should be writing this, Binod thought to himself, and then he asked, "What happens next? There is the fall . . . Is he sorry?"

Rabinder said, "You are the writer. You tell me."

Binod didn't say anything.

After a long pause, Rabinder spoke again. "He falls and, like his rise, his fall is also quick. Is he sorry? Maybe he is, but he doesn't want to show it because he knows that the people around him, people who are lesser than him, want to see him naked. Why give them that satisfaction?"

Binod said, "Yes."

Rabinder said, "Maybe he is not sorry at all. He thinks his biggest mistake in life was the last mistake he made, the one that got him caught. He thinks that it had been a dream run before that happened while everyone else wrongly thinks that everything he has done in the past has led him to this big mistake."

23

Rabinder arrived late on Christmas night, too late to be able to see some of the glitter of Bombay on a day like that, but he didn't seem to care. Binod was waiting for him at the airport and they went to Neelu's house, where they were going to have dinner. Shatrughan wanted them to have a drink first. Rabinder tasted the Johnnie Walker and said, "I can't tell you how sweet this is. Jai Bholenath!"

Shatrughan said after an hour, "Okay, we'll only drink till midnight."

But they went on drinking and had their dinner closer to two. At one point, Shatrughan began to praise Rabinder for surviving prison and for coming out with fresh plans. He said, "I admire you. There is no one in our family or among our friends who can compare to you. You are able to turn anything bad into good. I wish I were like that."

Rabinder's face was shining with emotion. He sipped his whiskey and, like an actor, allowed the pause to grow. Then he said, "The prison is a dark place."

....

That night in Bombay, when the others had gone to bed, Rabinder and Binod sat flipping the channels on the TV. A Hollywood film was showing on one of the cable networks. The hero was a Secret Service agent who had lost his memory. He had perhaps become useless, or at least dangerous, to his agency and they were now trying to kill him. But he was quicker and smarter. He was trying to escape with a woman he had met accidentally. She had a small battered red car. Although she was innocent she had now been drawn into someone else's drama. That is how life is. But she also didn't want to leave him; she was falling in love with the stranger.

He told her, as the police were approaching the parked car, "I'm trying to do the right thing."

She said, "Nobody does the right thing."

Rabinder laughed a loud, hollow laugh when he heard that. Then he rubbed his thighs and said, "I want to marry her."

He was still watching TV when Binod went to sleep on the sofa. Neelu had prepared a bed for Rabinder in their guest room, but he was sitting at the same place when Binod woke up early in the morning. His eyes were on the screen. Then Binod noticed that Rabinder had shaved and had taken a bath. His hair was glistening.

Rabinder said, "Good morning."

"How come you're up? It is not even ten."

Rabinder said in loud sing-song voice, "Prisoner number C 10954 follows all rules and regulations. He is always very punctual and his positive behavior is . . ."

Rabinder kept flicking the remote with his wrist in a manner reminiscent of feeding ducks in a pond. A bearded man on a yoga channel was teaching an audience spread around him the benefits of breathing exercises. "If you do this every day for only half an hour, you will never fall sick," he said. "And never drink Pepsi or Coca-Cola. Use them to clean your toilet instead. Stay pure. Eat vegetarian food and you will always be young." Rabinder liked his meat. He changed the channel.

Binod wanted some tea and looked in the direction of Neelu's bedroom, but no one else was awake. Rabinder returned to a news channel and the screen seemed to fill with dead bodies. There had been flooding in the sea around Madras. They were calling it a tsunami. It had started near Indonesia as a result of an earthquake and had hit India a couple of hours later. The news bulletin that followed said that in Sri Lanka the waters had rushed in and then retreated, leaving fish flopping on the wet sand. Children and older men and women had run to see what had happened. People were stooping and picking up fish by the armful when suddenly a new wall of water hit them and carried many into the sea.

In the area south of Madras, boats had been smashed and houses beside the beach had been flattened. Several thousand people were estimated dead. By the time Neelu and Shatrughan woke up, the stations were showing footage from Thailand and Indonesia. One segment from a place in Indonesia showed a man and his children grabbing the door of an ambulance even as it was quickly swept out to sea.

A tourist had filmed the swirling waters below the window of his highrise hotel on the Thai coast. Dead bodies were caught in the branches of tall palm trees with the receding water now just a few feet below. The footage was difficult to watch, but no one around Binod moved.

The storm had done greatest damage to kids because they weren't strong enough to hold on to pillars or trees. The channels began to show the faces of children bashed against walls, their small bodies bent, sand puffing their eyes and plugging their noses.

....

In the days that followed, as the news of the tsunami kept coming, Binod had more reason to think of Baba. He read a report that a Sri Lankan official had threatened legal action against people who were taking away the children whose parents or families had died in the disaster. The official had said that this was illegal and he had added that outsiders were using the snatched kids as domestic servants. Baba would have predicted this exactly.

24

There was a press conference in the Orchid Hotel next to the Bombay airport. Ten days had passed since the tsunami, and a group of film industry people was leaving for the Andaman and Nicobar islands; a government plane was going to fly them over and back so that they could then use their experience to raise relief funds. Binod went to the press conference and took Rabinder with him. The first person he saw there was the young director Karan Johar, who was casually dressed for the tour of a disaster area; sitting a little distance away was an old actress with faded good looks reading a paperback novel. The press conference was going to take time. Then, Binod saw Vikas Dhar.

Dhar was waving at him. He was wearing a white kurta and walked over, unapologetic about not having been in touch, simply saying, "Kyaa haal hai, bhai? How are you?"

Binod introduced him to Rabinder, saying that he was his cousin. He added, "Rabinder is a friend of Neeraj Dubey's. He used to act with him in school plays. They used to compete in elocution contests."

Dhar nodded at Rabinder. He said, "What do you do now—do you live in Bombay?"

Rabinder said, "No. I live in Bihar. I have recently come out of jail."

Dhar laughed, as if Rabinder had cracked a joke. Binod's face was frozen in an awkward smile. Dhar asked Rabinder, "Is it an interesting story?"

Rabinder smiled and said, "Every prisoner inside those four walls had an interesting story."

Dhar laughed again, this time with conviction. He turned to Binod. "Bring your cousin to the office sometime. I'm returning to Bombay tomorrow night."

Binod nodded. Dhar looked at the journalists waiting for the press conference to start. He asked Rabinder, "Is Lalu's party going to win in the Bihar elections?"

Rabinder said, "My mother is a senior member of Lalu's inner circle—anything we say on the matter will be very biased."

Dhar laughed louder. He said, "I asked the wrong question earlier. I am sure you have an interesting story. I will call you tomorrow night."

He did. They took a taxi to Juhu and all along the way Binod couldn't decide whether he ought to be thankful to Rabinder that Dhar had been in touch with them. In the taxi, Rabinder talked to Dubey on his mobile and told him that they were headed to Dhar's house. When the conversation was over, Rabinder chuckled. Dubey had told him, "Both you and Dhar talk too much."

....

The apartment building they were looking for was on A. B. Nair Road. An old servant led them into a large parlor where they were asked to wait. It was past ten at night. Binod caught a glimpse of Dhar's wife, Piya, as she crossed in front of the staircase. She had appeared in films about twenty years ago, and still looked the same, emaciated and sexy. After a while, Dhar came into the room. He had just bathed and was wearing a silk lungi and a blue silk kurta. He declared boldly, "The trip to the islands has changed my life. That is the simple truth. It couldn't have been otherwise."

He went on, "It is very terrible what has happened . . . I also met people from Bihar who have settled in that remote place. These are simple people, very good people. One woman told me that she felt that the gods were churning the ocean. She did not know whether the world was beginning or ending."

The farming people from places like Bihar who had settled in the Andamans had lost not only their homes, their papers, and all their possessions—even their land was now useless with all the saltwater drying in their fields.

When Dhar paused, Rabinder asked eagerly, "Are people getting relief?"

Dhar said, "Everyone's condition is wretched. I saw some of the tribals in the relief camp living in a broken church near Car Nicobar. One of them said that where his family lived the water didn't first come in a wave. The ground shook and then split apart. The sea water spurted up through the cracks in the earth."

Rabinder was making clucking noises and shaking his head. Dhar began to speak in a louder voice, first throwing back his head and addressing the ceiling, and then speaking directly to Rabinder. "Can you imagine it? You experience an earthquake. Then salt water that is white like chalk erupts from the ground under you. And mud. And then the deluge from the sea, taking everything away . . ."

Rabinder asked Dhar if he would make a film on the tsunami. The filmmaker shook his head. He said, "I had only gone there to learn what had happened. Someone called me from the prime minister's office and asked if I'd go."

Rabinder said, "Are the old prisons still there?"

Dhar didn't know. It is possible Rabinder had asked to remind Dhar of himself or to remind him why they were there. But his question appeared pointless to Binod and he became conscious that he was frowning. The servant brought tea. Rabinder was talking again. He said, "I asked you about relief because during the last floods in Bihar there was a lot of tamasha about giving help. The government provided crores of rupees on paper. But nothing reached the poor. My mother heard a lot of complaints about the district magistrate in Patna. He had been named a hero and a leader in *Time* magazine, but the man was a magician. He made crores of rupees disappear into thin air."

Binod had met the officer Rabinder was talking about, but he was unaware of the controversy. The floods had come some weeks before Baba's death; he had been in Bombay busy with his assignments. Dhar was listening, saying nothing, and Rabinder went on. He said, "The district magistrate was no doubt a smart man. He actually has a medical degree. He must be very talented. But he made money in the name of those who were poor and had been made homeless by the floods. Do you think there is any market for a film on a person like that?"

"Sure there is," Dhar said slowly, and added, "If you make a film well, people will pay to watch it."

Rabinder smiled. He said, "I was thinking just the other day that a film should be made about Satyendra Dubey, the young officer who was killed in Bihar after he wrote to the prime minister about the corruption there. I presented that idea to Binod, because he is a writer, but he said that viewers only want to see people making money in films."

"Making money or having sex, which is the same thing," Dhar laughed. "Binod is right. People appreciate a small piece of reality but not if it doesn't come wrapped in some attractive fantasy."

Rabinder was nodding his head. He hadn't touched the tea in front of him. He said, "Dhar saheb, no one has made a film about match fixing.

The motivations that must have fired an ambitious player like Azharuddin. The reasons for his fall. This is not simply about cricket. The filmmaker could be talking about politics or our bureaucracy. Let's go back to the example of the Patna district magistrate. Here's an officer who was trained as a cardiologist and he was making crores by stealing the relief money. He was signing false checks. Even before the flood, he was selling licenses for guns by taking thirty thousand as a bribe on each application . . ."

"There have been films on such themes," Dhar said. A note of tiredness had come into his voice. Rabinder stopped, his mouth ajar, wanting to say more. Binod was suddenly reminded of the evening when he had met Dhar, and he became more sympathetic toward Rabinder wanting to open his heart and spill out everything.

Dhar looked for a moment at Binod before turning back to Rabinder. He said, "Let me ask you a personal question. Why were you in prison?"

Rabinder said, "Bihar is a very corrupt place. In order to be successful there, you have to be a party to the corruption. Over the last few years, I made good money, but I also made some enemies. They got me."

"But under what charge?"

"I own a cybercafe in Patna. I was charged with the illegal sale of pornographic material because, unknown to me, my customers were downloading such materials on the Internet."

"Arre bhai, if people want to download porn, let them." Dhar said, and then added, "We are living in a democracy. At least we claim it's a democracy. We are not living, may Allah be praised, in Saudi Arabia."

Rabinder saw immense sense in what Dhar was saying. He said, "When we are not open-minded about such things, we leave the door open for blackmailers."

Dhar said, "Exactly."

Rabinder said, "I know of a case in Patna. A newlywed couple was filmed at the hotel where they were staying during their honeymoon—"

Dhar began to laugh loudly. He said, "Why would *anyone* want to spend their honeymoon in Patna?"

Rabinder said, "People stay in hotels so that they can keep away from their families. That is all . . . The hotel owner was a bad character. He began to show the film to some of his own guests as pornography. The couple was put in a false position. It was very damaging."

"How did the matter end?" Dhar asked.

"The couple was from an old Darbhanga family. They had contacts in the police and the man's uncle was a retired editor. They put the hotel owner behind bars."

Dhar said to Rabinder, "These are all stories that aren't only true in Bihar. People keep thinking it's only Bihar, but all of these stories will resonate in the rest of India."

Rabinder was nodding his head.

Dhar said, "You were talking about Satyendra Dubey. He was a noble fellow, no doubt. But you must have met more interesting characters inside the prison. Someone whose story will draw more viewers than a person like Dubey. No?"

Rabinder was silent for a moment. Then he said, "There was a man I came to know during my time inside. He was a lifer; he had killed a landlord thirty years ago. His brother is a professor at Stanford University. This man was also brilliant. But he had left his studies in Patna Science College to become a Maoist and fight for peasant rights. That was in the early 1970s. He had been in jail for three decades. When I met him in prison, he would keep himself busy by growing small tomato plants and reading the newspaper. I asked him if he missed his comrades; he said he didn't. Some of them must have become grandparents. The people he had hated were almost all dead—this in itself made him feel lonely. The man kept a pet mongoose and fed it milk. The mongoose was there to guard him against snakes. All prisoners slept on the floor and he was afraid of snakes. He was a man who gave up his home to free the world but who had been in prison so long that it had become his home and his world."

Dhar had listened to the story with attention. He said, "Yes. That is how life is. But you can't really turn it into a film. Where is the story that will make the people come to the theater to watch it?"

Rabinder was waiting for Dhar to elaborate. When he didn't say anything further, Rabinder said bravely, "There are a lot of stories in Bihar."

Dhar said, "I have been saying to your cousin that we need a good story. You discuss it among yourselves and come up with a powerful narrative about what people wanted from pornography in your cybercafe. This is the changing reality of Indian small towns today."

Rabinder joined his hands. He said, "Thank you so much, sir. The trouble in Bihar is that we do not get any encouragement. All we are left to do is run a bus service or own a petrol station. I have some capital that I'd like to invest, but . . ."

Dhar smiled beatifically at him and stroked his bald head. He said, "We'll make a film together."

When they were back in the taxi, Rabinder called Dubey again. He told him that Dhar had taken the bait. Binod heard him say, "No, not about Satyendra Dubey, but more general, a universal story." Dubey must have asked him to be more precise because Rabinder was saying, "Yaar, we will talk soon. I will give you details. We must once again have some rum and mutton."

....

Binod knew that his adaptation of Chekhov had been flushed down the toilet. He would now most likely be asked to doctor the details of Rabinder's career as a pornographer and produce a tale that would offer entertainment but nevertheless end on a note that was edifying. This was disappointing to him, but he also felt that a door had opened. A week later, Dhar was in the papers. When asked about his future projects, he had said he was planning a project in Bihar. When Binod showed the newspaper to Rabinder, he grinned and lit his cigarette. He was very happy and blew smoke like a gangster in Hindi films.

Binod's friend Ajay had also seen the report in the papers. He said on the phone, "The film will probably not be what you want but people will come and see it."

Binod told him that Rabinder had developed a good rapport with Dhar, and Ajay said, "That is good. Dhar is worldly wise. He is also not a hypocrite. Maybe what you will learn from this is that you cannot be in the industry and wear white all the time. If you will walk on the street, you are bound to get dirty."

Dhar called Rabinder nearly every day. They would discuss ideas about the shape that the story would take and then play around with other possibilities. In these conversations, Rabinder would frequently recall scenes from Dhar's other movies; he had worked out in his mind a calculus of repetition and change. This was also to Dhar's liking. Every time that Rabinder got off the phone after talking to Dhar, he was pumped and his energy would fill up the room.

Neither Rabinder nor Dhar really knew what the whole story was going to be about. There were times when Binod would be told about a scene and asked to imagine how the plot could advance. These were just imaginary scenarios with no reference at all to a larger narrative. When Binod was drawn into these conversations, his heart was not in it. He knew that

Rabinder wasn't telling his own story. If you could tell just any story you wanted, no demands ever needed to be made on your honesty.

If Rabinder noticed that Binod was not very enthusiastic, he hardly showed any sign of it. He had decided that he was going to stick around in Bombay till the project had assumed a definite shape. One evening Binod came home to find his cousin in front of the mirror: he had put on a new shirt and was applying gel in his hair. Dhar was to pick him up and they were going to meet Ajay Devgan to discuss plans for the future. Despite all of the reluctance he had shown during the past few days, a wave of immense disappointment washed over Binod. He saw that what he was feeling was envy. But he kept smiling. A little later, the bell rang. It was Dhar's driver, asking for Rabinder. Binod went down too. Dhar was very cordial and asked him if he was interested in meeting the film star. Binod begged to be excused. He said that he had just got back from work and there was pressure from his editor. The coming state assembly elections in Bihar meant that he would have to leave soon for Patna.

Rabinder's film project was growing without him. Bua would be very happy, Binod thought to himself, and then saw more reason to leave for Bihar. He would be extremely busy there, but he would also have the chance to be away from Bombay. When the car had driven away, Binod climbed back to the apartment and began to make tea.

Before the water had come to a boil, a memory came back to him from his childhood. Ma had bought a pet parrot for Rabinder when he had been left alone at home with her. He was ten at that time. Binod and Neelu had gone with Baba to Ratauli for a wedding. Bua was at her hostel. Buying the bird had been Ma's way of appeasing Rabinder, who had gone to sleep after feeding the little parrot a slice of tomato. That night, the boy was woken by what had seemed like a loud screeching. The sound was unfamiliar and at first he went back to sleep. But the screeching started again and he put on the light. It was then that he remembered the parrot, but its cage wasn't on the window ledge where he had put it.

Rabinder had gone around the bed and seen the green feathers on the floor.

The bird was still alive but rats had gnawed through the bamboo and chewed off one of its wings. There had been a lot of talk in the house about how the rodents used the drainage pipes in the bathroom to climb into the house from the sewers below. Rabinder didn't touch the parrot. He turned off the light and waited in the dark. When the screeching began half an hour later, he shut the bathroom door.

Ma was woken up when she heard the noise coming from the room in which Rabinder was sleeping. Her heart in her mouth, she opened the door. She saw the rat, its back broken, trying to creep away. Rabinder, hockey stick in hand, was going to bludgeon it to death. "There was blood on the floor," Ma said later. "On the other side of the bed, there were two more that were dead. They looked as big as well-fed rabbits."

VII

The Glass

Menagerie

25

The first report Binod sent from Bihar was set at a "line hotel" at Pipra-Kothi, perhaps an hour from Motihari. He had been sitting there at the dhaba waiting for his food when a jeep with green campaign flags stopped by. The campaigners were all young men barely out of their teens; they wore cheap sunglasses and had handkerchiefs covering their collars to soak their sweat. They ordered chili-chicken and roti—but first they wanted the bottled beer even though without electricity the beer was warm.

These were no doubt happy days for them, with black money pouring into everyone's pockets. The youth were discussing election strategy. Before long, he heard one of them say, "Bhai Ranjan, get it captured." Booth capturing was a Bihari staple, the term describing in a military idiom the condition when one candidate's goons have taken command of the ballot boxes. In the dhaba that day, the fellow named Ranjan, bearded and shallow chested, said, "He does not do this kind of work."

But the first guy was not to be put off. He said, "Why, he gets *girls* kidnapped all through the year."

When the piece was published, Rabinder called from Bombay to say that it had made him nostalgic for home. He had been a veteran campaigner for Bua in the past, but this time around Bua had decided to stay out of the elections. She was going to hold a senior post within the party itself, and, of course, head the government commissions on women's education and welfare. Then, returning to himself, Rabinder told Binod that he and Dhar had made a lot of progress. The screenplay needed to be written but the outline was in place. Rabinder said, "You have to help us when you come back."

Their story was going to be about a young single man, played by Devgan, who owns a cybercafe in Patna where people usually come to download porn. The Devgan character has a new, romantic obsession with a young woman, a porn star, whom he has seen on the short video clips his customers have been downloading to watch. A dance number, to be shown on screen entirely as a downloadable clip, would be the first song. One night the man makes an accidental discovery. A tiny videocam on one of the computers records the activities of some strange-looking customers in one cubicle in the cybercafe. Our hero suspects that a terror plot is being hatched via email. He goes to the police, but things take a wrong turn. The policemen are corrupt. The man is thrown into jail on the charge of trafficking in porn. There is a new twist in the tale at this point. In the prison, the man overhears a conversation that solves for him what had been a puzzle about the terrorists. He contacts the porn star on a mobile phone smuggled into his cell. The girl is enlisted to work as a decoy, and this time the police are led to the bad guys. Our hero, now free, sends an email to the woman saying that he doesn't want to play a game of make-believe any more.

The viewer would discover what the lovers did during a romantic holiday by watching a raunchy home video that the two made for themselves in the hills. The film would end with the credits appearing on the computer screen like pop-up ads while the couple exchanged fiercely loving notes through instant messaging.

....

Nearly every day during the lead-up to the elections, a Bollywood actor would join one of the main political parties. There were rumors that Neeraj Dubey would announce his support for the Congress. He was being billed as a future candidate from Bettiah. Binod called him, but Dubey just laughed it off.

When he went to Bettiah, Binod found that people were more interested in getting regular water and power supply than in choosing a candidate. He filed a brief report from that town, which he called an area of darkness because he had arrived in the evening and there was no electricity. All that he seemed to remember later were the ghoulish faces of the people talking to him. Faces lit by a smoky lantern. Or sometimes by harsh torchlight, the bright light turned away from him, as if the person holding it were pissing in the night. The people told him that they were happy, especially during summer, if they could get electricity for a few hours every three days.

His report was made up of interviews with people who were old childhood friends of Dubey's. A gentle, middle-aged man named Sudhanshu had told Binod that in school, back in the mid-1970s, Dubey used to recite one particular line from the Hindi film *Kuchche Dhaage*. The actor

Kabir Bedi played a dacoit in the Chambal ravines. His rival was Vinod Khanna. In one scene, Bedi said to his rival's mother, "Eh budhiya, dekh inn aankhon mein. Tumhe lakhon ki maut nazar aayegi" (Old woman, look into my eyes. You will see here the murders of many). But Binod had not been able to look into his interlocutor's eyes. It was already very dark. He had only heard the words, and the steady singing of mosquitoes.

The light from the hired jeep in which he was traveling bounced and fell on the shuttered doors of shops. Bettiah had been suffering from a spate of kidnappings. The dacoits slipped into the nearby forests and then made ransom calls on their mobile phones. This was the reason why businesses closed as soon as it was dark.

But there was one shop called Vaishnavi Jewelers that was still open. A Petromax lit its interiors. The shop was owned by Umesh, another old friend of Dubey's. He had been waiting for Binod. Umesh quickly closed his shop and they walked to his house in a lane nearby. His son unlocked the chains that were wrapped around the front door. Tea was served. Umesh said that the first film he might have seen with Dubey was *Gora aur Kaala* in 1975. This was at the inauguration of the local Priya Cinema. Umesh remembered the film. His eyes had looked hollowed by the dark, but Binod could see a twinkle in them. He said, "Rajendra Kumar in a double role. Opposite Hema Malini."

Umesh thought that despite Dubey's popularity it wouldn't be easy for him to win in an election there. He said that politics was a very dirty game and Dubey could only play a goon on screen, not in real life.

Binod was taken to Priya Cinema. Umesh's torch passed over the patches of cow dung in their path. At the movie theater, a loud generator was providing power. The film showing that night was a B-grade film from the previous year. The projector room was hot and the light that tunneled out of that room picked out the slow swirls of beedi smoke in the hall.

Umesh bought some sweets at a mithai store that he said had a fine local reputation. His host had high blood pressure but that didn't stop Binod from eating the rasmalai that was heaped on his plate. After a while, Umesh asked him, "Are you not related to Rabinder Singh?"

Binod said yes and asked if Umesh knew Rabinder.

Umesh said, "Oh, I know him, sure." He gave a short laugh and said, "He was a good friend of Dubey's. I remember back in school they had gone to watch a movie, the two of them. Rabinder pulled out a knife during a scuffle over a seat."

They got back in the jeep and went to meet Pawan, a building contractor, who was also a great childhood friend of Dubey's. But Pawan wasn't at home and they were asked to wait. In Pawan's front yard, two servants were busy, lanterns swinging in their hands. A black cow was about to give birth. The youths explained that the last time one of the cows went into labor it had been late in the night. No one was around to take care of the newborn calf, and in the crowded stall the mother had accidentally trampled the calf to death.

Within fifteen minutes, the calf arrived, its legs thin and crooked as in a child's drawing. The mother licked her young and would pause only to low loudly, her neck stretched close to the ground.

When Pawan didn't come for an hour, Umesh said they could go and look up another friend. The light from the jeep scoured the dirty walls in the narrow streets. In the vivid darkness of the night, their presence was an intrusion. Lives had been carefully constituted, out of sheer habit, around a routine of darkness. Whole families sat out on cots or on the steps of the houses they passed. Again and again, they surprised people who were eating or resting. Women turned their faces away and men shaded their eyes whenever the jeep turned a corner, headlights blazing.

Umesh rattled the door of a decrepit house. A woman appeared on the roof above. Binod didn't know it was a woman till he heard her voice. Her husband was not at home. Umesh asked her where he could have gone in the dark. She remained silent.

They made the trip back to Pawan's house. Once again the terrible embarrassment, the headlights tearing into shreds the thin cover of privacy that the night offered. Binod felt as if he was party to a crime.

Pawan was now back. He was a short, squat man with a thick moustache and mischievous eyes. He laughed a lot even though none of them was saying much. He spoke of the time when Dubey had come to town with Raveena Tandon. The film *Raat* was being made there. It was probably the only time that a film had been shot in Bettiah. Pawan was happy that Dubey had acted with him as if nothing had changed despite the years and the changes in fortune.

Binod had ended his report with the question he had asked Pawan. "Who will you vote for in the election?" Pawan had laughed again. He had waved his arm around and said, "In the dark, all our candidates look alike."

....

In Motihari, Binod went looking for Orwell's birthplace. The two lecturers in the English Department at the local college had not heard of the writer. One of them sipped tea and, clearing his throat, asked if Binod had meant Cromwell.

The district magistrate proved more helpful. His name was S. Anand. He was the grandson of an eminent economist from Mysore, a former member of the Planning Commission. Anand told him that Orwell's father had been the sub-deputy opium agent in Motihari and he took Binod to the Miscourt warehouse where the opium used to be stored. It was a shabby teachers' hostel now. There were three small bungalows, all of them painted blue, next to the warehouse. Orwell's family must have lived in one of those houses.

In front of them, pigs rooted around in a small mud pond next to some banana trees. An old man sat sheltered from the sun under a black umbrella, but neither the district magistrate nor Binod troubled him with any questions.

Anand said that there would be files in the office archives where Binod could find out about the duties of the British opium agent. Their main job, he said, must have been to enforce the forcible cultivation of indigo. Binod's own ancestors, peasants living in the villages near Motihari, would have followed those laws. He went to the record office. It was attached to the Revenue Department. There was a lock on the door where the records were kept and although there were three heavy rings with black keys in the office drawers none of them seemed to work. Then a peon poured some of the kerosene from a lantern into the lock and one of the keys finally turned. Bundles of paper tied up in cloth—rough white cloth with thin red stripes—were piled from floor to ceiling.

Binod pulled a bundle out. The paper, brown in color and brittle, dated back to April 1937. The dark room was airless and smelled of rot. Silverfish darted out of the sheets of paper that he unfolded. The notations in a cursive hand were related to the size of agricultural plots and an attached sheet showed forest areas owned by the Bettiah Raj. But the key to the past had been lost. And standing alone in that dank room Binod was no longer sure what it was that he was looking for. The bundles of files, heavy with the weight of years, seemed to be slowly marching down together, closing in on him in a way that touched a panic akin to claustrophobia. He pushed the door open and stepped out for some air. A koel was calling among the dusty leaves of the mango tree outside. Binod stood on the cracked cement of the steps for several minutes and then decided that he wasn't going back inside.

Later, while eating the vegetarian meal in the hotel's dining room, he asked the owner hovering nearby whether he had heard of a writer called George Orwell. He hadn't. He said he had gone to college to get his intermediate degree, as if that explained everything. The conversation turned to the coming election. The man had figured out that Binod belonged to an upper caste—all his talk, therefore, was about the lower-caste anarchy that had been unleashed by the ruling party. Binod didn't mention Bua's name.

Instead of the air conditioner in the wall, there was a rectangular shape of new bricks and cement. Binod pointed toward the brown patch on the wall and asked what had happened to the machine. The owner said, "As long as the air conditioner was there, local goondas thought it fit to stop by and demand money. So I had it removed. Anyway, the electricity was gone most of the time in the summer. It wasn't much help."

....

Back in Bombay, Rabinder and Binod were having dinner in a South Indian restaurant near Haji Ali one night. Rabinder was in high spirits. An astrologer in Patna with a good reputation had assured him that till March of the following year he would enjoy a tremendously "favorable period" and whatever he touched would turn to gold.

They ate their dosas and then asked for pistachio ice cream. Rabinder also wanted madrasi coffee. Binod was thinking of how much had happened in these brief few months. Rabinder had met Dhar through him at a time when Binod was himself hoping to start writing a screenplay, and now his cousin was making a film. It appeared as if fate had chosen Rabinder. What was remarkable was that Rabinder didn't seem too burdened by this fact; he had not, through any graceless word or boastful action, indicated that he had won or that he suspected Binod of harboring resentment. He had taken Dhirubhai's message to heart. He was staying true to his own orbit.

Before they left the restaurant, Binod said, "When I was in Bihar, I decided that I wanted to write a long story that would also report on the life I observe around us. The piece I wrote about Orwell's birthplace— I was trying to work something out for myself about what writers do as reporters."

Rabinder nodded encouragement. He said, "I liked your piece. You remember what the man in Motihari told you about the air conditioners in his hotel? That as long as they were there, criminals demanded money from him. There was no electricity in the summer anyway, and that those things were useless . . . I'm going to use that scene in my film."

Rabinder was going to Santa Cruz that night to meet a visiting Bihari politician in the bar at Bawa International. Before he let him go, Binod said, "There was a lot of poll violence in Saharsa, and I went there for a day. I didn't write about it because I didn't think I had a story. But I wanted to tell you something. The commissioner there was Banerjee."

He looked up at Rabinder's face, but it was impassive. He added, "It wasn't till I had reached Saharsa that I learned that he was there. I went to see him. I guess Banerjee let me into his office because he thought I had come on journalistic business. I talked a little about the elections. But when I mentioned Roma's name, he lost control. He took off his glasses and began to shout, asking me to leave his office at once. I don't know what I was thinking, but I had actually gone to ask him if he had ever had any inkling of the killers."

Rabinder stayed quiet. Then he waved down a taxi. He looked back at Binod and said, "Our family has destroyed his world. I'm surprised he doesn't want to kill us."

26

Rabinder found a flat to rent on Veera Desai Road in Andheri West. There was a large almond tree outside his window. When he phoned Bua in Patna she said she was very happy because she had never seen an almond tree before.

Binod was watching the news on a Sunday morning when Rabinder stopped by and said that Bua was also going to be in Bombay soon. When Rabinder had left, Binod called up Neelu and they agreed that Ma should accompany Bua. Ma had never been to Bombay. Everyone would get to be together in the city.

Both Ma and Bua stayed at Neelu's and then Bua bought some furniture for Rabinder's flat and moved there. She said she needed to teach the new servant how to cook. One day Rabinder borrowed Shatrughan's car and took Ma and Bua to Pali Hill to show them the houses of the film stars. Ma wanted to see the house in which Dilip Kumar lived. Rabinder called Binod in his office to find out the addresses where Aamir Khan and Rani Mukherji lived because Bua wanted to know what their houses looked like from the street.

....

There had been talk each day of visiting Neeraj Dubey too, but he was busy doing a play for the first time since coming to Bombay. A Hindi adaptation of Tennessee Williams's *The Glass Menagerie* was soon to open at the Prithvi Theater. It was being directed by Makarand Deshpande and had been previewed by all the newspapers in the city.

Dubey arranged for four passes and Neelu and Shatrughan bought tickets. At four in the afternoon, an extra hour in hand in case they got delayed, they left for Juhu.

At Prithvi, the audience could be divided into two parts: those who were there to be seen and those who were doing the seeing. The people from the film world were well-dressed and often hugged and kissed each other on the cheek. Ma recognized the actor Vijay Raaz, who had played a Bihari in *Monsoon Wedding*, and then she leaned toward Binod and asked in a loud whisper, "Tell me, who is that man with the beard?" "Dinesh Thakur." "And she?" The tall beautiful woman could be Sonali Bendre, but she could as easily have been any of the other female film stars. Ma's eyes shone, but Binod just shrugged and stayed silent. When Gulzar came in he turned and mouthed the word "salaam" to someone sitting in one of the rows behind Binod — but Ma had spontaneously raised both her hands in greeting. Gulzar saw that gesture and bowed, and then he glanced back at her, trying to search his memory for the name of the old woman who had greeted him. Binod quickly looked away.

There were only four characters in the play. The narrator was named Tom. He was played by Dubey, who filled the stage with his personality, an endearing mix of sensitivity and selfishness. Sonali Kulkarni played his sister, Laura, a young, painfully shy woman who was lame in one foot. Their mother was a loud, delusional woman called Amanda and that role was performed by a very emotional and cheerful Kiron Kher. The three-some formed a tight claustrophobic lower-middle-class family, their desperation sometimes seeming to suck the oxygen out of the space in which the spectators were sitting. In that atmosphere, there arrived a fourth character. He was the "gentleman caller" who came for dinner one evening, briefly setting alight Laura's hopes of romance before extinguishing them completely. His name was Jim, he was a former high school star, a classmate of Laura's, and although he had not achieved much in life, he had hectic plans for self-improvement. Laura had often thought about him in the past whenever she had been alone. In front of her, Jim projected a sunny blankness. They happened to kiss and then he revealed that he was already engaged.

The names from the original play had been retained, but along with the shift to Hindi the setting had also been changed to a chawl in Bombay. No one ever used the word "dowry" in the dialogue on the stage, but that is what a less urban or affluent audience than the one at Prithvi would have had in mind when watching the play. Binod thought of all of the women in his family, of the long list of cousins who with their arrival into puberty transformed the world outside into a battlefield where their fathers and brothers went out to wage battle. The men would return home and hold up their dented armor for display. Ointments and cold bandages would be put on their cuts and bruises. The wounds of those left behind at home were always less visible.

This play written about people in far-off America, if performed in Patna, would evoke in the hearts of everyone in the audience the same question, a question that could have been sung like a chorus in a tragedy—how will the dowry be found that will get this girl a husband? It was very much to Dubey's credit that he was able to draw attention to himself, as a man but also as an artist, struggling with the guilt of having to leave behind the women whom he loved.

Binod held his breath in the closing scene as Ma and Bua wept shamelessly. No one else was crying. The noise they were making was drowned when everyone stood up and shouted "Bravo" as the curtain came down.

....

In the crowded foyer, Vikas Dhar was engaged in intense conversation with a group of youngsters who appeared to have all dyed their hair shades of orange and blonde. He came over and asked Rabinder, "Bhai, did you get my message?" Rabinder bowed and said that he had but that he had been busy with the family. He turned to Bua and Ma and introduced them to him. Dhar must have noticed that the women had just been crying because he declared loudly, "The play was very moving, very moving. You see, in our society, woman is both a reality and a metaphor . . ." His eyes swept the room and he spread his arms wide as if he were going to take the world in his embrace. He said loudly and with great passion, "This is not anything new of course. But in the modern world, especially in India, this reality is our most revealing contradiction."

He turned to Rabinder and said, "Your Bihari friend did a great job."

Rabinder nodded and smiled, and when Dhar looked at Binod, he too couldn't help nodding his head.

Then Dhar's phone began to ring and he said that he was looking forward to talking to Bua at greater length during dinner about her experiences in Bihar. "You have survived in the system," he said, "I am sure we can learn from you." She was looking pleased and bowed her head humbly. Into their small company Dhar had brought wisdom and good cheer, and having accomplished this task, he turned and departed with his youthful entourage. While the rest of the family waited in the emptying foyer, Rabinder went backstage for a few minutes; he came back with the news that Dubey was going with his girlfriend to a party.

In the car Ma observed with great formality that the play had worked because it showed the truth.

In response to which, Bua said, "Didi, it worked because it showed its own truth. My truth is different from it. My brother never left me. I was a bigger weight around his neck than that lovely lame girl could ever have been."

No one said anything in response to that.

They were quite close to the sea and Binod liked the slightly salty air on his face. The highway was lit up by billboards advertising TV shows and fabrics worn by film stars. Binod felt the tragedy they had witnessed on stage had also made their own small sufferings pleasant and lyrical.

....

The previous week Binod had gone to a house in Cuffe Parade to meet a man who was an assistant income tax commissioner. He was doing a story on a set of properties owned by the superstar Shah Rukh Khan. During the conversation, they had found out that they were both from Patna and had common friends there. The man's wife had been listening to the two of them talking and suddenly interrupted them. "Were you married to Arpana Rai?" she said.

The sea was visible from the fifth-floor living room and he felt as if the water had washed away a part of the land on which he had stood for a decade. The woman said nothing more, but Binod knew the visit was over. He would ordinarily have found a way to get up and leave, but he was unable to. Instead he asked her how she knew Arpana. She said that they had been together in school in Patna. They were now in touch again.

Binod asked her whether Arpana was doing well.

Archly, she asked, "Jaan ke kyaa kijiyega?" (What will you do with that information?) Binod had looked down at his hands. He realized that he was doing this not because he was ashamed but because he wanted to slap the woman. He said, "When I could have done something, I did nothing. What could I possibly do now?"

In the elevator on the way down, the assistant commissioner said, "She is in Yemen. Her husband recently got a job there at a university. He will be teaching zoology there for a few years. . . ." He paused and added in English, "They were blessed with a daughter last month."

Binod had wanted to tell him that he had made him happy, but the man pretended to be looking for the doorman, who would get him his cigarettes.

27

Vikas Dhar had introduced Rabinder to one Mr. Iskander. He was a tall, extremely thin man, with wavy, hennaed hair, and a fondness for chocolate-colored clothing. Mr. Iskander was a poet; he wrote Urdu shayari and film lyrics. Dhar firmly believed that one hit song gave even a very bad film a strong chance to make money at the box office. Mr. Iskander was key to his plan.

He would call and recite couplets and Rabinder would quickly write them down on pages of the phonebook. Whenever Binod visited him, his cousin would cradle the thick white phonebook in his arms and read out romantic poetry about love and loneliness. When Bua once praised the poetry, Rabinder let it be known that Dhar had already signed up a young music director who was said to be the hottest thing in the industry.

In one of Mr. Iskander's lyrics, there were three or four lines devoted to the beauty of Kashmir's lakes and mountains. Dhar's family had ancestral links to that land. And Mr. Iskander's verses had given him an idea. He decided that the terrorists could be Kashmiris. The hero and the heroine of their film would have more run-ins with the bad guys when they went to Kashmir for their honeymoon. Dhar also felt that because summer was nearly here, it would be more comfortable to shoot in Kashmir. For days, Rabinder made plans about a visit to places like Gulmarg and Pahalgam. One of Bua's friends in the government gave the name of a man at the All India Radio office in Srinagar, and Rabinder and Dhar began holding discussions about filming a couple of cheerful folk songs in the valley. Mr. Iskander returned to his task with renewed zeal.

At eleven one night, Rabinder called Binod because Vikas Dhar had just left his flat after bringing him a story. An article from a Pakistani magazine had fallen into Dhar's hands. Seven young men, six of them Pakistanis and one Indian, had been killed by the police in Macedonia. These men were described by the Macedonian authorities as Islamic terrorists. Pamphlets had been recovered from the dead men. The Arabic-language pamphlets, the Macedonians said, provided the names of other terrorists and the dates of their previous meetings. This was seen as evidence of their link with the al Qaeda network.

The Pakistani magazine obtained copies of the pamphlets and found out that it was only an invitation to a *majlis-e-aza*, a Shia religious gathering, in Gujranwala, Pakistan, and the names on the invitation were the names of the meeting's organizers and speakers. The other "pamphlets" were nothing more than a verse from the Qur'an and a copy of *Nad-e-Ali*, which according to Dhar could be found in every Shia home.

The men had no identity papers on them. It was the pamphlet about the meeting that had led the reporter to Gujranwala, and he was then able to identify all of the dead within a week. The men had crossed into Greece illegally to find work. Some of them had been deported earlier from Iran and Turkey for trying to work as illegal immigrants. The brother of one of the men who had been killed said that the dead man had paid more than a thousand dollars to a smuggler to find entry into Greece. The men were in Macedonia because they had hoped to make their way into Greece. They would have had to walk undetected for some days through the mountain terrain. If they had succeeded, they would have saved nearly six hundred dollars.

Rabinder finished reading out the article to Binod and said that Dhar's brother-in-law was a Shia from Kashmir. Dhar was a Kashmiri Hindu, but his younger sister was married to a Muslim. It is also possible that Dhar had figured out that the audience in India, looking to the West for jobs, would be able to empathize with the young men. Rabinder said that Dhar had asked him to contact Binod. Would it be possible to marry a plot about terror with the murder of innocent migrant workers?

Despite all his misgivings and even resentment, once again, as so often during the past year, Binod felt a tight sense of exultation. The story would very quickly go out of his hands, but he could already feel the excitement of writing. He was still on the phone with Rabinder, but he walked over to his window and saw a row of three-wheelers parked at the crossroads.

Binod said, "It's late, but I'm going to come over right now. Wait for me. I can go to work from there in the morning."

. . . .

The film's release party was held at a luxury hotel in Bombay that had been built near the water's edge. Binod arrived late because Bua had wanted to stop first at Mahalaxmi temple. The cameras from the television channels were trained on the stars sitting in the front. A shaven-headed priest, a yellow silk shawl draped over his bare shoulders, was offering a prayer in a high, nasal voice. When he was done invoking 108 names of Lord Ganesha, he smashed a coconut under the screen. He was still whirling the ornate lamp for the last time during the aarti, tiny flames flickering in the air, when the electric lights were dimmed and the screen erupted in a red dawn.

Seven figures were walking over a sand dune, the silence suddenly broken by a shout, after which the men broke into a run. The camera jogged beside a youthful face half-wrapped in a blanket. He might have been told it gets cold in the nights in the desert. A tinkling sound was heard in the distance and the men stopped, panting. In the early morning light, the endless sand undulated like small waves in the sea. From a dip in the sand, a man emerged and then beneath him a camel. The long barrel of the rifle held by the rider raised the horizon to such a height that the air became thin and drew the breath out of the men's lungs.

But the man was smiling. He spoke in a Hindi that sounded foreign, "You are two hours late." His eyes were darkened with antimony.

The travelers were all young men. They were carrying very little and perhaps that is the reason why they looked all the more desperate. The wind carried sand, obliterating the landscape. The journey ended only when the long day had passed. The men had reached the sea by nightfall. The camel lifted its head and a lamp glowed brightly in its huge eyes. The seven youth were huddled beside a boat. The men around them were Arabs, wearing black or brown dishdashas. They had head-covers of red and white checked cloth, just as you would expect from having seen such things in movies.

The young men were given shiny passports. The books opened right to left. Their names were written in Arabic and in English. It was not till they were sitting in the tiny boat, their knees pressed against their chests, that one of them asked another, "What name does yours have?"

The boy took the passport out from his breastpocket. He smiled wanly and said, "Khalid Ahmad."

The first man addressed the same question to the youth who was furthest away from him. Only the back of his head was visible to the camera. When he turned, the darkness in the tight corner of the boat lessened. It was Ajay Devgan, playing the film's hero.

He said, "My mother had named me after her elder brother, who was killed in the 1965 war. His name was Prithviraj, although everyone in the village called him just Prithvi. Today I have changed from Prithvi to Bilal

Salim Saleh. You are born and you struggle to earn your bread. That is your only religion."

The screen turned black and the film's title appeared.

Prithvi. The Earth.

And then Rabinder's name. Until just eighteen months ago, he had been in prison. But now he had become a producer and made a mark in the film industry in Bombay. His film had been directed by a man who was known all over India. Stars were sitting in the audience tonight. Neeraj Dubey had played the role of the investigating police officer in the film. It was he who would appear on a nationally televised press conference at the end to give the news that the terrorist who had been killed was not a Muslim but a Hindu. He would say, "It was a case of mistaken identity. His name was Prithvi. He was a victim and not a villain."

Binod had still been standing by the door and he now edged outside. He had seen the film at least ten times during production, yet he had been excited all day, wanting to watch it with a new audience. But he now suddenly felt tired.

In the bathroom, small white flowers were floating in shallow bowls. He splashed cold water on his face. The man in the mirror looked like a stranger. Binod stood staring at himself, his face in his hands, when a stocky man in a white safari suit walked in. Embarrassed, Binod blurted out, "You didn't like the film?"

The man frowned. "What film?"

Binod apologized and stepped out. Two young women wrapped in silk saris were flanking the door of the hall where the film was being shown. Music leaked out. He knew what the music meant. The illegal travelers had now crossed into safe territory and were free to indulge in nostalgia. They were singing a song that described a tree that still remembers the weight of a boy's body on its branches. The ground under the tree misses the swift shadows that had flitted across it each afternoon. The girls in the village, and so forth.

Binod waited and then stepped into the room. On the screen, Prithvi was now working in a fish shop in Turkey. In a few weeks, he would make his way to a town in Leeds.

The story that was still to unfold on the screen was fairly straightforward by the standards of Bollywood. A young Hindu man, looking for work in the West, is taken to be a Muslim because of the name on his forged passport. He arrives in northern England and is arrested after September 11, possibly tortured, and then allowed to go free. A jihadi group contacts him after his release and the young man is too scared of being deported to tell them that his passport is fake. He is smuggled back to India with two others with instructions to carry out suicide bombings.

He hopes to make his break with the fanatics, but it proves impossible. Even at the moment that he betrays his comrades and causes their death he is photographed by surveillance cameras. In the eyes of the police, he is a terrorist. His face is in the newspapers, on television, and on posters in public places. The jihadis are also gunning for him. Once they are about to kill him along with many other innocent people on a train, but he escapes with a beautiful young woman who is grateful that he saved her life. The woman is Muslim. The two of them fall in love and together outwit the police and also battle the extremists for over an hour. Binod was painfully conscious of his failure with Arpana, and then also with Geeta; in the script he had written he pursued the idea of a romance that was immediate and urgent, driven by desperation and a hunger for survival. Success in love was also tied in his mind to success in writing. The contingencies he had invented gave his story a tautness that real life lacks, and Vikas Dhar had put together the love sequences superbly, cutting together scenes he had shot in Kashmir and then in Old Delhi.

In the end, the man who is known to the public only as Bilal is killed soon after he has removed a bomb put inside a mosque by jihadis. The film concluded with Dubey's press conference, which had been shot at the same hotel, and in the same room, where the release party was now being held.

Rabinder stood laughing in front of the microphones. Next to him was Neeraj Dubey, whom everyone had just seen on the screen in a police uniform. Vikas Dhar had put his arm around the starlet who was the film's heroine. She was the year's new face. (Her name was Mandira, and she was a local girl from Dadar. She was saying to the fellow interviewing her, "I don't believe in competition. For me, it has no place in art. I just want to do my work." Dhar laughed and hugged her tight. He said, "Where do you kids pick up such ideas? No one on the street, no ordinary man, is ever so pious. If you aren't competitive, you won't even be able to get inside the train at Dadar station.") There was also a thin white girl from London, Alice, who was writing a book on Hindi films. Alice was being introduced to one or two journalists. She was wearing an embroidered Rajasthani choli that ended an inch or two beneath her breasts; the photographers flashed their cameras at this single white face in the crowd and Binod too found himself looking at her. Was that a tiny silver ring in her belly button? The film stars were keeping pretty much to themselves, but Rabinder, with Alice smiling vacantly beside him, cheerfully went around the room from one group to another.

Binod had been told that the bhais, the dons in the Bombay underworld, had wanted to give money for the film. They had heard that the film showed Muslims in a good light. But Dhar had advised Rabinder against accepting anything. He had made vague noises about the bhais interfering with their freedom to shape the film as they wanted, but Rabinder suspected that Dhar was worried that the goons would demand their money back with high interest if the film became a hit.

· · · · · · · · · · · · · · · · · · · ·

When he was a boy, Binod had heard a story about his mother. Ma was eighteen and still unmarried when she had gone with her cousin Vijay to watch *Pyaasa* at Elphinstone Theater. A little after the intermission, the usher had come into the balcony section flashing his small torch. He was pointing the light on people's faces, one row after another, and the sound of angry hissing advanced up the aisle. Someone shouted, "Put it back in your pants, you joker." Another voice said, "If mine was that small, I wouldn't shine it in anyone's face." Then Ma saw that her nephew Munna was accompanying the usher.

As soon as they were outside, the boy said that everyone from Ara had come by train an hour ago. Ma's elder brother had a three-month-old baby whom Ma had named Chunnu. The child had contracted jaundice.

The hospital was less than a mile away and the young rickshawala rode very quickly. The baby died just minutes before Ma got there. Her sister-in-law sat at the side of a bed with a wild look in her eyes. Nurses at the hospital had taken the body away for the autopsy, but the mother kept saying, "I can hear him crying. Please bring him to me."

All those deaths, especially of children, when he was growing up. These days there were fewer deaths, even in films, and this could only be a good thing. That was the clear realization that came to him when he had first started working in Bombay. Criminals and cops in Hindi films still died violent deaths; but the fashionably dressed people you saw on the screen nowadays just drove around in flashy cars for a while and then went abroad for a holiday and were happy.

He had now been involved in the making of a film. The childhood association of the cinema-theater and death had been replaced by an idea of film and business. Vikas Dhar had said to him that every film is a hit till Thursday night; you wait till Friday to find out whether your movie is a flop. One filmmaker in Mhada called his company a factory. Material in, product out. There was democracy in the marketplace: everyone, regardless of talent, was like an animal with a ring in his nostrils. The ring was attached to a rope held by the one who had the money. There was no pretence of politeness, or boring talk about form and aesthetic ambition. At any moment, the man could yank the rope or reach for his lathi.

28

A little after midnight, Bua and Binod left the film release party accompanied by Neelu and Shatrughan. Rabinder's burgundy Qualis, which he had bought only a month ago, brought them to Neelu's house. Bua was extremely happy. On the way home, she said, "I wish Baba had lived to see this day." It was a line that had been spoken in the same manner in countless Hindi films.

At the flat, Binod dragged a cane-chair out into the tiny balcony. In the distance the lights of the houses in Azad Nagar twinkled in the dark and the small lights of planes crossed the sky above. For a few minutes, Binod wrestled with the idea of going down to the Nightingale Bar at the corner and having a drink by himself. But a sense of lethargy had taken hold of him. He wanted to stay focused on a feeling of calmness and not entertain any thoughts or desire.

He heard the screen behind him sliding. It was Bua.

"What are you thinking about?"

He smiled at her but said nothing.

Bua said, "What did you think of the film?"

He said, "I liked that the characters were people like us. Unlike us, their lives had found a story."

Bua was looking at the lights of the houses as they rose and fell in the shape of hills. She said after a while, "You were not very happy with Vikas Dhar. That is what Shatrughan said to me."

Binod looked through the door at his brother-in-law's face, which was lit by the glow of the television screen. He said with more force than he had intended, "It wasn't really a question of finding happiness by writing a story for Dhar. I can only get that by writing on my own."

"You are happy doing journalism?"

"I'm working on a long story right now," he replied and then, as if he were explaining something to her, he said, "Bua, please tell me whatever you know about the death of Romola Banerjee."

Bua sighed and said nothing. They had never talked about Roma before.

Perhaps he should have expected this. When she turned her back to him and looked out at the lights of the city, Binod quickly glanced inside into the living room and saw that Shatrughan was laughing at something on the screen. He was glad to be alone with Bua.

After a while, she began to speak to the little houses in the distance, houses with yellow windows that revealed, here and there, patches of white or green walls.

"Rabinder had given her his heart. This is not something that I wanted, but there was no arguing with him. So I tried to be nice to her. She was easy to like. She was very young. I never asked Rabinder about it, but I heard from people I can trust that she was fond of money. She liked it when men came to her at different times of the day and gave her money meant for Rabinder.

"I have often thought about this. Rabinder was very open with her. He talked to her about everything. I think she liked Rabinder because she felt she was choosing him over her husband. That it was her choice over what had been decided for her by others. It made her feel romantic.

"I don't need to hide this from you. I know that Rabinder is difficult to keep in check. He does many things that are wrong. I know that. Roma knew it. She was excited by what he did, I think, but she also tried to put a stop to it. I know this to be a fact because she told me to talk to him after she started getting phone calls at home. People were threatening her.

"For what it is worth, I'm convinced that Manik had a hand in her murder. If he hadn't been involved, this whole matter would certainly have been in the papers. It is as simple as that. The people he is with wanted to harm us. But they didn't want the matter investigated or even to stay long in the public eye. She became the sacrifice.

"I tried to do what I could to get the police to trap Manik. They did their bit, but you know how things are. I'm not the only one throwing around money. Just last month I heard that he had a seven-day celebration in Motihari because his only son was getting his sacred thread. Teams of Brahmins prayed and chanted nonstop under a shamiana around the clock. Laddoos from that puja were sent to everyone who matters in Bihar. There were public dinners for the poor, special dinners for the rich. Ministers flew in from Delhi. There was a Bollywood starlet who sang and danced at a party on the last night. Manik spent upward of eighty lakhs. They say he is going to get a ticket in the elections next time.

"Life is very cheap in Patna. Money won't even buy you peace. I'm relieved that Rabinder has moved here."

Bua was now standing with her face to Binod, her back pressing against the balcony's railing.

She said, "Now that you have asked me about this matter, perhaps I should also tell you this. In the beginning I had tried to get Banerjee posted elsewhere. Rabinder paid money to keep him in Patna so that Roma would stay close. During the time that Rabinder was in prison, there were nights when Roma would sleep at my house. Her husband knew this. She would come over late in the evening and just not go home. I wonder now whether it was also because she was afraid.

"You know, Rabinder couldn't survive without talking to her five times a day. Even in prison. He paid a lot of money to keep a mobile phone with him."

Binod let that statement hang in the air.

Then he said, "What did she like doing the most?"

She said, "She liked clothes, she liked to sing Bengali songs at women's meetings, she loved films. During the time that I knew her, she changed quite a bit. She grew up. A part of her became worldly but without that type of hardening that I see in women who are in politics."

It was as if Bua had given him an old photograph of a girl, her smiling face framed by two ponytails. One day you would take the photograph out of the drawer and you could see that everything had changed. Roma had become Mala Srivastava. And Bua? She was a survivor. Even someone like Vikas Dhar had seen that about her.

"What do you mean she became worldly?"

"I don't know whether you realize this but she was an educated woman. She had read many more books than Rabinder. She quickly learned about the world and accepted it as such. She knew that every bureaucrat in Patna was dishonest in one way or another. She knew the price that each politician commanded. Her husband is very much a spineless man. I once asked him if he didn't have any complaints against Rabinder. I put it as bluntly as that. All he would say was that Rabinder had borrowed a book of his on the boxer Muhammad Ali and had never returned it."

From where he was sitting on the sofa, Shatrughan looked up and then shuffled over to the screen door. He stuck his head out and sniffed the air. He must have sensed that Bua and Binod were talking about something serious—he stood with the remote in his hand and then withdrew without interrupting them. The living room appeared brighter now. Binod noticed that Neelu had bathed and was sitting next to Shatrughan, rubbing a towel in her wet hair.

Bua was not finished yet. She said, "Her death made me forget the things I didn't like about her. She was very young and only encouraged Rabinder in his crazy plans. They were going to open a boutique together in Delhi. More than once, when I praised her cooking, she asked me very seriously if I would help her buy a restaurant in Patna.

"She had met Neeraj Dubey once. She kept telling Rabinder that he should support Dubey in his projects. I think Rabinder lost some money trying to distribute a film that Dubey had partly financed. Well, I shouldn't complain about the poor girl—although we don't know what tomorrow will bring, here we are in Bombay and Vikas Dhar has made a film for Rabinder. In a way, she has made this happen. This is what she had wanted."

When Bua said this, Binod thought of Baba. A few years ago, a Chinese pilot had been killed when his jet fighter had crashed against an American spy plane. The pilot's death had caused an international controversy. But what had interested Baba about the episode was a report in the press saying that the Chinese Communist Party had quickly declared that the dead man had been a dedicated nationalist, a good cook, a fine singer, a flower arranger, and even a skillful tailor who had made a fashionable skirt for his wife on their wedding anniversary. Baba had saved the newspaper cutting and given it to Binod when he was home from Delhi. Binod now thought of the glory of Chinese pilots and of the words that surrounded Roma in death; he thought of rape and the coercion of ordinary love; he thought of Mala Srivastava and the great Indian middle class; he wondered if there was only hell for people who were second-rate and ambitious; he thought of Rabinder in prison and living triumphantly free in Bombay; he thought of how stories begin in one place and end in another place that is often altogether unexpected.

....

That night Binod didn't go back to his flat but slept on the sofa in the living room. He must not have slept longer than half an hour; he couldn't remember if it had been a dream that had brought him awake. He pulled at the screen door and it slid apart with a tiny creak. The air outside was cooler than in the room. The stutter of a scooter rose from the street below and when that sound had faded the silence returned.

He imagined that he was on a film set. This is what the viewer would see. A figure has come out on a balcony and the side of his face and shirt catch some of the light from the street. The viewer in the dark theater waits within that moment to see what will happen. The next scene or the one after that will reveal who this person is or what this film is about. It amazes Binod that in that brief moment the past is as much unknown as the future. It is strangely exciting.

....

He was lying on the sofa, his thoughts adrift, when his mobile phone beeped with a text message. Rabinder wanted to know if he was sleeping. Binod was unsure whether he should call him back, and then he did, and he immediately regretted it when he heard the bluster in his cousin's voice.

Rabinder was sitting inside Olive with Vikas Dhar, the English girl Alice, and Saif Ali Khan. Dhar wanted to get Saif to play the lead in his next film. Rabinder said, "I think you should be here."

Binod said, "Tell me, is Alice now going to write her dissertation about you?"

Rabinder began to laugh. He said, "She is an interesting woman. I want you to talk to her. She didn't believe me when I told her that George Orwell was born in Motihari."

The whole house was sleeping. Binod didn't want to disturb anyone by getting up and unlocking the door. He could imagine the chitchat around the table at Olive, and how, if he were to go there, he would find himself trying hard to impress Dhar and Saif. And Alice too, no doubt.

Everyone would make attempts to offer praise, not necessarily to each person sitting around the table, but at least to a chosen few. Through some invisible agency, some would be marked to be patronized, and some to be praised; the others would be ignored. The claustrophobia bred by the awkward, mechanical production of praise—a faint brittleness obvious in the reception of each remark because no one was convinced of anyone's sincerity—would be punctured by malice toward others who were not present in that company. Not that insincerity was unacceptable; it was flattering to you if someone was lying because it showed how badly he wanted to please you. Much of the conversation in the film industry was based on a clear understanding of this ordinary truth.

Rabinder said he was going to send his Qualis; it would be outside Neelu's house in fifteen minutes. When Binod again said no, Rabinder responded with greater urgency in his voice, "But you must meet Saif."

A few months earlier, while driving around Bombay in his Land Cruiser, Saif had hit a boy. Binod had done a small write-up on why the rich should always hire half a dozen drivers—two for each car, every man working twelve-hour shifts—and help reduce unemployment in the country. Then, the film star had run into more car trouble. His Toyota Lexus was impounded by the government because import duties had not been paid on the car. This time, what Binod really relished was Saif's telling a reporter on TV how he had acted after his car was taken away. "I did what anybody would do. I went out and bought a Mercedes."

When Binod said no a second time, Rabinder told him to be practical. Binod didn't respond and Rabinder said in a softer voice, "It will be good if you're a part of the new project from the very beginning."

But a stubbornness had crept into him, and a sense of clarity too. He didn't go.

Lying on the sofa in the dark, the window open beside him, Binod felt relaxed. He thought of his sister, asleep in the room nearby, who years ago had said no to her boyfriend, who had assumed that he was going to marry her. The two of them were very close to each other when Neelu had suddenly fallen ill; she was in college in Calcutta and had needed to be hospitalized, and the young man had taken care of her before Baba and Ma reached there a week or two later. But when she was better, Neelu had turned away from the boy, explaining to Binod that she had wanted someone she loved, not one for whom she only felt gratitude. He had met him once, a quiet, unassuming fellow named Deepak, who smiled often, his lips curling up nervously, revealing his gums.

Then, his mind drifted in the dark to his mother, who sometimes despite herself was kind to everyone. Baba's relatives from Ratauli, wanting to see a doctor in Patna, or needing to file a petition in the High Court, or looking for a groom for their daughter, would arrive at their doorstep at different hours of the day or night. Ma would silently knead more flour in the kitchen and roll fresh rotis. Her blouse was so often creased with sweat. The smell in his father's clothes, the smell of clothes drying in the sun mixed with the smell of the earth and grains, the same smell that he would always find in the bare, unfurnished rooms in the house in Ratauli, came back to him from his childhood. In Delhi, a red silk-cotton tree, the simul, stood tall outside the window in his hostel; each spring, red flowers with heavy waxy petals appeared on its prickly branches. An owl used to come and sit silently each night on a bough; he would watch the bird keeping its vigil on moonlit nights and even when rain was falling. During those summers, when he was a student at the university, waiting on the road for bus number 220 or 240, he could feel the tar melting under his heels. On the deep black of the road, the deeper black of the sticky tar. Life had seemed to offer such little refuge, and yet there was shade, and even comfort.

Five years earlier, he had spent an evening in the new Hasty and Tasty Restaurant in Motihari, listening to talk about planets and charts. Lattu Chachaji, the man who had attracted scandal by keeping a village girl as his mistress, had by then turned into a spiritualist and an astrologer. He had instructed Binod to recite the *Aditya Hridya Strotra* every day. The mantra's polynomial lines were written in Devanagari on a shiny card. On the top of the card was the four-armed Sun God, sitting on a chariot drawn by seven horses, bright rays shooting out into the blue clouds from a halo behind his head. For several months, on Lattu Chachaji's advice, Binod had worn black on Saturdays. Or was it Thursdays?

A young Bihari man from Samastipur had come to Bombay to become an actor, and not having succeeded in that attempt, began teaching in an acting academy. Binod had met him several times during his first days in the city; the actor's elder brother was a friend of Shatrughan's in college. There was little hope that the young man would find the kind of work he wanted, and yet in his conversations with Binod he seemed strangely confident and even serene. A few months earlier, Binod had received an email from him—one of those messages that are forwarded to a list of friends several times: "Life gives answer in three ways . . . It says yes and gives you what you want, it says no and gives you something better, it says wait and gives you the best!!! Have a good day." Binod had read the message before noticing who had sent it, and for a moment it had given him pleasure; he had accepted it like an anonymous message from the future. Then he saw the address from which the message had come and a shadow fell over him. Such delusion! Yet, he could never write to the boy and say that his faith in the future was baseless; it would be a bit like telling a believer that God did not exist. Who was he to do that?

He remembered the day when he had been taken as a boy to the hostel where Bua had just moved. She had kept her butter and jelly in small bowls of water so that they would remain safe from ants. Had Bua known then that she would fashion an independent life for herself? As he thought about it, he seemed ready to believe that everyone in his family had tried hard to find a semblance of order in their lives. Baba, Bua, Ma, Binod himself. And Rabinder too, no doubt, in his own special way.

In Bombay many months earlier, when Rabinder had come back to Binod's flat one evening after visiting his friend Neeraj Dubey, he said,

"Remember that sequence in *Aadmi* when Neeraj is torturing the man from the other gang, trying to find out who had given the guy the order to kill him? When I saw that, I thought immediately of the time when I beat up Shrikant. He was a cinema-hall owner. This was near the Teen Laltain Chowk in Bettiah. Neeraj had been with me that night. I had hit the man with the butt of my palm."

Rabinder held up his right hand, as if about to heave a shot putt.

He had said, "I hit him like this. One blow. And his cheek split right over the bone and the flesh fell open . . . That is what Neeraj did in the film. I remembered the incident in Bettiah when I saw the film, and today when I was with him I wondered whether somewhere inside Neeraj the memory of that scene had always remained with him. It must happen like that with artists . . ."

These were little details from Binod's life and he didn't know what they meant, other than that they made his solitude whole. They were all a part of who he had become—this was who he was.

He began to think next of the names of the books that he had liked when he was twenty, and the way in which he would touch their pages. They always appeared perfect to him, as if each printed line was a singular triumph. A life that had been narrated could be as complete as a book, white pages opening one after another in the dark.

Binod turned a page. In his dream, the dark line was a train cutting across the broad heart of the plains. The whole landscape appeared white in the bright sunlight. He must have been seated close to the engine because it was very hot. They passed a boat tilted on its side in a field. A woman sitting away from him in the train compartment was putting a piece of an orange into her mouth. But he remembered that he himself had just eaten: kheer, the rice and the sweetened milk scented with seeds of cardamom; he could still taste it on his tongue. The wind riffled the pages of the book he was holding, and passed its long fingers through his hair. The sky was cloudless, but he thought for a moment that he could smell coming rain.

AMITAVA KUMAR

is a professor of English at Vassar College. He is the author
of *A Foreigner Carrying in the Crook of His Arm a Tiny Bomb* (2010); *Husband of a
Fanatic: A Personal Journey through India, Pakistan, Love and Hate* (2005); *Bombay —
London — New York* (2002); and *Passport Photos* (2000). He is the editor of *Away:
The Indian Writer as Expatriate* (2004); *World Bank Literature* (2003); *The Humor
and Pity: Essays on V. S. Naipaul* (2002); *Poetics/Politics: Radical Aesthetics
for the Classroom* (1999); and *Class Issues: Pedagogy,
Cultural Studies, and the Public Sphere* (1997).

. . . .

Library of Congress Cataloging-in-Publication Data

Kumar, Amitava, 1963–
Nobody does the right thing / Amitava Kumar.
p. cm.
"An earlier, longer version of this novel was published
by Picador India in 2007 under the title Home Products."
ISBN 978-0-8223-4670-8 (cloth : alk. paper)
ISBN 978-0-8223-4682-1 (pbk. : alk. paper)
1. Motion picture industry — India — Fiction.
2. India — Fiction. I. Title.
PR9499.4.K8618N636 2010
823′.914 — dc22
2009049957